THE
ONE
WHO WAS
TAKEN

BOOKS BY KERRY WILKINSON

Kerry Wilkinson

THE ONE WHO WAS TAKEN

bookouture

Published by Bookouture in 2023

An imprint of Storyfire Ltd.
Carmelite House
50 Victoria Embankment
London EC4Y 0DZ

www.bookouture.com

ISBN: 978-1-83790-098-5
eBook ISBN: 978-1-83790-084-8

ONE

The pair of women nodded in unison towards Millie and Jack. It was what couples did when they passed each other in the woods. A little nod without breaking stride and everyone continues on their way. Only the real psychopaths said something like 'nice day for it'.

Millie nodded back at the women, although one of them eyed her a little too long, probably trying to place her. She'd either know who Millie was, because of the whole notoriety thing, or she'd wonder whether Millie was the daughter of a friend. There was that half-second or so of confusion and then Millie saw it click.

Ah, that's who you are.

A fraction of a second more and the two couples had passed each other. Give it a few metres and the woman would be cutting off her friend mid-sentence. 'You know who that was, don't you?'

Not that Jack had noticed. 'What I don't get,' he said, 'is if woods are called woods, then why aren't lakes called waters? Why aren't fields called grasses? Someone's just looked at a load of wood and gone, "Right, that's the woods."'

Ahead of them, Barry shot from one side of the path to the other. Light dappled across the trail but the gingery labradoodle wasn't too fussed about the proper route. He was too busy diving into bushes and hopping over logs. It was as if he saved up all his energy so that, when he was off his lead, he could go bananas.

'You've got too much time on your hands,' Millie replied.

'It's true though,' Jack said. 'It's like fruit. You've got bananas, strawberries, all that, then someone's seen something orange and gone, "That's an orange."'

A squirrel hurtled up a tree as Barry ran in a circle at the bottom. The squirrel stopped midway up and turned, cocking its head at the dog. Millie could've sworn there was a bit of side-eye in there. *Let's see you climb a tree.*

Another couple had appeared from nowhere. That older sort who had retired but were under strict doctor's orders to get some daily exercise. It was a warm morning but they were each wearing half a dozen layers and the man offered a cheery wave as the two couples neared each other.

'Great day for it!' he said.

Millie offered her usual nod of acknowledgement, alongside the narrow smile of dismissiveness – but Jack was far more sociable.

'Lovely, isn't it?' he replied.

Maniacs, the lot of them.

There was a short moment in which Millie feared the other couple would actually stop and try to have a conversation. Luckily, they didn't break pace, not until it was too late. It was the woman who noticed Millie. She slowed a fraction and squinted, then quickly turned away as they passed.

Jack noticed this time. He waited until they were out of earshot before asking, 'Don't you ever get tired of that?'

'What do you think I can do about it?'

'Wear a hat?'

'I'm not wearing a hat just to stop people staring.' She paused, then nudged him with her elbow. 'But I'm not surprised you're thinking about hats considering how quickly you're balding.'

Jack reached for the top of this head and patted down the thinning strands. 'I've always had an enlarged crown.'

'Is that a euphemism?'

That got a snort, just as Barry reappeared on the path. The dog trotted at Millie's side and looked up, wanting permission to dart away once more. Considering he wasn't her dog, he had better manners than many of the people Millie knew.

'Go on,' she said, waving a hand. Barry didn't need telling twice as he shot along the path and then veered sideways, where he disappeared into the undergrowth.

'The ghost tree is that way,' Jack said, pointing in the direction Barry had headed.

'You're always going on about ghosts!'

Jack didn't get a chance to reply, not with words anyway. Millie's phone cut through the silence as her friend yelped in surprise at the sudden noise. He caught himself, straightened, and then stared wistfully into the distance as if he hadn't been spooked.

Millie removed her phone from her bag, raised her eyebrows at Jack to let him know that she'd seen him jump, and then looked properly at the screen.

It was an unknown 07 number calling. Probably some scammer claiming there was an undelivered parcel, or someone saying she owed tax. It could all be figured out by giving her credit card number. She'd usually ignore unknown calls but it was early in the morning and it didn't feel as if fraudsters could be arsed getting up before lunch.

'Hello...?' Millie said.

There was a crinkling whisper from the other end, perhaps a gentle cough, and then a hesitant woman's voice. 'Mill...?'

Millie realised she'd stopped walking. Jack was a few paces ahead, turning back to face her. The only people who ever called her 'Mill' were friends. Good friends.

'Who's calling?' Millie asked.

Another rustle and then the sound of someone breathing. 'It's Nicola.'

Millie twisted away from Jack, not wanting him to see her face. She wondered if she'd known who it was simply from the 'Mill...?' The tone had been a bit scratchier – and yet it was the same as it had always been. It was hard to forget the voice of the person you sat next to in school all those years. The person who had been as close as a sister without actually being one.

'What's wrong?' Millie asked. They hadn't spoken in a long time – and, surely, the only reason Nicola could be calling was because something bad had happened.

The breathing was back. Like someone explaining why they were giving up smoking without having to talk.

'I found the shoes,' Nicola croaked.

Millie blinked and the woods were suddenly darker. The trees were curling down, creeping towards her. The bushes had edged closer, with leafy tendrils reaching and arching.

There was no need to ask *what* shoes. It could only be one pair.

The shoes a teenage Nicola had been wearing on the night she was kidnapped.

TWO

Millie and Nicola stood at the patio doors, staring across the garden. A neat, trimmed hedge ringed the bowling green lawn, with a square of intricate paving closer to the house. On the patio, four lounge chairs were angled around a matching table, with a large umbrella over the top.

'Charlie's got a gardener who comes every two weeks,' Nicola said.

Millie momentarily wondered why she'd said it – but then remembered it had been a habit of Nicola's when they were growing up. Anything that could be seen as an extravagance had to be explained away, as if money shouldn't be spent on anything other than necessities.

It was long after they'd fallen out that Millie had heard the term 'working-class guilt' and realised what she'd missed for so long.

Millie had barely noticed the tidiness anyway. She was focused on the washing line that stretched from the furthest corner of the garden to the opposite side of the house. It was empty, except for a pair of shoes, tied together by the laces, hanging in the centre.

'When did they show up?' Millie asked.

'I was at the gym first thing. I got home and went upstairs to shower, then saw them from the top window.'

Millie took a half-step forward, away from the doors, and looked up to the window above. It was central to the house, offering the most perfect of views of the garden.

'What did you do?' Millie asked.

Nicola was blank, staring somewhere into the distance. 'Nothing. I've not touched them. Charlie's on a course and doesn't get back 'til tomorrow.' A pause. 'I called you.'

'Does he know what happened?'

Nicola didn't reply, which was enough of a response. Only Millie knew what had happened – which is why Nicola had called her, even though they'd barely spoken in fifteen years. They avoided one another at weddings and, though they didn't cross roads to dodge each other, they made sure to be on opposite sides of the room if they were in the same pub.

This was the closest they'd been physically in a very long time.

Millie stepped back and stood in the doorway once more, staring out towards the shoes. There was the gentlest of breezes and the washing line was ebbing from side to side.

It was a crossroads. Millie could leave and let Nicola deal with whatever this was. Except a lot had happened in the years since they had stopped talking.

Nicola must have sensed it too. 'I almost called when I saw what happened to your mum and dad,' she said. 'I wanted to say sorry. I didn't know if you wanted to talk about it, or if you had someone else around. In the end, I just, sort of... left it.'

Millie wasn't sure how to reply. She didn't answer calls from numbers she *did* know back then, let alone those she didn't.

'How did you get my number?' Millie asked.

Nicola blinked for a moment, taken by the question.

'Charlie had it somehow,' she said. It sounded like a lie, and perhaps it was. Perhaps it didn't matter. They'd all been friends back in the day, and somebody might have passed it on to him.

'How have you been?' Nicola added quickly.

There was still a huskiness to her voice and Millie almost laughed at the absurdity of the question. It was so vast.

'Do you mean the last fifteen years? Or the eighteen months since Mum and Dad?'

Nicola breathed in. They were standing side by side, not looking at each other. 'Both, I guess.'

Millie didn't reply. There was a lot she could say but so much she wouldn't. How could either of those timeframes be summed up into a tidy sentence?

'I didn't want to fall out,' Nicola said, more quietly this time.

Perhaps it was the solemn tone but Millie was suddenly furious. The hair on her arms stood up as she clenched her teeth. 'What did you think would happen when you slept with my dad?'

There was no reply, not at first. Millie was still staring across the lawn, not allowing herself to look at her old friend. Even with that, she felt Nicola sag a fraction.

'I didn't plan it,' Nicola said. 'Not the first time.'

'So you did the other times...?'

Millie already knew the answer, of course. She'd had a long, *long* time to think about it all.

'I was only twenty-two, twenty-three. Charlie was still at uni and I didn't know if he was coming back. Your dad was—'

'I know what my dad was. I know *who* he was.'

Nicola was quiet at that and Millie wondered if *she* knew, too. Whether she'd heard the news about Millie's parents' deaths, and the subsequent rumours, seen the Facebook posts where people said Millie was a suspect. Where they said *she'd killed them.* And, after all that, whether Nicola had thought about who Millie's father actually was.

The spell was broken.

'Did your mum know?' Nicola asked.

Millie almost replied 'about what?' but then realised Nicola was talking about her affair.

'I think Mum never let on about a lot of things she knew,' Millie replied.

Nicola took a deep breath and Millie could *feel* what she was about to ask before she did.

'Did they really kill themselves?'

The question hung and Millie almost turned to walk out. She stared across the lawn, towards the dangling shoes, picturing the moment a lifetime ago that she'd found her barefooted friend.

'How else would they have died?' Millie replied.

'I know, I didn't mean—' Nicola stopped herself, although Millie suspected that *was* what she meant. 'I know what people say about you. I tell them it's not true. I got into an argument with a woman at the office a while back.' As if anticipating a question that Millie wasn't about to ask, Nicola added quickly: 'I'm assistant office manager at Grants. It's—'

'I know what it is.'

Millie instantly regretted cutting off Nicola. Grants was a construction and lumber yard based a little outside Whitecliff.

'I was in late last night,' Nicola added. 'There's a stocktake so I got the morning off. I thought I'd go to the gym, then have lunch in town. Quiet morning, y'know?'

They stared together at the shoes on the washing line for a few seconds more. Not such a quiet morning any longer.

'What do *you* do now?' Nicola asked. 'I know you used to put on events. Charlie and me went to a few and they were always really well organised.'

Millie didn't know if it was true and, in many ways, it didn't matter if it was. It felt like a life that was somebody else's. She had left the job when she was forced to move back in with her parents, a couple of months before their deaths. After that, she had become front-page news and it was impossible to do anything other than hide.

'I groom dogs,' Millie replied – and it sounded almost pathetic on its own. As if owning and operating her own business wasn't enough.

'That sounds interesting,' Nicola replied. There was a forced politeness, for which Millie didn't blame her. It was the sort of thing people said to each other when they had no idea what the other's job entailed.

It was all small talk, of course. A delay in facing the inevitable. They could stand for hours and talk about nothing, because the alternative was in front of them.

To break the cycle, Millie moved quickly, striding away from the house, across the patio, and over the lawn. When she reached the shoes, she stretched on tiptoes and flipped them up and over the line, where she caught them. The Converse Hi-Tops were a faded purple, with a felt-tip heart drawn on the canvas side of the right shoe. The red ink had bled over the years, seeping deeper towards the sole.

Millie had been there when Nicola had sketched the heart. They'd been sitting underneath the pier, in the spot against the curved wall, where the tide only reached a handful of times a year. Learning how to smoke or drink in that spot was practically a rite of passage for the youth of Whitecliff.

Or it had been when they were young.

Millie carried the shoes back across the garden and offered them to Nicola. The other woman stared at them in the way a mouse might stare at a snake. She reached a hesitant hand forward and stroked the heart, before taking both shoes in her hands.

'What do you want to do with them?' Millie asked.

Nicola continued ogling the trainers for a moment. When she looked up, she was starry-eyed. 'I don't know. I... didn't think I'd ever see them again.'

Millie almost suggested calling the police – except she hadn't had great experiences with them in the past. Nicola read her mind anyway.

'We didn't call them back then, did we?' she said.

'No...'

'What would I say? Someone's returned my stolen shoes twenty-odd years after they were taken? Twenty-odd years after...'

The sentence wasn't completed. Not properly. Not out loud.

'I don't want Charlie knowing...' Nicola added.

That answered one of Millie's questions. In the time since everything had happened, she wondered if Nicola had told Charlie about it. They had got married in the end. After he'd gone to university and come home. After Nicola and Millie's dad had done what they'd done.

With all that, Nicola had still kept this from him.

'Did you ever tell anyone?' Millie asked.

'No.' Silence and then: 'You?'

'No.'

Their secret, then. Just the two of them... plus whoever was responsible for what happened.

Nicola put down the shoes on the kitchen table and closed the patio doors. Millie crossed to the other door that led into the hall and took in everything she'd missed first time. The kitchen was spotless: all stainless steel and granite worktops. The cupboard doors were a bright white, the sink was empty, and everything had the general sense of not being used. Like a show home. Millie thought about Nicola's guilt over the gardener and wondered if there was a cleaner, too. Not that it mattered.

'Can we be friends?' Nicola asked.

It hovered in the air, like the moment before someone throws themselves down a slide. The weightlessness of time, where, for the merest fraction of a second, everything feels possible.

Millie thought back to school and an English lesson in which their old teacher had them recite a sentence where putting the emphasis on a different word would change the meaning.

Can we be friends? was asking about an indeterminate future, where there was a possibility of them being friends at some point. Can *we* be friends? was specifically asking if they could be friends in the moment.

Millie didn't know the answer to either question.

'I think I know someone who can help,' she said instead. 'Not the police.'

'I don't think I want anyone else to know.'

Millie looked up from the shoes and waited for Nicola to do the same. She was the same but different. Still with the absurdly straight hair and the freckles near her ears – and yet there were crinkles around the edges of her eyes. Perhaps a few grey hairs, too. It came to them all.

'If someone left the shoes,' Millie said, 'then it's someone who knows what happened to you. Or it's the person who did it. What can we do with just us? We already lived through it once.' A pause. '*You* already lived through it.'

Nicola didn't reply for a while. She shifted from looking at Millie to watching the shoes, as if they might jump to life and come for her.

And then, eventually: 'Who do you think can help...?'

THREE

Millie double-checked the address on her phone's maps app and then turned off her car engine. She was definitely in the right place – and it was one of the few areas of Whitecliff she didn't really know.

On the way out of town, most of the way up the hill but not quite on the cliffs, was an estate that hadn't existed when she'd been born. She remembered the billboards from when they were being built, plus the various cranes and cement lorries that would appear sporadically. Nobody she knew lived in any of the houses, so she'd never had a reason to visit.

That was until now.

She got out of the car and felt the warmth of the summer day tickling her skin. Further up the road, she spotted the rickety shape of the Volvo in which, even from a distance, she could see the moss growing around the window frames.

Millie walked up the gentle slope, to the driver's side of the car. The window was down, although there was a decent chance it was because it had broken and couldn't be rewound up. She crouched to look at the man inside, who was reading something off a notepad. As her shadow crept across his light, he turned and blinked towards her – then cracked half a smile.

'Barry was particularly exhausted after his morning's walk,' the man said. 'He drank a bowlful of water and then I found him in the kitchen, lying in a sunny spot. I'm not sure he's moved since.'

'It's hard work chasing squirrels.'

Millie stepped away from the car and allowed Guy to clamber outside. His height always surprised her, as if he was a short man in a tall man's body. He was over six foot, broad and wide. The sort of man who might end up spending half his life in other people's personal space, whether or not it was on purpose. Despite that, since they began working together, it always felt as if they were on the same level. That they were equals.

Guy shut the door behind him – although it took three attempts to actually stay closed – and then he rested against the car.

'You'll have to start letting me pay for your dog-walking services,' he said.

'Don't be silly,' Millie replied. 'Although I do need a favour. Two actually.'

That got a smile. 'What sort of favours are we talking?'

'Can you meet someone I know? An old... *friend*?'

'You don't seem too sure about the "friend" bit?'

Millie didn't know whether she'd actually phrased it differently but, with Guy, she wasn't sure it mattered. He might not be imposing with his size – but he was certainly annoying with his perception. That was the gift a lifetime of asking people questions had given him.

'It's complicated,' Millie replied.

'Why would you like me to meet her?'

'That's complicated, too. Things from years ago. It's probably better if she tells you herself. She's working now but maybe tomorrow morning...?'

'I think I can manage that...'

He waited – and it was Millie who broke first. The second favour was the main one on which she'd been holding out. 'Eric turns eight on Saturday,' she said. 'There's going to be a party. A few of his school friends, plus parents. Alex is hosting in our back garden—' She stopped herself. It wasn't *their* house any longer. 'In *his* back garden. Eric's never met you and I'd like him to know you're my godfather, if that's OK...?'

Guy had been nodding along. Across the previous six or seven months, she'd spoken to him more than anyone and she suspected it was true of him as well. It felt strange to her – and likely him – that, despite that, he'd never met her son. Their lives had been separate for decades even though, unknown to her, he was her godfather.

Not just that. Millie's former husband had custody and she only saw Eric every other weekend.

'I think I'd enjoy that,' Guy replied, although Millie hadn't finished.

'Rachel's going to be there,' she added. 'Alex's parents, too. I think I just need someone who...'

She wasn't sure how to finish. Someone who... didn't *hate* her? Wasn't a massive nob? It felt a bit extreme and yet her ex-husband, his parents, and his fiancée were all going to be at the party. The other parents would know who she was and why she and Alex were no longer together. There wouldn't be much sympathy.

'I see why that would be uncomfortable for you,' Guy said. 'Though I do wonder how you'll explain who I am. Godfather is more of a symbolic thing...'

He was right and yet...

'It's not as if I have any *actual* parents,' Millie said. 'On my side, you're the closest thing Eric has to a grandfather, so it would be good if he knows who you are.'

She didn't add that Guy would be a bit of backup on the day, compared to the *actual* grandparents being around.

Guy was nodding again and she thought about how they'd never quite got around to discussing his own lack of children. His wife had died a little while after he'd been made redundant from his job at the local newspaper. He'd spoken about her – and yet Millie knew nothing else about whether he had more family. It felt rude to ask, invasive even. If he wanted to tell her something, he did – and vice versa.

'I'm sure I'll be able to make it,' he said. 'Is this the sort of party that has cake?'

'What sort of party *doesn't* have cake?'

'Bad parties.'

Millie was in full agreement, which was when she noticed the notepad in his hand. It was open roughly halfway through the pad, with lines of squiggles across the page.

'What's that?' Millie asked.

Guy glanced at the page and then held it up for her to see properly, not that it helped. The shaky symbols weren't English.

'Shorthand of an old planning meeting from almost nine years ago,' Guy replied.

Millie was only half-surprised.

She rolled her eyes, making sure he saw it. 'I knew you were a nerd but I didn't know you were such a *big* nerd. Who goes to planning meetings? Who makes notes, *keeps* them, and then reads them back years later?'

Guy half-turned, indicating the street behind them. He was smiling. 'That meeting led to everything here.'

Millie stepped around the side of the car and took in the view he was motioning towards. Behind them was a near perfect sight of the town below and the ocean beyond. Rows of houses and hotels, stretched to meet the pier, which ate into the

sea. Far beyond that, boats were bobbing near the horizon as
sunlight glinted from the shimmering surface.

It was a far cry from the massive, spaced-out houses around
them. There were high walls and spiked gates, with CCTV
cameras on even taller poles. It was as if the owners thought
they lived in some sort of ghetto, even though that couldn't be
further from geography, or the truth.

'I've never been up this way,' Millie said, wondering why
she hadn't. If nothing else, it was probably the best view in the
area.

'It started with one house about sixty years back,' Guy
replied.

'I didn't know it was that long ago.'

'It was and it wasn't.' He tapped his pad. 'Everything was
built one at a time over decades – and then, at this meeting,
someone wanted to buy one of the old houses, knock it down,
and build a newer, bigger mansion. They needed permission –
and then, once it was given for one, it couldn't realistically be
denied for the others. The last nine years has seen a lot of old
houses demolished and now...'

He finished the sentence with a half-pirouette. The results
were around and in front of them: a series of huge, soulless
buildings, hidden behind needlessly giant walls. It was a town
within a town. A community of people who paid for the view
and then blocked it out.

Millie spent a few more seconds taking in the houses, then
the view, before she realised Guy had taken a few steps away
from her.

'You said something about a party the other day...?' Millie
said.

'That's why we're here.'

'Will there be cake at this one?'

He grinned. 'Let's hope so.'

Millie caught up to Guy's side and then they walked along

the length of a wall taller than she was, and around a corner. The faint sound of music was on the breeze: something new and auto-tuned, where whoever was singing sounded thirty per cent robot.

They crossed the road and then Millie realised where they were going. With all the talk of knocked-down houses and rebuilds, there was one place that stuck out like Guy's Volvo in any car park. Among the mansions was a regular-sized house that looked as if a giant had sat on it. There were tiles missing from the roof, a gutter hanging from the wall and a wooden board across one of the front windows. A vast garden of weeds and ankle-high grass stretched from the front door to the road with an upturned wheelbarrow sitting neatly in the middle.

In contrast to the neglect, there were rainbow streamers pinned to the front windows, with a ring of colour around the front door.

Guy stepped onto the path and then checked to make sure Millie was still behind. 'I wasn't sure this would be my scene,' he said.

The music was louder as they got closer and, when they were almost at the front door, it opened to reveal a man who was probably eighteen or nineteen. He had a bare, hairy chest, nothing on his feet, and a glazed, glassy look of someone who was either on drugs, or who had spent an entire afternoon watching daytime television. He grinned and chuckled to himself as he passed them.

Millie almost told Guy that this wasn't *her* scene, either. She might be a generation and a bit younger than him – but her days of leaving parties while missing clothes were long, long gone.

'What sort of party is this?' Millie asked.

'From what I can gather, it's a reverse housewarming.'

Millie didn't get a chance to question that, because Guy opened the unlocked front door and led them into a dark hall. A string of white fairy lights were taped to the ceiling, with a cord dangling down the wall and plugged into a four-gang that was snaking its way up the stairs. There was no bulb in the *actual* light fitting and, as Millie's eyes adjusted to the gloom, it was impossible to miss the dents and holes in the walls.

She followed Guy into what turned out to be a kitchen. The sink was filled with grubby dishes, while the floor was covered with soiled footprints. There were more dents in the walls and the curtain rail was hanging diagonally across the window. On the other side was a dining table loaded with more dirty dishes.

Guy had stopped, waiting for Millie to reach his side. 'And you reckon my study is cluttered,' he said.

'This is like living in a landfill.'

Every surface Millie could see had a thin coat of dust or dirt, while the fridge had a power cord hanging at its side, with the plug cut off, exposing the wires. She felt dirty simply looking at it all.

In an attempt to escape, Millie edged through the door at the back, into the garden, which was even bigger than the one at the front. The grass was shorter and the music louder, with a row of tables off to the side that had a Bluetooth speaker sitting on top. There were paper plates, plus platters of sandwiches and bowls of crisps. At least thirty fairy cakes were lined up next to jugs of something purple. Guy had seen the cakes too and they smiled at one another as they realised they were thinking the same thing.

Despite the mess of the inside, the back garden was like a normal summer party. There were groups of people milling around, chatting and eating. Laughter and chatter was in the air, along with a sense that it really was a party. The atmosphere couldn't have been more different than the grimness of the inside.

Millie spotted some likely in their seventies, plus others who were teenagers. The mix of ages was so noticeable that

Millie found herself wondering about the last time she'd been anywhere similar.

Millie was about to ask Guy why they were there when she realised she was being watched. A man with a shaven head was at the drinks table, batting away a wasp when he'd stopped mid-waft and started to stare. He seemed vaguely familiar, although Millie couldn't quite place him. As they looked to one another, he took another swipe towards the insect and then filled a glass with the purple liquid before crossing towards her and Guy.

Even though he'd been looking at her, it was Guy to whom he offered his hand.

'You must be Guy,' he said.

Guy shook his hand enthusiastically, as if they were old friends. 'You must be Will!'

Millie suddenly knew who it was. 'You're Will Harper,' she said.

The man turned to her with a half-smirk. 'Hi, Mill.'

That shortened name again.

Mill and Will. He was another face from the past, the second in a matter of hours.

Millie again found herself examining his features, searching for that link to their teenage selves.

'You used to have such...'

He finished the sentence for her: 'Long hair? I know. Baldness runs in families, apparently – so I blame Dad. He reckons he got it from his dad, so I think it's a family tragedy.' He laughed to himself and then his eyes crinkled. 'What are *you* doing here?'

Millie looked to Guy, not quite sure how to explain it herself. It was Guy who'd been invited.

'We work together,' Guy said – which was an explainer of sorts. Since being made redundant after decades on the local paper, Guy had used his payoff to set up his own website to report on Whitecliff. Millie had fallen into writing bits and

pieces for the site after he'd decided she was a natural at, well...
sticking her nose into things.

The explanation only seemed to confuse Will more. He
eyed Millie curiously. 'Are you a writer?' he asked.

'Not really,' she replied, too quickly.

'She is,' Guy said, 'she just doesn't know it. She wrote a
piece a couple of months back about how the men's changing
rooms were being upgraded at the leisure centre – but not the
women's. They rewrote their budget because of Millie.'

Millie found herself hugging her arms across her front,
relishing the praise but simultaneously not wanting it.

'I saw that story,' Will said. 'Someone put it on Facebook
then it was everywhere.'

'Made the TV news,' Guy said. 'Then the politicians got
involved and it was sorted out.'

'Guy's the real writer,' Millie added quickly, wanting to
change the subject. 'He's got his own archives and contacts. I
just get in the way now and then.'

Will looked between them curiously, probably wondering
what exactly they were to each other given the low-level bickering. Telling him that Guy used to be a good friend of her dad's
didn't feel like something he needed to know. If anything, it
made their relationship seem weirder.

'Didn't you used to run events for the council?' Will asked.

'It didn't work out,' Millie replied. She said it firmly enough
that it was clear no further questions were welcome.

There was a second or two of awkwardness and then Guy
chipped into the centre of it: 'How do *you* know each other?' he
asked.

Millie had started to answer but Will cut across her.
'School,' he replied. 'We were in the same year. Had the same
friends.'

He was right but it sounded a little more clinical than Millie
remembered. They had always been friends of friends who

hung around in the same circles. If she'd answered first, she would have said they were old friends.

Perhaps sensing the difference of opinion, Guy cleared his throat and then moved things on. 'Anyway,' he said to Will, 'you're the one who emailed me...'

'Yes!' Will raised his glass, remembering why they were there. 'It's time to celebrate and I thought someone should be here to mark the occasion.'

When he got little reaction, Will's face fell a fraction.

'Have a drink,' he said, angling towards the table. 'Hannah made the punch and there's loads of it.'

The purple abomination didn't seem too appealing to Millie but Guy was ahead of her anyway. 'It's a bit too early for me,' he said.

'I don't drink any more,' Millie added.

That got the deepest frown yet – although Millie wasn't too surprised given Will knew her at a time when she certainly did.

'What are we celebrating?' Guy asked, although he spoke with a tone that made it sound as if he already knew.

Will sipped from the glass and didn't bother to hide the gentle wince from whatever it contained. 'It's a year since they issued the section twenty-one,' he said. 'One whole year and we're still here.'

He was excited as he turned as if to show off the garden beyond. Millie had little idea what he was talking about – but Guy did.

'A year's a long time to stay in a place after you've been told to evict,' he said.

'Exactly! That's why we're celebrating. That initial paperwork was missing a signature, so they had to re-file the whole lot.' He pushed onto his tiptoes, as if looking for someone, and then lowered himself again. 'This way.'

He turned and led them back into the house, through the bomb site of a kitchen, partway along the hall, and into the living room. The windows were open at the front and side, with sun beaming through onto a brown fabric sofa that had flowery patches sewn across it. Apart from the sofa, a couple of plastic outdoorsy tables, and three rolled-up sleeping bags underneath the window, there was almost nothing else in the living room.

Almost nothing because Will crossed to where a series of papers had been blu-tacked to the wall opposite the window. He scanned the pages and then removed one that he handed to Guy.

'See,' he said. 'No signature.'

Guy looked through the page he'd been handed and then passed it to Millie. 'Section 21' was written at the top, with 'notice of possession' underneath. As best she could tell, it was ordering the tenants of the house to evict. The date was exactly a year before – but Millie had to look closely to realise the signature that was supposed to be in place was actually a stamp.

She passed the page back to Will, who re-tacked it to the wall. 'One of our friends is doing legal work for us for free,' he said. 'She noticed it and they had to restart all over again.' He handed over a second set of paperwork to Guy. 'We ignored this one. When the move out date passed, they went to court to get an order of possession. That took a few more weeks for a court date and then we had a fourteen-day deadline to go.' A pause. 'We ignored that, too.'

Guy passed across the second set of papers but Millie didn't bother to read them. The pattern had been set, even as Will retrieved a third set of papers that he gave to Guy.

'They had to get another court date after that to ask for a warrant of possession. That was about three months ago. Someone said the bailiffs are backed up with too much to do, so here we are.' He spread his arms high. 'A full year. Victory!'

Guy gave Millie the next set of papers, which she scanned, before handing the lot back to Will. He re-pinned everything to the wall and then turned to face them.

'I'm not sure what's going on,' Millie said. 'You had to move out a year ago – but you're still here...?'

Will shrugged, not understanding her point, while she didn't understand his. 'Exactly,' he said. 'We still pay rent, the full amount, on time. We've never missed a payment. We've not even asked for repairs, even though the electricity only works upstairs.'

He sounded joyous and Millie turned between him and Guy, wondering what she was missing.

'I still don't get it,' she said. 'If the electricity doesn't work, why don't you move out? Or ask for repairs?'

She hadn't finished the sentence when she realised she'd said the wrong thing. The sun continued to burn through the open windows but a cloud had fallen across Will.

'That's not the point,' he said sharply. 'Rich folk come here, buying our houses and only coming for a holiday a few weeks every year. Meanwhile, people who were born here, who *live* here, can't afford anywhere.' He spun, jabbing an angry finger in the vague direction of town. 'You know those flats by the bay? We have proof that at least forty per cent are owned by people who don't live here. Parasites relying on *us* to pay off *their* mortgages.'

Will spat the final few words – and he wasn't the only one. A woman's voice came from behind Millie.

'...So we're taking a stand,' she said. 'Some rich prick who works in the city bought this place and wants to knock it down. Wants to build some massive weekend home that's empty most of the time. But we were here first – and we're not going anywhere. We don't care how many notices we get. They'll have to knock down the place with us inside.'

Millie and Guy were in the middle of Will and the newcomer. The woman was somewhere around Millie's age, perhaps a little younger. She had tight red dreadlocks past her shoulders and was wearing a black T-shirt with 'PEACE' in big white letters across the front.

'This is Hannah,' Will said. 'We're, um... housemates. A few of us live here.'

Hannah was standing in the door that led to the hall, her arms now crossed over her front, scowling towards Will.

Guy hadn't said anything for a while and he stepped past Will to the wall, where he removed the page they hadn't been handed. He scanned it and then looked up, speaking to Hannah.

'This says you have to be out on Tuesday...?'

Hannah shrugged. 'We've had demands before. They're all there. It's another bit of paper.'

Guy looked to the page again and took a few seconds to read it. 'This is a final notice,' he said. 'The bailiffs are coming *on* Tuesday. They already have a warrant of possession. There is no more paperwork.'

A look passed between Will and Hannah that was hard to read – but only for a moment. Suddenly, Millie realised exactly what was going on.

'That's kinda why I contacted you,' Will said, speaking to Guy.

'What do you think we can do?' Guy replied.

Millie clocked the use of the word 'we', even as Hannah skipped straight past it.

'We want you to help us stay,' she said.

FOUR

Guy laughed, though more to himself than anyone else. Will and Hannah both had their arms folded in defiance.

'I think you're overestimating my powers,' Guy said.

Another glance passed between Hannah and Will – and Millie knew they'd been arguing over this precise thing in the recent past.

Will dug into his back pocket and pulled out a roll-up. He grabbed a lighter from the windowsill and lit the cigarette.

'Want one?' he asked.

It wasn't clear to whom he was offering but Millie and Guy each said 'no' at the same time.

Will perched in the windowsill, making a minimal effort to blow the smoke outside.

Nobody spoke for a short while, until Millie cut in. 'If you're struggling to find somewhere to stay, we can probably—'

'No,' Will said.

The silence deepened and, even though he'd said there was no power downstairs, electricity crackled in the room.

'This is a war,' Hannah said firmly. 'We didn't start it, *they* did.'

'Who did?' Guy asked.

'Rich people,' Hannah said. 'Old people. Coming here and wanting to take over. They want to sit in *our* cafés, telling all their posh friends what a lovely area it is. But they'll happily make it so expensive to live that no one can actually afford to work there. Then they chuck a pound coin on the plate as a tip and spend the rest of the day telling themselves they're the good guys. They're driving this town into the ground and they don't even know it. Don't even *care*.'

She thumped the wall as she finished and her stare burned with such fury that Millie didn't risk a reply. Not that she knew what to say. This very much felt like Guy's type of situation.

He defused things, if it could be called that, by taking more time to re-read the document. 'I think it's too late for that,' he said, calmly. 'The bailiffs are coming.'

Hannah shook her head. 'Nothing's ever final. We want you to tell people what's happening here. We want a big turnout on Tuesday. Get loads of people down to tell them lot this is *our* town, not theirs.'

She was so angry that she could barely get out the words, which left it to Will to finish. He wafted a hand towards the ongoing party at the back of the house.

'We've got a few supporters already, plus we're on Twitter and TikTok, all that. We were hoping you might, um, be able to get us a bit more, um... *diversity* on the day...?'

'You mean older people,' Guy replied.

Will shrugged. 'Yeah. I mean, it's not all about age. This is *class* warfare. It's not old versus young; it's rich versus poor.'

There was something about the way he said it that left Millie wondering how much of the militancy was Hannah's and how much was his. The real venom had come from her, not him. She had also specifically mentioned 'old people' barely a minute before.

'Capitalist pigs versus non-capitalist pigs,' Hannah spat.

Guy returned the paper to the wall and stepped away. Millie knew what he was going to say before it came out.

'I don't write pieces on demand,' he replied. 'I am here out of courtesy, to hear you out. I really think you're overestimating my reach.'

Hannah slapped the wall, sending a booming clap echoing around the room. 'I told you this was a waste of time,' she said, talking to Will. 'Told you boomers are only in it for themselves.' She nodded at Guy. 'All the same, you lot.'

Without waiting for a reply, she turned and stomped into the hallway towards the back of the house. When the door slammed, Millie turned back to Will, who was still smoking on the windowsill. Guy caught her eye and offered a minuscule, barely there nod towards the front. It was time to leave. Will must have spotted it, too, else he felt the shift in the atmosphere. Before either Guy or Millie had moved, Will said: 'Can you give us a minute?'

Millie thought he was talking to her, asking if she'd leave him and Guy alone. Instead it was the opposite. He was talking to Guy.

Guy glanced curiously from Will to Millie, silently asking if she was OK. Millie was intrigued more than anything. She wasn't sure she and Will had ever had a conversation where it was only the two of them.

'I'll catch you up by the cars,' she said.

Guy's forehead creased momentarily and then he broke into a calm nod. 'See you soon.'

He ambled across the room, into the hall and then out the front.

Will waited, still smoking, until the front door clicked back into place. He leant backwards out of the window and continued to watch until Guy was presumably far enough along the path so that he couldn't quickly return.

'Do you reckon he'll help us?' Will asked, twisting back to Millie.

'Maybe if you'd told him what it was about before getting him here...'

That got a shrug.

'I don't think the talk of "war" helped, either,' Millie added.

That got a second shrug as Will mashed the remains of his cigarette onto a plate that was already piled with ash. He didn't stand.

Will nodded towards the front of the house. 'Is he your boyfriend?'

It took Millie a moment to realise what was being implied. 'Why would you even ask that?'

'Old guy hanging around with someone twenty years younger. Maybe he's got a bit of money, or something?'

Millie stepped towards the door but Will called her back with a laugh.

'C'mon, I'm only joking.'

'Doesn't sound like a joke.'

'C'mon, Mill...'

'Don't call me that.'

Will huffed something that was half-snort, half-laugh.

'What do you want?' Millie asked, even though she had an idea.

'I thought...' he tailed off and then bit his lip. He seemed almost amused. 'There's something *you* want to ask me, isn't there?'

Millie almost walked away... except, as she thought about it, she realised he was right. There seemed a degree of fate to it all. She'd seen Nicola after so long apart and now, from nowhere, somebody else she knew from the same time was in front of her.

'Do you remember the battle of the bands?' She'd wanted to ask it the moment she'd seen him.

Will stared wide-eyed for a second and then snorted again.

'Wow. That's going back a bit. Can't remember the last time I thought about it. How old were we? Seventeen? Eighteen? We were doing our A-levels.'

'Right...'

Will rocked back and forth on the windowsill. 'I remember Matty's band was on – and they finished third? Fourth? We all went to the park after and sat on the bandstand.'

Millie knew that much. She had thought about that night perhaps more than any other.

'Do you remember anything else?' she asked.

Will pouted a lip and shook his head. 'That was probably the last time we were all together,' he said.

'We weren't all there,' Millie replied.

Will began counting on his fingers. 'You, me, Jen, Alex, Rach—' A pause – and Millie wondered if it was because he knew Alex was her ex-husband. That Alex was currently engaged to Rachel. It was quite the triangle. The pause lasted a moment too long and then: '—Matty, Charlie, Nic...' He tailed off: 'Are Charlie and Nic still together?'

Millie thought of seeing Nicola that morning. 'Yeah – but Charlie wasn't at the park that night. He was working at the pier and we left him behind.'

Will nodded along. 'Right...' He blinked. 'It was so long ago and I was ratted anyway. I think I was already out of it before the bands started, let alone after.' He laughed. 'They were the days, right? Pound a pint and all that.'

Millie wasn't sure they *were* the days... but there was something nostalgic about the times when life was simpler. They were all living at home, without rent or bills. Where any side money they earned could be spent on cider and cigarettes.

Will was also partially right about something else, even if he didn't know it. It *wasn't* the final time they had all been together – but it was the final day of their collective innocence. Some people evolved slowly into adulthood but Millie could pinpoint that single evening as the first time she fully felt like a grown-up.

Will wasn't done: 'Didn't you cut Nic's hair sometime around then?' he asked, laughing again. 'You cut the whole lot off. It looked... *mad*.' He gave a shake of his head, as if he couldn't quite believe what he was saying. 'I thought *I* was drunk that night. What were you thinking?!'

Millie didn't reply and she certainly didn't laugh. She shouldn't have brought it back up.

He looked at her curiously for a moment, likely wondering why she'd wanted to know something from so long before. Then his face hardened as he remembered why they'd ended up in the same space.

'D'you reckon you can get your mate to help us?' he asked.

'Guy? I already told you. If you'd been honest with him, he might—'

'Are you still in contact with Pidge?'

Millie froze at the mention of the name. It was a stupid nickname for a lad who used to go to their school. George had once spilled paint in a primary school art lesson. It ended up on his trousers in the shape of something that looked a little like a bird poo. Someone called him Pigeon, which became Pidge – and thirty-odd years later, that was still his name.

Of course she knew Pidge, everyone at their school did. Some of the teachers even called him that. One day, it would be his funeral and people would still have forgotten his real name.

But Millie shivered, because there was no way Will could've brought up that name by accident. Not when he was asking her for a favour.

He must know.

'Why?' she asked, not wanting the answer.

Will smirked as he poked a thumb towards the front of the house and, presumably, Guy. 'No reason... but maybe ask your mate if he can help us...? Might be better for everyone.'

FIVE

The 'no reason' was still rattling around Millie's mind as she finished off blow-drying her client's dog. It was only two words but there was a threat she and Will both understood. If Will knew about her and Pidge, then he knew about...

The tub of beef chews scattered across the floor as Millie had been trying to reach for a towel. The dog, who'd previously been calm, leapt off the low table. He was only stopped from scoffing as much as possible by Millie clasping onto his middle. She half-held onto the dog, while stuffing the chews back into the tub.

It was the snigger that let her know she was being watched.

Jack was leaning on the doorframe, grinning. 'Is throwing dog treats on the floor all part of the service?'

'Is being a sarky sod part of *your* service?'

Jack laughed as he took the tub from her and returned it to the shelf. 'Rish threw me out of the kitchen, so I thought I'd see if you wanted any help.'

Millie rubbed the dog between his ears and he curved his body, leaning into it and groaning gently with pleasure.

'I'm done,' she said.

She poked her head out of the shed at the back of her house, taking in the smell that was drifting from the kitchen.

'Rish can *really* cook,' Millie said.

'He's been practising. Seems to think it might make a difference with the adoption...'

Millie turned back to the dog, keeping her feelings to herself. At least it explained why Jack and his boyfriend had offered to come to her house and cook for her. She knew what was coming.

'Are you still all right for Monday?' Jack asked.

'What's Monday?' Millie asked.

'The woman from the adoption agency is—' Jack stopped as Millie turned to raise an eyebrow at him. Of course she'd known.

'I told you I'd be there,' she said.

'It's just—'

'I know how to be polite,' Millie said.

She got a raise of his eyebrow this time.

'I didn't say I'm *always* polite,' Millie added. 'I said I *know* how to be polite. It's not like I'm going to tell her about the time you were so drunk you fell over a bollard and ended up rolling around in the gutter outside a chip shop.'

Jack didn't crack. 'I wasn't *rolling around*. I was trying to get up – and you were taking pictures on your phone.'

That was true. 'It was like watching a man try to tap-dance with both shoes tied together,' Millie said. 'On ice.'

That didn't get a smile either. The issue of the adoption application was not a topic for anything other than outright seriousness.

Millie checked the time on her phone. The dog's owner was late and hadn't called or messaged. She gave the dog one of the chews it had been craving, before levering herself up onto her workbench. She craned to get a look at the house, making sure

Rishi was still visible inside the kitchen, before lowering her voice.

'Are *you* ready for Monday?' she asked.

'What does that mean?' Jack replied.

'You know what it means.'

He stood rigidly, acting as if he had no idea what she was on about, so Millie pushed on.

'I was ten or eleven when Mum signed me up for these after-school ballet classes,' she said. 'I hated them at first. Not my thing. I couldn't balance and didn't like the clothes—'

Jack couldn't resist: 'I guess no patience is a long-running thing...'

Millie allowed herself a smile. 'I had *very little* patience. But they'd paid for the classes, so I had to go twice a week. But it wasn't only ballet. I did that Monday and Thursday, then band on Tuesday, drama on Wednesday, athletics on Saturday mornings in the summer. There was always something. With the ballet, I got better over time, then a lot better in the end. I don't think I ever enjoyed it but it was something I could do. After about two years, I was the joint-lead for a recital at the big school's amphitheatre. We did three successive nights. D'you know how many times Mum and Dad came?'

Jack shifted uncomfortably, perhaps having an idea of where she was going. 'Three...?'

'None. Not once. And I realised the reason I was in so many clubs wasn't anything to do with me. It was them. They'd sign me up for everything, pay whatever it cost, buy all the instruments, or kit, or shoes – and it was because they didn't particularly want me around.'

Millie had got louder but she was past caring. From nowhere, her nose was full, her eyes puffy. She blinked it away as best she could.

'They were happier at their dinner parties and their black-tie things.'

'Mill...'

Jack reached towards her but Millie shook him away. It wasn't him, it was her. She didn't want touching.

He waited as the dog crept onto Millie's feet and pawed at her ankle. She crouched and he found his way onto her lap.

'Wasn't your mum a primary school teacher?' Jack asked.

'She liked *some* children...'

Jack was stuck for words. He mumbled a few things and then stopped.

Millie hadn't been quite sure where she was going when she'd started talking – but she had suddenly spilled something she'd never said in full to another person. Not even Alex – and they had a child together.

'What are you saying?' Jack managed.

'Do you *really* want me to say it out loud?'

Jack turned away, staring off towards the end of the garden. Millie stroked the dog's head, whispered a thank you, and then stood again. Jack knew exactly what she was saying. He and Rishi had almost broken up a little over six months before because Rishi wanted children and Jack didn't. They were back together now and on their way through the adoption process.

'It's not like that...' Jack said, although Millie thought he was trying to convince himself more than he was her.

'I'll talk to whoever you want,' Millie said. 'I'll tell them you and Rish are a great couple, that I love the pair of you, that you'll be great parents. I'll say that you're smart, that he can cook, that you can eat, that you watch trashy reality shows every night – and that your Spotify playlist is ninety per cent disco. I'll do all that – but if you're going to adopt a child, you have to want him or her. *Both* of you.'

Jack was still avoiding her stare. He gasped a big breath and blinked rapidly. 'I didn't know your parents were like that,' he said quietly. 'You never really talk about them.'

Millie was already regretting doing just that. He was right

that she didn't talk about them. The only reason she'd slipped is because she couldn't face another poor kid realising his or her parents didn't really want them.

Millie's phone started to buzz and she checked the screen before holding it up for Jack to see. 'The owner's here,' she said.

SIX

Rishi's efforts in the kitchen were, as ever, delicious – but his offer to cook had come with the ulterior motive that Millie had expected. As they ate, he went down the full wormhole of 'If the woman from the adoption agency says *this*, you should say *that*.'

Millie listened and nodded in the right places, while Jack poked aimlessly at his food, only chipping into the conversation when Rishi specifically asked something.

Jack had been friends with Millie first, and she'd met Rishi through him. Although they were also friends, it wasn't quite the same as it was with her and Jack. She could wind up Jack about various things and know he wouldn't take her seriously. There was always an edge with Rishi, as if he might think something was a personal slight, as opposed to a silly joke.

With that, Millie let Rishi continue with the speech he'd planned. He told her about the way they'd made their flat more child-friendly. There were now soft corners on edges, plus a significant number of new cushions. It sounded like he'd gone berserk in the textiles section of IKEA.

Then he started panicking that the guy in the flat at the end might start playing his 'sweaty gangster rap', whatever that was, during the visit. He told Millie to tell the woman from the agency that she'd never heard the music before and that it must be a one-off. Then he wondered if he or Jack should hang around at the end of the row, so they could knock on the guy's door if he did start playing music.

He had just got to the bit about re-grouting the bathroom when Millie's phone mercifully started to buzz.

'It's Eric,' she said, as she grabbed the device from the table. Alex's name was on the screen as their son was too young for a mobile of his own. 'I've got to take this.'

Millie pressed to answer, said 'hang on' and then hurried through the house until she was upstairs, in her room, with the door closed. She loved Jack and Rishi – but some things were only for her.

'How was school?' Millie asked.

There was excitement in her son's voice. 'I won a spelling competition!'

'Did you?'

Millie couldn't hide the surprise in her voice – mainly because this was not a skill that had come from her.

'I told Miss Briggs I want to be a writer, like you.'

'I mean... I'm not really a writer,' Millie said. 'I write a bit sometimes but—'

Eric wasn't listening. He started listing some of the words from his test, and, although Millie had never thought of herself as an *in my day*-type, she couldn't get her head around the phonics that was now taught in schools. When it came to Eric's homework, it often felt as if he was teaching her, rather than the other way around. It was impressive that he'd managed to spell 'mention', 'possession' and 'imagine' correctly – so something had to be working. There was a short lull after he finished teaching her and then:

'Are you excited about your birthday?' Millie asked.

'Dad said you're coming to my party.' He sounded even more excited.

'I am!'

'Are you bringing a big present?'

Millie laughed: 'I'm bringing *a* present. I can't guarantee the size.'

'Is it stickers? Auntie Rachel said I have to buy my own stickers from now on.'

Millie bristled at 'Auntie' Rachel laying down the law but there was no point in letting her son see how annoyed it made her. Instead, she listened as her son regaled her with a long story that involved a series of intricate sticker swaps, involving multiple schoolmates, few of whom she knew. His knowledge of how the stickers had passed through numerous sets of hands before ending up with him was unquestionably impressive, if ultimately useless.

Her phone was on speaker and Millie simply listened. With her lack of access, it was good to hear her son speak, even if it was to tell her about a lengthy chain of trades. She threw in the odd 'that's nice' and 'that sounds good' until she realised he'd asked her a question.

They were back onto the subject of birthday presents.

'Will you buy me a dog?' Eric asked.

It took Millie a moment to realise what he'd asked. 'It's, um... not really up to me,' she replied. 'You'll have to ask your dad and Auntie Rachel.'

There had been some talk of a cat at some point, though that had seemingly gone away. Millie usually found out about such things either through Eric, or with a good bit of social media stalking.

'They already said no,' Eric replied.

Millie couldn't stop herself laughing at that. 'If they said no, then I can't say yes. Besides, I don't think dogs make good birthday presents.' She couldn't believe she was saying it but the words came out anyway. 'A dog is for life not just for presents.'

She was so old.

'But you *always* have dogs at your house,' Eric said.

'That's my job.'

'Auntie Rachel says dogs are dirty...'

Millie might not have custody of her son but she knew him well enough to know when he was stirring. That was something he probably did get from her.

'They can be,' Millie replied, tactfully. 'I make them... not dirty.'

'So can I have a dog that's not dirty...?'

She'd walked into that one. 'I really can't answer that,' Millie said. 'You'll have to ask your dad.'

There was a moment of silence as Eric thought of what to say next, while Millie considered the phrasing of what she'd said. She always assumed there was some sort of call recording app on Alex's phone that meant her talks with Eric would be documented. There was no evidence for that – but Alex was a lawyer. She knew her ex-husband well enough to think he'd be amassing evidence if there was ever another custody challenge. Perhaps that was the other reason she let Eric talk so much when there was a phone line between them?

Millie looked up to the clock on her wall, where it was quarter to eight.

'It's almost your bedtime,' Millie said.

'Five more minutes...?'

'We can talk tomorrow – and then it's your birthday on Saturday and I'll see you then.'

There was a reluctant grumbling from the other end – but this was the routine now. Off the phone at quarter to eight, pyjamas, teeth brushing, bed.

'Dad wants to talk to you,' Eric said.

Millie managed to avoid sighing, as it wouldn't be anything

good. There was a goodbye and then a muffled rustling until Alex's voice sounded. 'I'll be back in a minute,' he said.

Millie said 'OK' but could tell from the echo that he'd put down the phone and was already off somewhere else. It was hard to make out what happened over the coming minutes. There was a man's voice – presumably Alex's – then a woman's – presumably Rachel's. A couple of doors slammed and there was an angry shout that sounded like it might have been Eric's. Millie almost hung up a few times and it was almost fifteen minutes before Alex was back on the line. He was breathless as he immediately launched into it.

'We've got to stop these nightly calls before they become the routine,' he said.

Millie had been listening to muffled sound for so long that she jumped when he spoke. 'It already is the routine,' she replied.

'That's the problem. It's got to stop. We can talk properly at the party.'

He spoke in his lawyerly way. A decision had been made that was final – and it didn't matter what she thought. It was only after they separated that she realised he spoke to her like that a lot. He always had.

'It's not my fault he wants to tell me about his day,' Millie said. 'I am his mum.'

'Yeah, and you made your decision, didn't you?'

Alex left that there and Millie could sense him wanting her to bite back. She really did wonder if these phone calls were recorded.

'I'm not going through it all again,' Millie replied.

'Fine. But I'm the one with custody, so this nightly thing is going to stop.' He paused, breathing heavily. 'I'll let him call you tomorrow – and then we'll talk on Saturday.'

Millie moved away from the phone as she sighed. In the

moment of silence, there was the vague sound of crying in the background. 'Is that Eric?' she asked.

There was the cloaked muffling of something covering the phone at the other end. After that, there was an indeterminate sentence or two, spoken by Alex presumably to Rachel. When his voice was loud again, Alex was short. 'I've got to go,' he said.

'Right, but—'

Millie didn't get any further – because the call had dropped. She stared at the screen for a second and took a deep breath, then counted silently to ten.

Saturday didn't feel as if it would be much like a party.

SEVEN

In the fifteen minutes that Millie had been sitting in Nicola's kitchen, her friend... or, perhaps, her *old* friend, had rattled through two coffees. Nicola had one of those bells and whistles, pipes and tubes, chrome machines that made an awful lot of noise considering the teeny little drinks it banged out.

Millie's own coffee still sat on the table in front of her, untouched except for a single sip. Nicola had already started on her third when the doorbell sounded. She looked up, wired and wide-eyed, as Millie stood.

'I'll get it,' she said.

It was strange to be opening the door in someone else's house but Millie headed along the hall and welcomed Guy inside. He was in a shirt that was only a size too big this time and was carrying a large paper bag as Millie ushered him in.

'She's in the kitchen,' Millie said, pointing Guy in the right direction.

He headed past her as Millie locked up and then stopped for a moment to take in the picture board on the wall. It was old-fashioned in many ways, especially in the age of smartphones, but a couple of dozen photos had been pinned to a large cork board. They'd been cut into shapes to cover every free space. Some had crinkled zigzags around the edges, some were circles, some hearts. There was a smiling Nicola and Charlie in various places around the world, with captions written underneath in tidy capital letters.

AT THE BEACH!

IN A FIELD!

ON A ROLLERCOASTER!

Millie would have spent longer looking through them – except Guy's voice was coming from the kitchen.

He could be crotchety sometimes, and certainly sarcastic. On occasion, it almost felt as if he wanted trouble – as with Will at the squat the day before – but this was his other side. This was where charm oozed from him, where everything was said with a sideways grin and a look that felt as if he might have winked, even though he hadn't. As Millie got into the kitchen, the paper bag had been opened and Guy was removing croissants.

'I brought these,' he said. 'I didn't realise it would be such a beautiful house. What a wonderful surprise.'

Nicola was on her feet, dragging plates from the cupboards and accepting the compliments as Guy listed half the contents of her kitchen and told her how wonderful it all was.

Suddenly, Nicola had transformed into the welcoming host. The coffee machine was bubbling and she was talking about milk and sugar. Guy accepted whatever was offered, even though Millie knew tea was his drink – and that he would usually whack seven or eight sugars into a mug. By the time they'd settled, Nicola was halfway through an almond croissant and her caffeine intake had mercifully slowed.

It wasn't what Millie had expected – but then expecting

anything with Guy was a mistake. He had a way of making people feel comfortable, if that was what he wanted.

'I hope I'm not imposing,' Guy said, which was a bit late considering the three of them were already around the kitchen table – and Nicola had almost finished a croissant.

Nicola caught Millie's eye momentarily and, though she didn't speak, Millie knew it was OK to start. The smell of rich coffee and warm pastries was in the air – but that wasn't why they were there, after all.

'We were all seventeen,' Millie said. 'We had a group of friends and it was the summer holidays. We were about to go back and do our final year of A-levels, so it was our last definite summer together. After that, there'd be proper jobs, or uni, or travel, or years out. Nobody really knew what would happen after we all went back to college.'

Millie glanced across to Nicola who, partly unexpectedly, started to speak: 'You work your way up to the bandstand,' she said. 'When you're fourteen, fifteen, or whatever, the older kids get first dibs on all the places to hang out. It was our turn that summer because we were the oldest.'

Millie hadn't ever thought of it like that – but there was a truth to it. Each age group had its single summer of monopolising the park benches, or taking over the war memorial. They'd sit as a group and drink cider, or pass a cigarette around the circle – and then, as soon as it had started, it was over. Back to college or school, then to the real world. After that, the next year group would get its turn.

She was momentarily lost in those thoughts until she realised Nicola was watching her.

'There was a battle of the bands on the pier,' Millie continued. 'Our friend Matty had a band and they were in it.' She risked a little glance at Nicola, hoping for a smile that wasn't there. 'A bunch of us went and Matty's band was...'

'Bad,' Nicola said.

Millie laughed, humourlessly. 'They were all sixteen or seventeen, in these massive green jackets, like they'd just been kicked out of the army for having long hair. They'd written these songs that rhymed things like "love" and "above" – and they took it all so seriously.'

Another glance to Nicola, who was staring through the window, out towards the washing line where the shoes had shown up the day before. 'We looked like such twats,' Nicola said.

'Speak for yourself! I've still got the dungarees I used to wear.'

That got a laugh, a proper one, and – for a second – it was as if she and Nicola had never stopped being friends. They were seventeen again, deciding whether those dungarees looked better fastened properly, or with one strap unhooked.

And then she was back in the kitchen, remembering why they'd stopped being friends. Remembering that sense of betrayal and disgust when she realised her best friend and her dad had done what they did.

Guy sipped his coffee and there was a minuscule wince that he couldn't quite hide. Nicola hadn't seen it but Millie knew he really didn't like it.

'Our friend Charlie,' Millie said, 'Nic's husband now, was clearing glasses. He kept slipping us free drinks, so we were all hammered by the time they announced the results. Matty's band was fourth, I think, which tells you how bad everyone else was. Charlie had to finish his shift but the rest of us wanted to carry on, so we all went up the hill to the park.'

'How many of you?'

Millie started to count on her fingers the way Will had the day before. 'Nic, me, Jenny, Alex, Rach, Will and Matty. I think that's everyone. Seven.'

Something crossed Guy's stare, though he didn't say

anything. He'd definitely clocked the name 'Will' in the list – and realised that was the person he'd met the day before.

Millie looked across to Nicola, wondering if she'd missed anyone.

'Matty always looked older than he was,' Nicola said. 'He got some cider at the Spar. He never had a problem getting served'

Millie wondered if Nicola was going to continue. She didn't remember the cider but she did know he'd bought a bottle of vodka for them to share.

Guy was nodding along. 'You were one of the bandstand kids,' he said.

'What's that?' Millie asked.

'Every council meeting I ever went to had people complaining about kids drinking on either the bandstand in the park, or the cenotaph.'

'We did a fair bit of drinking at the cenotaph, too,' Millie replied. It didn't sound too clever nowadays, though she doubted there was a single war memorial in the country that hadn't had teenagers sitting on it while sharing a two-litre bottle of White Lightning. It was almost a British tradition. What better way to honour the fallen soldiers than by hurling back, and then possibly up, the cheapest cider going?

Nicola was back to staring out the window.

'Do you remember the park that night?' Millie asked.

A shake of the head. 'Not really. Only the cider and I think I shared a ciggie with Matty. We chatted. The usual.'

That was the problem for Millie when it came to remembering the middle part of that night. All those afternoons and evenings at the park blurred into one. The whole summer, until it culminated in the night she'd never forget.

'I was the first to leave,' Millie said, talking to Guy once more. 'Mum and Dad didn't mind what I got up to, as long as I was home before dark. The sun had gone past the trees and I knew that gave me about twenty minutes to walk home. Nic said she'd walk with me, so we left together...'

Nicola was still staring out the window. A browny-grey rabbit was sitting on its hind legs somewhere towards the middle of the lawn, sniffing the air. The three of them watched it together for a few moments as Millie wondered if Nicola would continue the story. It was hers to tell, after all. When she didn't, Millie continued.

'We were about halfway back to my house,' she said. 'Just past the Fox and Hounds, when Nic said she wanted to go back to the park...'

Millie waited this time, because this was something she couldn't explain.

In the garden, the rabbit was nibbling at the lawn.

The silent hint was eventually taken as Nicola spoke: 'I wondered if Charlie was going to the park after he finished work,' she said quietly. 'I figured someone would've told him where we were, or he'd have guessed anyway. I wanted to see him.'

There was a lengthy quiet after that. Millie watched Guy, who was holding his coffee cup, not drinking.

'I went one way,' Millie said, 'Nic went the other. I got home and went to sleep. It was a normal night for me...'

She looked across to Nicola once more, who was still watching the rabbit. It was at the back of the garden now, sheltered under the hedge.

'I don't remember much of what happened next,' Nicola said. 'I was on my way back to the park and I sort of remember the gates... but maybe I'm remembering when we were there earlier. It's all...' She swirled her hand in the air.

It was Millie who continued. 'When I woke up, I had a text from Nic. We'd only just got mobiles and used to call each other to chat about... everything I suppose. Nothing as well, though. We used to say nothing half the time. We'd be watching the same thing on TV and have our phones there so we'd hear each other laugh at the same time...'

The memory felt so close, so real, that Millie was back in her bedroom, as it was then. She'd be laid on her bed, phone at her ear, *Big Brother* or something like that on the TV. Nicola and her would be watching the live feed of the housemates doing not very much while they also did not very much. Sometimes they just breathed to each other for minutes at a time. All these years later, it felt odd and yet satisfyingly comforting. Who else had there ever been in her life with whom she could do such a thing?

'We had to count how many minutes we used,' Nicola said quietly.

It brought Millie back into the kitchen. She'd somehow forgotten that. There were no unlimited minutes or unlimited texts back then. Everything was paid for. Millie would frequently be over her monthly minutes, leaving her dad to shout about how phones didn't pay for themselves.

'Everyone had Nokias,' Millie said. 'All our texts had to be typed out by pressing the keys two or three times.'

It felt like another world, even though it wasn't *that* long ago. Had life always moved so quickly for people?

She'd momentarily forgotten what she was talking about but then remembered that single text she'd received overnight.

'The text was just a place,' Millie said. 'It said something like, "Past the Kissing Tree, near the field".'

She stopped, trying to remember if that was what it *actually* said. It was so long ago. When she looked out the window, the rabbit had disappeared.

'What does that mean?' Guy asked.

Nicola's eyes were closed.

'I didn't know at the time,' Millie said. 'The Kissing Tree is near the edge of the woods, by that stile which opens onto the big field. The one that's covered in hay at the end of the summer. I think the tree got hit by lightning at some point and it's all hollowed out. People used to go there and, well... kiss.'

Guy had a curious, almost amused, look on his face. 'I guess you learn something every day.'

'I had no idea why she'd texted me that,' Millie said. 'We'd message times to meet, or dumb bits of gossip. There were these pictures you could make out of letters that we'd send and would cost 50p. It was a weird message, so I replied with something like "what do you mean?" Nic's parents were on holiday, so we'd been spending the days at her place. I didn't get a reply, so went over that morning and rang the bell. I'd done it every day that week – but there was no answer that day. I think I texted Alex to ask if he'd seen her – but he hadn't. Nobody had. I was still messaging Nic through the morning, asking where she was, but there was never any reply. Then I read her message back and figured I'd go where it said.'

Nicola had rotated in her chair at some point and was facing the cooker on the other side of the room.

'There was no one there,' Millie continued. 'Not at the Kissing Tree, anyway. It was off the main trail, the sort of place you'd only know if you'd ever been there. When you're there, you can either walk back towards the town, further on towards the cliffs, or over towards the field. So I started walking towards the field and then... I saw her.'

Millie needed a moment for the next bit, even though it still wasn't really her story to tell. So long had passed that it sometimes felt like she'd dreamt it, or watched it on a TV show.

'Nic was tied to a tree,' Millie said. 'Not tied, I suppose. She was facing it and her arms were around the trunk and attached by this set of fluffy pink handcuffs. Like something you'd get on a hen do. She'd, um...'

Nicola picked things up, still facing away from them. 'Someone had cut my hair,' she said. 'They left it on the ground around me. Chunks of it. They took my shoes and my phone...'

She tailed off, then spun and looked to Guy. 'They didn't do... *that*.'

She bit her lip as Guy gave a gentle nod to let her know he understood what '*that*' meant.

'Nic never sent the text,' Millie said. 'Whoever left her in the woods wanted me to find her. We didn't have passcodes or facial ID then. Whoever took her phone either knew to message me, or contacted the person at the top of her texts list.'

Guy looked from Nicola to Millie. 'I'm not sure I understand...?'

Millie waited for Nicola – who had her elbows on the table and her head in her hands.

'That's pretty much it,' Millie said. 'There were keys on the ground, close to Nic's hair. I unlocked the handcuffs and... we don't know a lot more than that.'

Millie tailed off and, for a second, she was back in the woods. Nicola was wide-eyed, blinking and relieved. Millie herself felt as if she was living through a movie, like she'd seen what was happening, rather than experienced it.

A blink and she was back: 'I asked Alex what happened in the park the night before,' Millie added. 'After me and Nic had left. This was before we were married, before we were even going out. He said that people started drifting off in ones and twos. Some old guy came and said he'd call the police if they didn't leave. Nicola never made it back to the park after we'd gone our separate ways. Everyone said more or less the same thing. Jenny – Genevieve – said she and Rach left right after us. Matty left with Will. Charlie never went to the park. He headed home after work. That was it. And then Nic didn't want to make a big deal of it...'

Millie looked to her old friend, whose face was still cupped in her hands. She understood the decision then – although, as time had passed it seemed less real.

In a small town, nobody wanted to stand out. Millie knew

that better than anyone after her very public divorce from Alex, and then her parents' deaths. If Nicola had been known as the girl who was left in the woods, it was something that would live with her forever. She'd have to escape the town because she'd never escape the way people saw her.

'Someone must have noticed your hair...?' Guy said. It was kindly and inquisitive.

'Mum and Dad were in France,' Nicola replied. 'They went every year – but this was the first time they'd left me alone. I didn't like it there because there was nobody my age and I didn't speak French. I think they'd been sick of me moaning the year before. I begged them to let me stay home by myself – and they said it was fine but that I had to look after the house and all that...'

She tailed off momentarily and glanced to Millie.

'I didn't want them suddenly thinking I needed supervision all the time,' Nicola added. 'I didn't want people *knowing*. I didn't want to be *that* girl. I bought a new phone and got a new number. I wanted to forget.'

She turned to Millie, who took the cue.

'We told everyone that I helped her cut her hair,' Millie said. 'She wanted to try something new and we were drunk, so it went wrong. Whoever *actually* cut it, didn't shave it all off. They cut out chunks and left them on the ground – so it wasn't an obvious lie. There was a hairdresser in town who tidied everything up, even though it was short. There were kids in our sixth form who had mohicans, so it wasn't that out of place.'

Guy nodded along. 'I'm really sorry for what happened to you.'

Nicola mirrored him, nodding along herself. What else was there to say? They sat quietly for a little while, thinking through it all. For Millie it was a moment in time that was largely someone else's. It wasn't something that had specifically happened to her.

After a few moments, Nicola scraped her chair back and crossed to the sink. She crouched and opened the lower cupboard door, then strained to the back. There was the sound of things being shuffled around, and then Nicola stood with the Converse in her hands. She placed them on the table in front of Guy.

'These were the shoes I was wearing that night,' she said. 'Somebody must have taken them when they tied me up. I've not seen them in twenty years – but, yesterday, someone left them hanging on the line.'

EIGHT

Guy looked at the shoes, though he didn't reach for them. The red ink of the heart was facing him as he pursed his lips. For the first time since Millie had known him, he seemed genuinely unsure what to do.

'Who knows what happened to you?' he asked.

'Just us,' Nicola said, nodding to Millie. 'And you. And whoever left me in the woods.' She stopped and picked up the shoe with the heart on the side. When she turned it over, the sole was dark with decades-long dirt. 'I sometimes dream about it,' she added. 'I try to remember what happened after Mill and I separated. I think I remember the corner, by the park, and the gates. But I'd drunk so much and then...' She glanced up to Millie. 'I thought I got back to the park but I don't remember and nobody Mill asked said I was there.'

It felt a little too definitive. 'I didn't ask outright,' Millie said. 'Nic didn't want people knowing, so I couldn't go up to our friends and say, "What happened to Nic that night?" I was careful. I asked what happened after we left, that sort of thing – but I never *specifically* asked if Nic got back to the park. Nobody said they saw her after we left the first time.'

Millie realised she knew what Guy was thinking. It was the same thing she'd thought at the time but had never been brave enough to say out loud. She certainly hadn't said it to Nicola. Cutting someone's hair, stealing their phone and shoes, then leaving them in the woods was the cruellest of pranks. But it wasn't the sort of thing a stranger did to an unknown victim – especially not in a place like Whitecliff. Whoever left Nicola there didn't want her to die, else they wouldn't have texted her location to Millie. There was a good chance that whoever did it knew both Nicola and Millie.

Millie hadn't dared say it back then. She hadn't wanted to upset Nicola. They were about to go into their final year at college anyway and those friendship groups were shifting. Some were readying themselves for university; others were already looking for jobs. Millie figured someone might own up to it one day, though they never had.

If Nicola had thought the same, she'd never said it to Millie. Their deliberate ignorance had provided a degree of bliss to them both. They could pretend it had never happened, or that it had been done by a stranger who offered no threat. Months passed, then a year. Then another. It never went away, though they also never talked about it.

And then they stopped being friends anyway.

Nicola spoke quietly. 'Matty's dead now,' she said. 'He died a couple of years back in a car crash. He was Charlie's best friend. The best man at our wedding. He married Genevieve about six months after our wedding, and Charlie was his best man.'

It sounded so incestuous. Their friendship group of eight had spawned three marriages: Nicola and Charlie, Matty and Genevieve – plus Millie and Alex. When Millie and Alex had separated, he and Rachel had got together. It was only Will who'd not ended up with one of the others. Millie sometimes wondered if that was normal, or if it was only in a small town that groups of friends all ended up together.

Guy brought them back into the room: 'Did you ever fall out with your friends?' he asked.

Nicola snorted. 'All the time! Especially me and Jenny. Genevieve. She liked Matty but Matty and Charlie both liked me. I wasn't into either of them at the time, not really. Maybe Charlie a bit – but I didn't want *him* to think I was.' She pulled at her hair. 'We fell out over stupid things every day. It all seems so childish now. You think you're in love, then you're convinced you're not. Then you are. Then one boy looks at you the right way and it feels like you're flying. Then a different boy does and you can't make up your mind. It's all so... *intense.*'

She was breathless in the end – but it summed them up well enough, especially when they'd been teenagers. Except for one thing.

'We never *really* argued,' Millie said. 'We hung around and drank cider or vodka. We smoked when it wasn't such a bad thing. Sometimes things got said but nothing big. Nothing to cause... *this.* It was mainly the boys who'd end up half-fighting, half-shouting. Everything was always forgotten the next day.'

Millie looked to Nicola for support, wondering if they saw things the same way. Nicola had returned the shoe to the table and was staring out the window again.

If Millie was honest, she had been more jealous of Nicola than the other girls. It wasn't because she had any particular interest in Matty or Charlie – but she used to wonder why two boys liked *her friend* and not her. What did Nicola have that she didn't? She and Alex hadn't been together then, and she didn't think she even thought of him in that way.

A couple of decades on and it all felt so inconsequential. It was hard to remember quite why those feelings had been so intense.

Nicola suddenly sat up straight, back in the present. 'Charlie can't know any of this,' she said firmly. 'I've never told him. We got together around Christmas that year, a few months after it all happened. He went to uni and we got married after he graduated and came back. If I didn't tell him then, I can't do it now.' She glanced across to the clock on the microwave and then honed in on Guy. 'He's back from his conference tonight and you have to *promise* not to tell anyone.'

'Of course,' Guy replied.

Nicola was suddenly alert and interested. 'Mill reckons you might have some ideas. You might know how to find out who left the shoes...?'

Millie was watching Guy from the other side, trying to tell him telepathically that she hadn't *quite* said that. She'd said she knew someone who *might* be able to help, which wasn't the same thing.

It felt as if he knew that anyway. 'I've got decades of newspaper archives at my house,' he said, talking to Nicola. 'I know a lot of people around town, across every generation, that lives here. I probably know the person who organised that battle of the bands and, if it was in the function room on the pier, I definitely know who would have rented the room. I'll be discreet and I can ask around – but I don't want to promise anything. If I'm honest, if you're trying to find out who left those shoes, the best bet might be to ask your neighbours about whether they have security cameras facing the street...'

Something crossed Nicola's face and it looked to Millie as if this was the first time the thought had occurred. There was something there.

'I wouldn't know what to say to them,' Nicola replied.

'Maybe say you saw someone hanging around?' Millie said. 'If someone got into your garden, it's not even a lie.' A pause. 'Do you have any cameras?'

That got a shake of the head. 'We've never needed anything like that.' Nicola glanced up to the microwave clock once more and then to the trainers that were still on the table. 'I've got to get ready for work,' she said. And then, almost as an unrelated afterthought: 'I just want it all to go away.'

NINE

Guy stopped when he reached his car, which was parked a little along the street from Nicola's home. He scanned the nearby houses, which Millie had been doing as they'd walked. She'd not seen any obvious cameras outside – but that didn't mean some of Nicola's neighbours didn't have a doorbell cam, or something similar.

'This is a curious one,' Guy said.

Millie leaned on the back of the car, wringing her top. It was a warm day, with the sun searing thought the hazy blue. There would often be a cooling breeze from the sea but not today.

'I think about it sometimes,' Millie said, 'about finding her and not understanding what had happened. I assumed we'd go to the police but she wanted to go home and have a bath. I tried to sort out her hair but only made it worse.'

Guy hmmed for a moment and she thought he was going to ask why they hadn't gone to the police. Perhaps why they hadn't told *anyone*.

Except it hadn't been Millie's decision to make. If Nicola wanted to keep it quiet, what sort of friend would do the opposite? Plus, now more than ever, Millie really did understand the reason for keeping something between them. It wasn't fun to have people staring in the street, or whispering as they went past.

'I'll do a bit of digging,' Guy said. 'It won't be easy but you know what year it was, so I can look for anything from August and see what's in the archives. I suppose I don't really know what you're asking me to do...'

It felt like a question.

'I'm not sure I do, either,' Millie replied. 'Perhaps there's something obvious from that week that we didn't know about at the time? Or there was a different event on the same night...? I don't know...' A pause and then: 'I guess we want to know who did it...'

Guy seemed to accept that as enough of an explanation as he patted the top of his car. 'I'll let you know if anything comes up.'

Millie thanked him and stepped away. Then, even though he didn't need to know, she found herself telling him anyway. 'I'm going up to the squat,' she said. 'I'll talk to Will and see if he remembers anything else from that night.'

Guy's eyes narrowed a little. 'I'm not your dad...' He left that sentence where it was, then added: 'Be careful. I've seen things like this before. All that talk of "war". If that's what they want, and the bailiffs show up knowing that, they'll probably get one.'

Millie had been thinking much the same thing – except that wasn't the whole picture.

'Maybe they're right?' she said. 'Maybe there *are* too many rich people buying houses they don't live in? Maybe they *should* build cheaper houses for locals?'

She wasn't sure what she believed but Guy simply shrugged. 'People made those exact same arguments thirty years ago. Probably thirty years before that. I think it's a bigger problem than a local council can deal with. Perhaps a bigger problem than any local community can handle.'

'Maybe that's why they're right to take a stand?' Millie replied.

Guy bit his lip and Millie wasn't sure if it was to stop himself saying something. 'If you want to write something, you know I'll publish,' he said. 'But I don't think this is my battle any more. You have to learn to pick them at some point.'

Millie didn't know what to say in return. It felt like he was probably right – but she really couldn't leave things with Will the way they had been. She'd have to tell him that Guy wasn't going to write something, no matter how much Will tried to blackmail her regarding Pidge and what he thought he knew.

'Are you still coming tomorrow?' she asked.

'To the party? Of course! Shall I bring Barry? I know you said Eric loves him…?'

Millie thought for a moment. 'Dogs are a point of contention in that house at the moment – so maybe not.'

Guy said that was fine and added that he'd be in contact if he found anything he thought she needed to know – and then they went their separate ways.

Millie was still sitting in her car a few doors down when Nicola pulled off her own drive and headed to work. Millie watched the vehicle disappear around the corner, wondering why this was happening now. Holding onto someone's shoes for the best part of twenty years was strange enough as it was – but the timing of returning them felt random. Nobody was seemingly asking for anything from Nicola and there was no outward and obvious threat. There was no ransom, no blackmail attempt. There might be something implied but it was hard to know what to make of it all.

She'd told Guy she was heading up to the squat to talk to Will but Millie was barely at the end of the street when she decided she couldn't face him. That snide mention of Pidge was meant to unsettle her, which it had – but she didn't want him to know that.

Instead, she drove the other way, heading into the centre of Whitecliff. It was a place she rarely visited in the middle of summer, let alone since her very public divorce and the death of her parents.

Whitecliff in August was different to any other time of year. Holidaymakers packed themselves into the caravans and chalets outside the town, while the hotels and bed and breakfasts were rammed for a minimum of three months. What she hadn't realised until she began walking around was that the bedlam gave her an anonymity she hadn't had for a while. Nobody bothered to give her sideways glances, because the pavements were so packed that people were only interested in getting themselves from one place to the next. Not only that, locals were vastly outnumbered by visitors who had no idea who she was, or why she might be recognised.

The high street was bulging. Tourists were wearing very little in the way of clothing and there were red-raw shoulders, pasty strap lines, and uncovered hairy bellies in all directions.

Onto the main promenade, near the pier, and the smell of chips and vinegar was almost overpowering. People were clasping ice creams and occasional pints, weaving around street sellers trying to shove cheap sunglasses into their hands. A woman was bellowing after her husband, telling him he was walking too quickly – but he was already off down the road, hands in pockets. In the meantime, a small group of lads in matching bucket hats were walking in the road, waving angry hands towards the cars that were weaving around them.

The hordes of people took up the entire width of the pavement on both sides of the street, with even more forced to walk in the road. Millie snaked her way through the chaos until she was at the entrance to the pier. She had set off without much of a plan but, as soon as she'd arrived in the centre, she knew where she was going.

The arcade at the front of the pier dinged and fizzed in much the same way that Millie remembered from her youth. The sparkly lights from the inside barely cut through the brightness of the day but, come night-time, they'd burn into the darkness and be seen from the highest point of the cliffs above.

She passed the arcade and continued along the pier, narrowly avoiding a wayward stick of candy floss that a girl was waving around as if it was a magic wand.

The ballroom halfway along the pier had been refurbished around ten years before. That's where the battle of the bands had been held, back in its grungier days. There was a series of posters across the walls, largely advertising cover bands, or shows from local comedians that were probably getting away with the same set they'd been doing for thirty years.

Millie stopped for a while and scanned the posters, not quite sure what she was looking for. It might have been more a feeling than anything else. Something that could trigger those memories of the night they'd all been on the pier, watching Matty's band.

Past the ballroom was a cluster of small booths, with rows of benches in front. There was a puppet show happening – but there was none of the Punch and Judy that used to be advertised when Millie was young. Instead there was something called Alice and the Tiger, which had a captive audience of thirty or so children. There were parents at the back of the benches, almost all on their phones, and Millie found herself slotting in to the side of them. She watched as puppet Alice tricked the tiger into eating her wicked godmother, which got a cheer from the children and a couple of sideways glances from the parents.

Then Millie remembered the last time she'd been on the pier. It had been with Eric a few months before her marriage had fallen apart. She'd brought him to town and he'd wanted to watch the puppet show. They had sat and watched something about a frog and a footballer, with a plot that Millie couldn't remember but that definitely included a helicopter puppet.

She was lost in those thoughts of Eric and a time when she could see him every day when she realised the show was over. A few adults were arriving back with coffees or bottles of pop, as puppet Alice told the kids that a collection bucket was going around. There were a series of reluctant reaches into pockets, plus a couple of conversations about 'not carrying cash'. Most seemed to drop something in as the bucket made its way around the crowd as the audience drifted back towards the arcade.

As the crowd thinned, there was a flutter of a curtain next to the booths, and then a sweaty woman appeared. Her brown hair was in a tight ponytail, which she flipped from side to side as she hovered in front of a fan, letting it blow the back of her neck. She grabbed the collection bucket and started sorting through it, before giving a stiff shrug to the young man who'd started the collection.

'Tight lot today,' she said.

'They were saying you need a card machine,' he replied.

That got a roll of the eyes before the woman noticed Millie was hovering behind the benches. She squinted at first and then stood, stepping away from the fan and wafting a hand in front of her face.

'Why are you here?' she asked, talking to Millie.

'Can I buy you lunch?' Millie asked. 'Old times' sake.'

Genevieve – Jenny – raised a sceptical eyebrow. All these years on and Millie still felt as if she was in the judgemental shadow of someone she barely knew.

There was a moment in which it felt as if Genevieve was going to tell her to get lost but, after a second or two, she shrugged. 'Fine. But I'm picking the place and I'm not queueing.'

TEN

Genevieve was an expert at negotiating crowds. She weaved and ducked around families and groups with the calm prowess of a veteran ninja. Albeit one who was sweating profusely, carrying a backpack full of puppets, and muttering a string of swear words under her breath. Millie was sometimes at her side, sometimes a few steps behind. She marvelled at the guile of the woman who slotted seamlessly from the pier, across three roads, past all the tourist traps, and down an alley into Whitecliff's inner sanctum.

They ended up two or three streets away from the bustle, inside a sandwich shop slotted between a hairdresser on one side and a vintage clothes shop on the other. Genevieve waved at the owner as she entered and then pointed at an empty table, before being given the nod. It all happened so quickly that Millie was in the seat opposite before she properly knew where they were. A huge menu board was across the counter, with a lengthy sandwich list written in multicoloured letters on the dark background. A few of the other tables had one or two people sitting at them – but the café was more than half-empty.

Millie started to scan the board as Genevieve shrugged the backpack away and rubbed at her shoulders.

'Matty's cousin is the girl behind the counter,' Genevieve said.

Millie could see the resemblance now she knew. Matty had sandy hair, brown eyes and a resting amused face – as if he was always on the brink of laughing about something. The young woman had longer hair but the eyes were the same, and so was the sense that she'd just been told a joke.

'The turkey and ham is good,' Genevieve said. 'They do something with the mustard, assuming you eat meat nowadays.'

Until she'd said it, Millie had forgotten that she went through a vegetarian phase when she was a teenager. Someone on the high street had given her a flyer about how pigs and cows were killed – and she'd stopped eating meat for a few years until gradually falling out of the habit. Or back into the habit, she supposed. Nicola had gone through the same stage and they'd frequently tell their parents they were disgusting for eating meat. That went down as well as any adult would have suspected.

'I'll have a camomile tea with that,' Genevieve added, which reminded Millie that she'd offered to pay.

She was back on her feet, at the counter ordering two of both things, largely for the simplicity.

By the time Millie got back to the table, Genevieve was on her phone. She spoke without looking away from the screen. 'Why are you here?' she asked. 'I've not seen you since Matty's funeral, so I'm assuming you want something.'

Millie started to answer but Genevieve continued talking.

'Still, I guess you've had your own problems since then.'

It was true but sounded harsh, perhaps harsher than she meant, because Genevieve lowered her phone and looked up to Millie.

'I was at your mum and dad's funeral,' she said. 'There were so many people there that I don't think you saw me. I couldn't get into the main church, and was in that alcove bit.'

'I saw you,' Millie said.

Genevieve angled back a fraction. 'Oh...'

'I should've said thanks for coming,' Millie replied. 'It was a long day and there were so many people who wanted to talk to me...'

They sat quietly for a moment, listening to the bustle around them. A woman behind was telling her friend about how her neighbour's son had taken up the drums and that she was thinking of complaining to the council. On the other side, someone's bottle of Pepsi had sprayed across the table and they were busy trying to mop it up with a single napkin.

'I saw Nic this week,' Millie said. 'First time in ages. I also ran into Will by accident. I thought of you and I knew where you worked, so...'

It was true, though not necessarily why Millie was there. Or, perhaps it was? She wondered if she should have kept better friendships over the years. If she had done that, perhaps her life would have been easier when things happened the way they did with her failed marriage.

Genevieve didn't reply at first, not that there was a question. 'Didn't you and Nic fall out?' she asked.

'Yes.'

'You always seemed so tight when we were younger. Always together. I used to see the two of you in the pub long after we'd left school – and then, all of a sudden, it was like you hated each other.'

Millie didn't reply to that. It was more truth. She'd never told anyone why she and Nicola had fallen out and, as far as she was aware, neither had Nicola. It suddenly felt as if they shared too many secrets.

'Did something happen?' Genevieve asked. 'Matty and me used to talk about it. Charlie didn't seem to know either – and he's married to her. If Nic never told him, it must've been bad...'

Millie listened to the woman behind, saying how she didn't buy a house only to end up living next to a Glastonbury stage.

'We fell out,' Millie said.

'But you're friends again now?'

'Maybe...'

Millie was saved by the woman from the counter arriving with two lots of tea. The cups rattled on the saucers as she put them down, next to a teapot that had a pair of bags hanging over the side.

'I figured I'd make you a whole pot, seeing as you're sharing,' the woman said.

Genevieve and Millie each said thanks – but, if Millie hoped the moment was gone, then it was immediately clear it wasn't.

'I always wondered if there was something with her and Alex,' Genevieve said. 'If they'd... you know...'

'You think Nic slept with Alex?'

Genevieve reached for the teapot, lifted the lid and gave the two bags a bit of a dunking. Psychopathic behaviour.

'Did she?' Genevieve asked. 'It'd explain why you two stopped talking.'

'Alex and I weren't even properly together back then.'

'That's not answering the question.'

There was a smirk on Genevieve's lips as she stirred more than one pot.

Millie waited until she looked up. 'They didn't sleep together,' she said.

Genevieve swished the teabags around a few more times and then poured the liquid into both cups. A few drops ended up on her finger and she winced at the heat, before drying her skin on a napkin.

'It would make sense,' Genevieve added, still pushing. 'It

was always Nic who had the boys twisted around her fingers when we were younger. She ended up with Charlie but it could've been any of them.'

They were getting into uncomfortable territory and Millie couldn't quite remember why she'd sought out Genevieve. There was an inevitability that things would end up like this. There was a hostility, too, because Genevieve and Matty had been married – but Genevieve always knew that her husband's first crush was Nicola.

'Weren't you ever jealous?' Genevieve asked.

'Of what?'

'Of her.'

She didn't say 'Nic', or 'Nicola', as if she couldn't quite bring herself to, even after all these years.

'All the boys fancied her,' Genevieve added. 'Even though we were there, too. You, me and Rach. We never caught them looking at us, while pretending to be doing other things. Only her.'

There was a truth there, although one that Millie had long since put to one side. It felt like such a teenage thing to care about.

'I don't remember it like that,' Millie replied, even though it was untrue, and partly because she knew it would annoy Genevieve.

And it did.

'Oh, come on!' Genevieve said.

She'd spoken so loudly that the conversation about drums went momentarily silent.

Genevieve reached for her tea and had a sip while she waited for everyone else to continue their conversations.

'*We* should have been best friends,' she said.

'Huh?'

'It was us in those drama classes when we were kids. *We* did ballet together. But then, as we all fell into our group, it was you and Nic who were always together.'

Millie had somehow forgotten that Genevieve had done many of the same evening classes as her. They *had* been in the same clubs together. They'd not been friends in any way at the time – and they were only marginally closer as they got older and slipped into their group of eight.

She'd never thought of their missed friendship in the way Genevieve described. Perhaps they *would* have made better mates? They certainly had more in common. Millie wondered if Genevieve had been hanging onto such thoughts for all these years.

'She always strung the boys along,' Genevieve said, 'and I wondered if that's why you were friends. If you were there for her cast-offs.'

'It wasn't like that,' Millie said.

'It was. I wasn't even the third wheel. More like the fifth, or sixth. Hanging around and hoping to be noticed.'

The bitterness was impossible to miss.

It felt so... inconsequential. Millie hadn't thought much about being fancied by boys in a long time. A *really* long time. And yet that probably wasn't why Genevieve was annoyed. Not really. It was being left out.

Genevieve patted her forehead with another napkin, dabbing at the sweat that hadn't cleared since she'd got out of the puppet booth.

Before anything else could be added, the server was back with a pair of plates. She put one each in front of them and asked Genevieve how her morning had been. They chatted for a minute or two, until someone else entered the café and headed to the counter.

Once they were alone, Genevieve bit into her sandwich and then nodded towards Millie's, that hadn't yet been touched.

'It's good,' she said.

Millie had a bite herself – and, though Genevieve had been right about something being different with the mustard, Millie wasn't sure she liked it. They sat across from each other, eating slowly and listening to the bustle around them. The woman behind had moved on from complaining about her neighbour to complaining about her son-in-law. He apparently needed to get a better job, which would mean her daughter could give up her job and get pregnant. There was a lot of talk about how she wanted 'grandbabies' and not a lot of talk about whether her daughter wanted to have them.

It was hard for Millie not to remember her mother's delight after Eric was born. She suddenly wanted to visit more often and there were always offers to babysit. There was a time in which it felt as if having a child had brought Millie closer to her parents, her mum in particular. In reality, it was Eric with whom they wanted a relationship.

A good ten minutes had passed since Millie and Genevieve had spoken properly.

'I didn't know you felt like that back then,' Millie said. 'I would've tried to involve you more.'

Genevieve didn't react as she continued chewing her sandwich.

'Things only changed when Nic cut her hair...' She stopped, then added: 'When *you* cut her hair. I always wondered how drunk you had to be to do that. I remember Matty saying she'd had some sort of breakdown when her hair ended up that short.'

There was definite amusement in her voice.

'She didn't have a breakdown,' Millie replied, suddenly feeling defensive over the friend with whom she'd not been close in such a long time.

Millie stuffed the final part of the sandwich in her mouth to stop herself saying anything more. Anything she might regret.

'It's interesting that you came to see me today,' Genevieve said.

'Why?' Millie replied.

'Maybe not *specifically* today – but I always think about us at this time each year. When it's sunny. When the bay is busy. When there are groups of kids hanging around the war memorial and at the park.' Genevieve was looking right at her. Staring through her. 'Is it like that for you?' she added.

There was a sadness there and Millie couldn't hold the stare. It was the sense that, for Genevieve, perhaps those few years of teenage friendship had been the best of her life. That was even if she thought of herself as the fifth or sixth wheel.

'Sometimes,' Millie replied, wishing it wasn't the truth. 'After me and Alex broke up, I thought about those summers a lot...'

Genevieve finished her own sandwich and then dotted her finger around the plate, collecting the final crumbs. 'I always thought it was a bit odd that you and Alex got married,' she said.

It was Millie's turn to stare. 'Why?'

'Because Nic could've had her pick – and she was probably always going to end up with Charlie. I was always into Matty, but you...' She tailed off, then picked it back up: 'I wondered if you were a lesbian for a while. Would've explained why you and Nic were always together. Boys didn't seem to be your thing...'

Millie couldn't stop staring – but it was Genevieve who was now deliberately avoiding it.

'That's a bit direct,' Millie said, although she really meant to say it was a bit rude. It sounded like Genevieve was implying Alex was too good for her. If only she knew the truth about him. Millie had told Guy but barely anybody knew.

'I assumed getting all this out is why we're here,' Genevieve said.

Millie was confused and stumbled over the start of a

sentence or two. 'Me and Alex... it wasn't instant like that. It was gradual. He went to law school and I only saw him a couple of times in the summers. We didn't get together until after...'

It felt as if she was justifying something that didn't need justifying. She and Genevieve *had* been part of the same group and yet seen their friends in totally different ways. Millie hadn't felt left out because she never had been. She hadn't been jealous of Nicola, not really. It wasn't that she had no interest in boys, simply not *those* boys. She also didn't know what Genevieve meant by saying this was the reason for them talking. Alex was nothing to do with it.

'You said you saw Will...?'

Genevieve was talking again, bringing Millie back to the moment.

'He's in a squat up on the hill,' Millie replied. 'They're protesting against eviction. Someone's bought the house but they're refusing to go.'

That got a derisive snort. 'He always was a bit Greenpeace. He used to organise those Vote Green rallies when we were all in sixth form. Then it was pro-marijuana. Then something about the ocean, or cleaning the ocean, or general ocean stuff. I think there was something about saving rhinos in there, too. Maybe koalas? Who knows?'

Somehow the bulk of Will's activism had passed Millie by – even when they'd been part of the same group of friends. She wondered how many other things she'd either forgotten, or never noticed in the first place. Was she that self-absorbed as a teenager? It was beginning to seem like she was.

'When did you last see him?' Millie asked.

'I see him semi-regularly around town. He was with an older woman last time. Heather, or Harriet, or—'

'Hannah,' Millie said.

'Ah, you've met her too. She didn't like him talking to me and seemed a proper horse's-head-in-the-bed-type.' She laughed at her own joke, then added: 'I always thought he'd end up in a commune somewhere, but I guess he's stuck here like the rest of us.'

'Do you really feel stuck?' Millie asked.

Genevieve sighed. 'Dunno. Sometimes. Matty liked being close to his mum and dad, which is why we got a place here. I thought about leaving after his crash.'

She took a breath and, for the first time since they'd started talking, Millie wondered if the brashness was a front. Genevieve was a widow who wasn't even forty. Her husband had got in the car one day and never come home. It was a lot for a person to go through.

'Maybe I should leave Whitecliff?' Genevieve added, a little more quietly. 'We were trying for a baby when he died and I was off work. Afterwards, I couldn't get back into it. I ended up doing this.' She reached for her bag of puppets but didn't pick it up. 'There's not a lot of money in doing shows for three months and then scrabbling around for arts grants the rest of the year. I do a bit of bar work at the Legion, plus I had some shifts at Royal Mail last Christmas. They're always after people for the warehouse.'

There was a definite bleakness about the way she described her life. Millie didn't know what to say, but Genevieve was still going.

'I'm surprised Will stayed,' she added. 'He always seemed the most likely of us to get away.'

'He was the one I knew the least,' Millie replied.

That got a snorted laughter. 'He *hated* you!' Genevieve said.

Millie needed a moment to process that, wondering if she'd misheard. 'What do you mean?'

'Maybe not *you* so much – but he *really* hated Nicola. By default, he didn't like you either. Whenever he got drunk, which was a lot, he'd always end up telling me how Nic would get her comeuppance one day.'

This really was new.

The woman behind was onto complaining about how her husband bought her the wrong bag at the last birthday but Millie wasn't listening any longer.

'What d'you mean?' she asked. 'Comeuppance for what?'

Genevieve held up both her hands, as if she was about to explain how two and two made four. 'How did you not see it? Nic had her pick of the boys and used to flirt all the time with Matty, Charlie and Alex. I don't think she even knew she was doing it half the time – but she *never* showed any interest in Will. Of course he hated her for that. Wouldn't you? He'd always go on about how she thought she was better than anyone else.'

Millie started to reply, then stopped. She'd never seen their group friendship in such a way. Nicola probably had been a bit of a flirt – but that was who she was at the time. The boys in their group liked her – but so did loads of others around the school. Outside of it, too. Millie was convinced there was a teacher or two who had an eye for her as well.

Not to mention Millie's own father...

Millie needed a moment to blink away the thought. 'Did Will ever do anything about it?' she asked.

She wasn't sure what she expected but Millie received something close to derision. 'To Nic? Like what? He was always all talk. Why do you think his campaigns never got anywhere? Why do you think he's still here?'

Millie didn't know how to respond to that. She'd not specifically meant that Will might've left Nicola in the woods that night – but she was learning a lot about her old friendship group, even some things about herself. Little of it was good.

They settled for a moment. Genevieve sank a little lower in her seat, the fight gone.

'Can I ask you something?'

Millie had an inkling of what was to come. People only ever

wanted to ask about two things in her life. What *really* happened to her parents, or—

'What's it like being on the front page?' Genevieve asked.

Millie blinked. That was definitely the second thing. People wanted to know why she'd had an affair that had ended up being revealed so publicly. They wanted to know what it was like to be famous for all the wrong reasons. It was only Guy to whom she'd spilled her secrets about why she'd done it. Nothing was as straightforward as it seemed.

'What do you think it was like?' Millie replied, keeping her voice low and suspecting the women behind were now listening to them. 'I lost my son and husband. I had to move back in with my mum and dad. I lost my job. Everyone was talking about me on Facebook and sending me messages.'

Genevieve's features didn't shift. She probably knew most of that, if not all. 'Someone must have tipped off the paper,' she said. 'I told people that at the time. You obviously didn't mean to get caught, so someone must have told them where to look. It must've been one of your friends, mustn't it? It wouldn't have been his. He's an MP. He has too much to lose.'

There was a lot to take in, not least the implication that he had more to lose than Millie – when it was Millie who'd lost everything. He'd carried on with his job and family as if nothing had happened. But Genevieve was right about the other thing. Millie had no idea who'd tipped off the photographer. There was no way he got the photo of her with Peter Lewis, MP, by accident. No photographer would have cared about an inconsequential politician enough to be following him about. Not unless they already knew what he, what *they*, were up to.

Genevieve was the first person who'd ever brought it up and it was as if she'd reached into Millie's thoughts and found the deepest question, then said it out loud.

'I was just wondering,' Genevieve added.

Millie didn't answer. *Couldn't* answer. The words were

stuck, even if she knew what to say. She wanted to be some-where else and, as she started collecting her things together, Genevieve seemed to catch on.

'Sorry,' she said. 'I didn't mean anything by it.'

Millie swept her phone into her bag. 'Maybe we should do this semi-regularly?' she said, surprising herself as she spoke.

Genevieve clucked her tongue and it felt as if she was about to laugh, or say 'no thanks'.

'Maybe we should?' she replied.

Millie hooked her bag onto her shoulder and stood. They said their goodbyes and there was an awkwardness where Millie wasn't quite sure how to leave things. Should she apologise? Was there anything to apologise for?

In the end, they swapped phone numbers and made vague promises about staying in contact. Millie didn't know if any of that would happen but it was better than making an enemy.

Millie was almost back at her car when she realised the obvious thing she had missed. With all they had talked about, with the way Genevieve had instigated so much of the conversa-tion, it was almost as if she'd expected a visit. *It's interesting that you came to see me today*, she'd said, before switching to add that she thought of the group during the summer. It was almost as if she knew something had happened that would bring at least one of her old friends out to find her.

ELEVEN

Ingrid might have been well into her eighties – but she could certainly shuffle a deck of cards. She flicked them from one hand to another and then riffled the set, before splitting them into two and repeating the process.

The nursing home's rec room was cool as conditioned air blasted through the hallways like a sneeze through a tissue. Despite the heat of the outside, it was so cold that Ingrid was wearing a cardigan over her usual cardigan as she flicked seven cards in Millie's direction.

When Millie checked her hand, there was an ace, four, five, seven, nine, jack and king, all spread across the four suits. Not a lot to work with in a game of rummy.

Ingrid sorted her own hand into some sort of order. She then took a card from the top of the upturned deck, before doing some more rearranging in her hand. The three of diamonds she discarded was of no use to Millie.

'You seem as if you have something on your mind…?' Ingrid said.

'Huh?'

'I've done all the talking – and although I'm happy to tell

you about Elsie's son-in-law having a secret gimp suit hidden at the back of his wardrobe, you seem a bit distant...'

Millie took a card from the deck. It was a useless three of clubs, which she dumped on the pile. She tried to think of a better way to phrase a sentence that wasn't, 'What's it like being old?'

'I've had a lot to think about recently,' she said instead. 'About friends and growing up. How a lot's passed me by. There were eight of us who used to hang around together when we were kids. Six of us coupled up and married. There's one death and one divorce. Even with the divorce, *my* divorce, he's gone straight on to someone else in our group.'

Ingrid picked up Millie's three of clubs and put down the king of clubs in its place. Still no use to Millie.

'When I was young,' Ingrid said, 'you'd meet someone at sixteen or seventeen, and get married. If you didn't have a child on the way by the end of the year, everyone would think there was something wrong with you.'

She nodded at the pile of cards and Millie picked up the queen of hearts, that she kept in place of the seven she'd been holding.

'My gran had these virility potions,' Ingrid added. 'A mix of stuff from the back of her cupboard. God knows what was in them. She made me and my sister drink them on our wedding days – and then every time I saw her after. Tasted like a spoonful of sick. She reckoned it'd get you pregnant.'

'Did it?'

Ingrid picked up the seven, which was annoying, and put down the three of hearts. 'I did get pregnant,' she replied. Millie laughed as Ingrid quickly added: 'I don't think it was the potion, though.'

'Maybe your gran was on to something?' Millie said.

A smirk: 'Luckily, she's not around to hear you say that.

She'd have been injecting you with her home-made Worcester Sauce.'

Millie smiled as they continued to play. Around them, the television blared in the corner. It was permanently set to BBC One and never changed, in an attempt to stop arguments before they began. Switching it to Channel Four would presumably start some sort of war.

Millie had been volunteering at the nursing home for almost two years – and Ingrid was the resident to whom she spoke the most. When she began volunteering, some people she knew would behave as if it was a great act of charity. Especially recently, Millie wondered if the residents got as much from her time with them as she did.

Perhaps sensing there was more on Millie's mind, Ingrid picked up the conversation. 'Did I ever tell you I played tennis?' she asked.

Millie's hand of cards was a disaster. She'd thrown away cards that might have already got her to four of one and three of the other – and was stuck with a hand that was worse than the one with which she'd started.

'No,' she replied.

'I took it up after having my two girls,' Ingrid said. 'My husband wanted me to be a housewife, which I largely was, but Mum would look after the children for a few hours here and there. I lived along the road from a tennis club. I walked past it every day for years and didn't think much about it. I never went in. Then, one day, I decided to see what was there.'

Ingrid picked up the top card, switched it with another in her hand, and then laid down a full run of seven to king. She gave a little smile, as if to tell Millie she'd been playing with her for the past few minutes.

'I didn't have any equipment and no shoes to play in,' Ingrid added. 'The only other woman I saw there gave me a racquet and said I should give it a go – which I did.'

'Were you playing men?'

'Anyone. Sometimes teenagers, sometimes men. The occasional woman, although there weren't many of us. You know those things in your life you can just do? You don't know why, or where it all comes from, but you can just do it? That was me and tennis. I was decent to start with and really good after a while. I'd beaten every other woman at the club – and then I started beating the men, who really didn't like that. One of them was on the committee and, after that year's AGM, there was suddenly a new rule about men and women not being able to play each other.'

Ingrid laughed at that, though there was unquestionably an edge.

'He changed the rules because you beat him?' Millie asked.

'They changed them "for everyone's safety" – but, basically, yes – because I beat him easily.'

'What did you do?'

Ingrid picked up the cards and started shuffling them effortlessly and without looking. Millie wondered if Ingrid had an unmentioned career as a poker hustler that would come out one day.

'Not everyone agreed with the new rules,' Ingrid said. 'One of the members would let me play on the private court at his house. A couple of others would sneak me into the club for games. I once had half a chance to play the qualifiers for Wimbledon – but it didn't come off for various reasons. I was getting a bit older by then and it was one thing to be a woman but another entirely to be a women *in her thirties.*'

She said it as a joke but they both knew it wasn't.

The cards continued to fly between the older woman's fingers. Ingrid sometimes told of her arthritis and the stiffness – but, when there were cards in her hands, she seemed as nimble as a child.

'I guess what I'm saying,' Ingrid added, 'is that when you

think life is one thing, it can still be something else. I was supposed to be a housewife and a mother – and then I was playing tennis against the best people in the area. You don't have to be tied to one set thing. Friends don't have to be friends forever. Husbands don't have to be husbands forever. If you're unhappy, you can try to change things.' A pause and Millie felt Ingrid weighing her up, perhaps considering whether to finish the thought. 'Sometimes you have to be ruthless in letting go of things... or in trying to keep hold of what you have.'

Ingrid had put down the deck of cards without dealing any.

Millie looked towards the corner of the room, where a handful of other residents were staring at phones or iPads, while the TV played above them. The room was bright with sun but cold from the air conditioning. The chill was suddenly biting.

'Do I look unhappy?' Millie asked.

'I'd never say such a thing... but you should probably get more practice at cards if you ever want to beat me.'

It came with a chuckle that Millie couldn't avoid joining.

'Any more secrets?' Millie asked. 'Were you actually Home Secretary in the seventies? One of Concorde's first pilots?'

That got a laugh.

'Yes to both,' Ingrid replied. She yawned and something cricked as she stretched her arms. 'I'll tell you about those another day – but I think I fancy a lie-down, if you don't mind.'

Millie obviously didn't.

She helped Ingrid back to her room and then returned to the rec room and continued in a loop; saying hellos, fetching drinks, playing the odd game and offering a small amount of tech support for how to turn off the sound on someone's iPad.

Before she knew it, hours had passed and Millie said goodbye to Jack, who still had a few hours of his actual *paid* shift, before she returned to her car.

The unknown number in her phone still had no name

attached, so Millie corrected that by adding it to her contacts, along with the name 'Nic'. She tapped out a simple text.

> How are you?

It was only as she pressed 'send' that Millie realised it was the first time she'd sent something like that to Nicola in the best part of fifteen years.

Three dots appeared and then a series of short replies landed.

> Feeling better!

> Thanks for asking

> Charlie got back ok

> How ru?

Millie was considering how to respond, or whether to reply at all, when her phone began to ring. It wasn't Nicola, it was Guy. He was always more of a caller than a texter – and most of those calls came from his landline.

'Have you got photos of you and your friends from back in the day?' he asked.

He also wasn't one for hellos.

'Somewhere,' Millie replied. 'Why?'

'Because I've found someone who remembers you and your friends – and I think he might have something we need to hear.'

TWELVE

Guy's Volvo was already parked in front of the detached house on the corner as Millie pulled up behind it.

The house was the sort of place that didn't get built in modern times. Instead there'd be three or four new-builds on the same plot, each with tiny patches of grass at the back. That and some sort of critical plumbing issue that would end up with everything being knocked down again after a decade or two.

As it was, the giant front lawn was more dried mud than it was grass. An old washing machine was leaning against the fence, with piles of mangled metal blocking what would have been a path to the side of the house. It was across the road from the park gates, with three storeys – and a top window that was probably tall enough to see over the trees into the park itself.

Guy was waiting in his car and clambered out when he saw Millie. She nodded towards the house. 'We all used to think a witch lived there,' Millie said.

'Not quite,' Guy replied. 'Augustus has lived in that house his entire life. His dad bought the patch of land sometime in the nineteen-twenties.'

'Augustus?'

That got a shrug. '*Millicent?*'

She laughed. 'Touché.'

'His dad was also called Augustus,' Guy continued. 'Must be a family thing. I've no doubt that, if he had children, any sons would have the same name.'

They turned together to take in the house. The trees from the park were casting a shadow across much of the front. It looked dark and mysterious in the gloom, especially as the rest of the street was bathed in glorious sun.

'The thing about Augustus,' Guy added, 'is that he *really* enjoys the quiet – and he really *doesn't* like children.'

A vague thought swirled through time. 'Is he the man that used to threaten to call the police about the noise?' Millie asked. She remembered the haggard bloke in a massive coat that would come into the park most evenings and start flailing his arms around. He'd make far more noise than they ever did as he shouted about 'police' and 'the law' and 'you lot'. She vaguely recalled him saying he was going to contact the Queen if they didn't shut up and go home.

'He also used to come to the news office every week and demand we do something, because the police weren't bothered,' Guy replied. 'We used to make him a cup of tea and let him sit in the corner and rant, to get it out of his system. It wasn't only kids in the park. He had it in for British Telecom, the water company and Richard Branson, for some reason.' That came with a little half-smile. 'Every town has an Augustus.'

Millie nodded to the house: 'And he lives here...?'

'Correct. We swap Christmas cards every year and he writes me a long letter to say who's wronged him over the previous twelve months. They're quite enlightening, really. I've got them going back years.'

'Are you friends?'

Guy took a step towards the house. 'In a manner of speaking. I've found it's best not to burn too many bridges, if you can avoid it. If indulging his letters and sending him a Christmas card once a year means he's willing to help when it's needed, that seems like a small price to pay...?'

It sounded so obvious when he said it like that. Just as Millie had been wondering about her own friendships, Guy had explained things as if it was simple.

She was still thinking on that as they headed towards the large house. Voices were carrying on the breeze and Millie turned, almost expecting to see someone walking at her side. It took her a moment to realise the sound was coming from the park. Perhaps Augustus really *did* have a point all those years?

When they entered the garden at the front, Millie realised there was even more clutter than she'd first seen. As well as the rusting washing machine and the pile of scrap metal, there was a pair of crusty lawnmowers, what looked like the front half of a shopping trolley, and two fat-backed old televisions, with the screens busted. There was plenty more, far too much to take in, as Guy knocked on the door. A croaky 'I'm coming' came from the other side and then the door squeaked open.

The smell hit Millie almost immediately and she had to turn away to get a breath. It was like being punched by whatever lived at the bottom of a bin. Even Guy gasped and took a small step backwards.

When Millie felt able to turn, a short, old man was on the doorstep. His grey beard was at his chest and it was impossible not to notice the sheer amount of ear hair sprouting sideways from his head. It looked like stuffing being squeezed from a cushion.

'How are you doing?' Guy asked, as if talking to an old friend – which Millie supposed he sort of was.

Augustus eyed Millie with suspicion and then focused back on Guy. He was wearing a heavy tweed coat that came down to his knees. Millie was almost certain it was the same one she'd seen him in twenty and more years before when he'd come to the park to complain about the noise.

'This is Millie,' Guy continued. 'Like I said on the phone, we wanted to talk to you about the park and the noise. About everything you've gone through over the years.' He paused and gulped. 'I wondered if we could come in...?'

Millie was suddenly unsure about the whole endeavour. The smell was already bad enough that she could taste it.

Augustus glanced to Millie once more and then stepped back into the house. The door closed momentarily and then almost immediately swung back open. It was dark inside the house but the smell was so strong that Millie felt strangled by it. Beyond Augustus were mounds and mounds of boxes and various other items that were hard to make out. There were so many things that Millie couldn't see any actual route through the hall. The junk was floor to ceiling – and the only parts of the ceiling she could see were crusted with mould.

It was like someone had fly-tipped a house inside another house.

Guy was clearly thinking along the same lines as Millie. He abruptly changed tack and angled back towards the outside. 'Maybe it would be better to walk around the park?' he said. 'It'll be easier to place things then...?'

He took another step backwards, making it clear enough what he thought.

Augustus didn't seem too fussed. He mumbled something Millie didn't catch, moved back onto the step, and closed the door behind him. He fished around in the coat pockets for a key that ended up being inside one of the inner pockets. It was attached to a long piece of string that appeared to be tied around the man's waist.

The three of them crossed the road together, heading through the tall gates and onto the cracked, uneven, tarmac path that ringed the park. Guy led the way, taking them off towards the tennis courts. It was early in the evening but the sun was still high. A series of games of football were happening across the near side of the grass. On the furthest side, couples and families had laid down their towels to claim their small part of the town. On the actual courts, a dad was on one side, playing tennis against what were likely his two daughters on the other. As one of them served underarm to him, he thrashed the ball through the centre of them. As it hammered into the cage at the back, he called 'love–forty', before taking his place on the other side of the line.

A husband and wife pair of joggers clip-clopped past them as Millie, Guy and Augustus reached the far end of the courts. The woman was upright with a bottle in her hand; the man had a hunched back and a drenched T-shirt. He seemed fully on the brink of ruin at keeping up with the pace.

Guy and Augustus were doing much of the talking, which was fine by Millie. Augustus had a near encyclopaedic memory for everything that had happened in the park over the past seven decades or so. He pointed towards where he said there used to be an old toilet block, which was apparently pulled down in the eighties. He went on about the running track that was replaced, the bandstand that burned down. He talked about the annual fetes and the celebrities he'd met. Bobby Davro once shook his hand, apparently. He'd also handed Gail from *Coronation Street* a portrait he'd done of her that sounded borderline terrifying.

By the time they reached the current bandstand, it was unsurprising to see a group of young people spaced around it. Their music was playing quietly through a Bluetooth speaker and there was no sign of cigarettes or booze on show. That all gave Millie a *kids today* moment of wondering if things really had changed so fast.

Augustus told them about something he described as a 'full-on rave' that involved the police turning up with riot shields and a helicopter. Millie wasn't convinced but Guy nodded along, even as Augustus predicted that it would definitely happen again.

'I kept saying it would happen,' Augustus warned. 'Did anyone listen? No.'

One of the things Millie had learned from Guy was that if she wanted information from someone, the best thing to do was let them speak as much as possible. They would get there in the end as all people really wanted, according to Guy, was to be listened to.

And so listen they did.

On a second loop, Augustus told them how men used to meet at the toilet block every night, so he'd got that shut down. He was almost on to the next complaint as Millie cut in, unable to stay quiet any longer.

'How?' she asked.

Augustus had seemingly forgotten she was there as he stopped on the path and turned to look at her. 'How what?'

'How did you shut that down?' she asked.

'I'd wait in there with a camera, wouldn't I?'

He made it sound as if it was the most natural of behaviours. That anyone would have done the same.

'Doesn't that mean you were one of the men in the toilets you were trying to stop...?' Millie asked.

Augustus coughed and blustered as he tried to explain that, though he had been in the toilets, he wasn't *actually* in the toilets. Even though he definitely was.

On another day, Millie wouldn't have let it go but Guy caught her eye and raised a single eyebrow. *Not now.*

Millie shut up after that, as Augustus pointed to various places around the park where he'd popped kids' footballs with a knife he used to carry.

'Do you know what happened?' he said. 'Someone reported

me! The police questioned *me* for carrying a knife! Can you believe it?'

Millie certainly could believe it – but she said nothing.

Guy tried to steer the conversation but they were soon talking like old men in a pub about how more bobbies were needed on the beat and things like that. Augustus was one step away from lurching on to how hanging should be brought back when Guy finally got him on subject.

'Has it *always* been noisy?' he asked.

Millie could almost hear the *ding-ding-ding* from Augustus as they reached his favourite topic.

'Always!' he declared. 'You used to be able to clip kids round the ear back in the day but not any more. There was a time when you could call the police and they'd send someone out – but that's stopped too. The chief of police once gave me his home number and said I should call if I had concerns. I did that a few times but then there was some sort of problem with his phone and I couldn't get through after that.'

Millie suppressed the snigger.

'You must have chased off a lot of troublemakers over the years...?' Guy said.

'Hundreds. *Thousands*. I never forget a face. Told you that on the phone, didn't I?'

Millie wondered if he remembered hers from the times she'd been sitting on the bandstand with her mates. Or if he knew her anyway? Enough people around the town did.

'I learned that at the beginning,' Augustus was saying. 'The police would come round and want a description, so I taught myself to remember what everyone looks like.'

He tapped his forehead and, as Millie realised Guy was looking to her, she knew it was time. She took out her phone and found the photo of which she'd taken a picture before coming out. It was of the eight of them, taken by someone she didn't know, maybe a month or so before the battle of the bands.

They were on a wall somewhere that she didn't recognise but was probably near the college.

Millie had been in a period of growing her hair – although her dress sense was borderline deranged. Why was everything they wore back then so big? Why were there so many rips? Why were *dungarees* a good idea? She was sure there were mirrors in her house, so what happened?

There were so many questions but she showed Augustus the photo anyway and asked if he remembered any of them.

Augustus went through what seemed like all his pockets until he found a pair of glasses. One of the arms was held on with a piece of Blu-tack that he rearranged as he put them on his head. It felt as if he wanted to take her phone but Millie clasped onto it as he jabbed a finger towards Matty. There was an arc of filth wedged until his nail.

'That one I do,' he said. 'Used to see him here all the time. Matthew-something. A very rude young man with a foul mouth.'

Millie could definitely see why he thought that. Of them all, Matty was definitely the one most likely to stand up to an adult. His choice of language ranged from industrial to sailor when he wanted. He'd been fearless but reckless – and it had been impossible for Millie not to wonder if that's what had led to him being the one who died in a car crash. Of their eight, if it had been anyone who'd lost control on a bend, Millie would've gambled everything she owned on it being Matty.

Augustus was still looking at the photo when Guy spoke. 'Do you remember the battle of the bands that used to happen each year?' Guy asked. 'It was always the last Saturday in August.'

Augustus looked away from the phone. 'Not my thing. Too loud.'

'But you do remember them?'

'Course I do. I was ready 'cos they'd all come up the hill and create a right racket after.'

'What do you mean by "ready"?' Millie asked.

He looked at her as if she'd asked what came after the letter 'A'. He had a way of making it seem that every crazy thing he thought, said or did was the most natural way of doing things. That all the other people were the nutty ones.

'Ready with my camera,' he said. 'Took it everywhere back then. I remember a face but the police can't argue with evidence.'

Millie knew the answer before she asked. She'd seen his house and the tiniest fraction of what was inside. 'Do you still have the photos?'

'Of course. I never throw anything out. You never know when the police might want to round up some of this lot.'

THIRTEEN

There was no avoiding Augustus's house now. No way of preparing for it, either. He led Millie and Guy the rest of the way around the park and then back over the road to where he lived.

The noise here was unquestionably loud; a mix of voices and music that had felt like background when they'd been in the park but was now dominant. Something about the breeze, or the angle of the trees, seemed to send all the noise careering towards the house.

Augustus fiddled through his pockets once more, looking for his key before finding it in the same place he had first time around. It was still on the string, still tied around his waist, and still in that inside pocket as he stretched the cord and unlocked the front door. Not that Millie could imagine anyone wanting to rob him. Where to even begin?

Guy's place was messy with all the newspapers, notepads and other clutter – but there was at least some degree of order to it. The smell of old paper wasn't unpleasant and, on occasion, Millie even found it satisfying.

None of that was true of Augustus's house.

Millie almost gagged as she followed Guy and Augustus over the threshold. When she was a child, she had once found a dead badger in the road – and the smell had never left her. Augustus's place was similar. A haunting, cloying stench that hit the back of the throat and burrowed until there was nothing else.

The hall was wall-to-wall, floor-to-ceiling junk. There were a pair of bicycle wheels, some table legs, at least six fans that didn't look like they worked, cushions, packs of printer paper, a pile of empty milk cartons, coat hangers – plus dozens of other things she couldn't identify.

She held her hands high, desperate not to actually touch anything as Augustus showed them what he called 'the path'. It wasn't really a path, more trampled ground. As they moved, Augustus seemed desperate to tell them how useful it all was. He claimed the bike wheels were the same type that won the Tour de France at some point in the eighties – although, from the way they were bent, it didn't seem as if they had been much used any time recently, especially with no sign of a frame on which to put them.

She wondered what kind of life it was to live alone in such a way. Whether a person wanted to be helped, or if they even knew they had a problem.

Not that there was time to say such a thing.

Augustus was busy telling Guy how he had a matching set of table legs to the ones they angled around, although there was no mention of an actual table.

Millie followed the two men over to a low table in what would have once been a kitchen. She took one look at the black ceilings and forced herself not to look up again. Not that down was much better. There were mounds of old cereal boxes, plus cartons, plastic bottles, wrappers, packets and everything else that belonged in a bin.

Mercifully, the kitchen window was open, which provided at least some respite from the smell.

Millie tried to find a spot to stand that wasn't on top of something and, as she looked towards the cereal boxes for a second time, she noticed the nibbled edges.

She shuddered and tried to get Guy's attention. They had to get out.

But Guy was not paying attention to her. He was acting as if he'd walked into a house like any other. He was busy agreeing with Augustus' lunacy that, yes, those crooked and useless bike wheels might be good for winning a race forty years after they were new.

Augustus was in the corner, close to the fridge that was humming like a cow-sized bee. He reached onto a shelf and pulled down a stack of tins that had 'Danish Cookies' written on the side. The sort of thing that cost a fiver before Christmas and 99p from the moment supermarkets reopened afterwards.

There were at least forty of them but Augustus knew precisely what he was after as he pinged the lid from one of the tins and put it down in the sink. It was there, or on a pile of junk.

He passed Guy a clear bag that had a series of six by four photographs inside. The sort of thing that Boots used to develop in an hour.

'That's July 30, 2005,' Augustus said proudly.

Guy took the bag and unclipped the top, before flitting through the photos so that Millie could see. The quality looked like the pictures had been taken on a cheap disposable camera. She wondered if Augustus would hide in the bushes to take his shots.

As far as she could tell, it was a bunch of normal-looking kids hanging around the bandstand chatting. There were forty or fifty photos in total, none of which showed anything more offensive than someone who was probably underage necking a bottle of Bulmer's.

Augustus was still hunting through his tin, as he took back the initial bag of photos and passed across another. 'May 28, 2002,' he said. 'Was hot that day.'

He spoke with such pride and Guy didn't acknowledge the clear madness as he took the second set. 'Battle of the bands stopped a bit before that,' Guy said. 'I was wondering if you have any of Matthew…?'

There were more tins, more bags of photos, more dates, more years. Augustus was handing them over, even though they were outside the timeframe in which they were interested. They were trophies to him. Prized pieces that he wanted to show off now someone had finally shown an interest. Guy went through a few, seemingly to be polite, but there was little difference between any of the scenes. Millie recognised a couple of people from the photos. The odd couple from the year or two above, more from the year or two below. Normal teenagers doing normal things while not knowing some creepy hoarder was hiding in a bush taking their photo.

There were boys trying to shimmy up the pillars of the bandstand, something Matty had definitely attempted a couple of times. Millie remembered him falling and splatting on his back on the grass, then jumping up to insist he was fine and *ha, ha, ha,* wasn't that dangerous fall hilarious?

There were girls sunbathing; some reading, some chatting. None doing anything wrong. Was this sort of intrusion illegal? It probably should be. Millie tried to remember if she, Nicola and maybe the others had ever worn bikinis to the park. It didn't feel like the sort of thing she'd have done – and yet there was a lot about those years she had apparently missed, or forgotten.

Not that she had time to dwell.

There seemed to be no order to the bags of photos, or the tins themselves. Augustus would pass over something from

2009, and then from 1992. Sometimes he'd have collections from four or five days in a row – and then nothing else, as if he'd got bored that particular year.

And then Guy handed her a picture. There were two of them in the middle of the bandstand, leaning towards each other and laughing. Matty and Charlie were so young and thin. They were tanned, with clothes too big. Millie remembered they used to like wrestling and would practise moves on each other while offering loud, over-the-top commentary.

As Millie stared at the pair of them, she longed for the days when everything was easier. When all she really had to bother about was getting home before it was dark.

In the next picture, Charlie was on the ground as Matty stood over him, arms raised in apparent victory.

'What's the date?' Millie asked.

'July,' Guy replied.

It wasn't the right month but that didn't matter. Millie took the entire bag and started to sift through the pictures. There was a girl she didn't recognise in the next, half-sitting up with her elbows supporting her as she spoke to someone out of frame. Millie had no idea who it was at first, assuming it was a different group, then she realised it was Rachel. She'd forgotten Rachel's hair used to be that big, that curly. The woman who was now engaged to Millie's ex-husband didn't look like that any longer. For one, from the look of it, she straightened her hair like a steamroller on a bumpy road.

In the next photo, Rachel was still there, in a similar pose – but she was staring sideways towards Alex. Towards Millie's ex-husband.

Alex was bare-chested, slim with youth, and tanned from the long summer. His hair was darker than she ever remembered and she was dumbstruck by how attractive he was. They hadn't gone out back then and Millie didn't remember noticing him until years later.

Rachel had certainly noticed him.

It was only a still shot, taken at a distance on a cheap camera – but the body language and the gaze was impossible to skip over.

More photos came from the same summer. There was no Charlie or Matty in the new set – but all four girls were together, sitting in a semicircle, each with a magazine on their laps. There was Rachel with her huge frizzy hair, Genevieve scowling at whatever she was reading, Nicola looking flawless in her massive sunglasses... and then Millie on the end.

She stared at herself. She would've been sixteen, maybe seventeen, but she looked like a child. She was so skinny – and not because of diet or exercise, simply because she was all elbows and knees. Millie could see the self-consciousness in herself. Her arms weren't fully crossed. She was trying to force herself to sit up straighter, to seem taller, to push out her chest further.

From nowhere, the old, deep feelings of inadequacy were back. She'd told Genevieve she'd never had them but she had. Genevieve had described herself as the fifth or sixth wheel, but Millie had felt like an outsider, too. She was the one with the famous dad, the newsreader, who couldn't quite escape his presence over the town.

Some things had never changed...

'You OK?' Guy asked quietly.

Millie nodded, not quite able to speak.

She moved onto the next photo, which was focused tightly on Nicola. The idea that Augustus was simply documenting bad behaviour was ridiculous given the way he'd zoomed in as close as he could on the teenager's chest.

There were more photos from another date – and all of the group were together in frame. The eight of them: Matty, Charlie, Alex and Will, then Nicola, Rachel, Genevieve and Millie. They were sitting in two lots of fours, split along gender lines, with Matty's mouth wide open as he seemingly did the talking. It felt about right. He was often the centre of attention. Millie looked at her younger self in those dungarees and couldn't remember why she would have worn them to the park.

Then, finally, Augustus passed over the bag for which they'd been waiting. He continued hunting through the tins, not knowing what he'd found or why they wanted it. The bag contained a smaller stack of pictures, fourteen or fifteen – and there were seven of them on the bandstand, as Millie had remembered. Charlie was the only one missing, because he'd been at work. Matty was on his feet, arms wide, telling some sort of story or joke as the others looked up to him. Nicola was sitting with her legs crossed, almost achingly beautiful. Her tanned skin was glowing as she smiled.

As Millie looked closer, she realised Matty wasn't talking to the group, he was talking *to Nicola*. The other boys were staring across to her as well. *She* was the centre of attention, even though she wasn't in the centre.

Millie wondered how she'd missed it at the time. Genevieve had spelled it out as if it had been obvious but it hadn't been to her.

There were some people Millie didn't recognise in the next two photos. As well as the seven of them, there was a couple maybe a year younger, probably trying to blag a cigarette, or something like that.

In the next, Millie was on her feet, Nicola at her side. Then they were halfway across the park, just the two of them. Nicola's purple shoes blazed bright against the dark green of the grass as the light faded. Millie felt as if she was *in* the photograph. A part of it.

She remembered saying she was leaving and then Nicola saying she'd go, too. She remembered walking in that exact direction across the park and heading out of the gates through which she'd walked with Guy and Augustus barely minutes before.

After those two photos, there were only five people in the next one: Will, Alex and Matty, along with Genevieve and Rachel. One of the boys' tops was around Genevieve's shoulders. The sun was behind the trees and the photo was drenched in gloom. Augustus wouldn't have been able to use a flash, else he'd have been caught – so Millie's friends had turned into silhouettes.

There was no Matty in the next photo, leaving just four of them. They were all standing, angling in different directions. Some sort of goodbye, probably. Back then, none of them seemed to know quite how to leave it, so saying it was time to go could take an hour in itself.

And then it was only Will. The last man standing – or sitting, as it happened. He was alone on the bandstand in the final photo. Nicola either never made it back, as everyone had said, or Augustus had given up taking photos.

Millie restacked the pictures and returned them to the bag. Guy reached for them but Millie clutched the pile tightly.

As well as the original set of biscuit tins Millie had seen, there were at least a hundred more against the other wall. Thousands of photos across hundreds of bags. Invasion after invasion after invasion.

Guy touched her hand and the gentleness of his warm skin on hers made her realise she was trembling. It was only a raised eyebrow as he silently asked if she was OK. Millie didn't want to answer. She *wasn't* OK. She was furious. She was raging with such fire that she wanted to grab the random cordless iron that was lying on the draining board and hurl it through the grubby window.

The sheer audacity of this man. The absolute *nerve* of him. This grown man, this *actual* adult, spying and invading the privacy of teenagers because of what? And not just once, for *years*.

Millie pushed the fury down deep and was polite when she spoke. It took everything she could muster but her tone was level. 'Can I keep these?' she asked, holding up the bag.

Augustus tensed. He'd just removed a lid from another tin and was holding it in the air. The photos couldn't possibly hold any actual value to him but she knew it wasn't about that. There was a control about taking the pictures and then hoarding them.

'I'll bring them back,' Millie said, knowing she wouldn't. 'I just want to make copies.'

Augustus eyed Guy, wanting approval from the older man. It was like he thought Guy was her dad and that she couldn't speak for herself. If he was asking whether she could be trusted, then he shouldn't – because there was no chance he was ever seeing these photos again.

'I'll make sure she returns them,' Guy said – and Millie was suddenly venomous towards him as well.

It was only that which changed Augustus's mind. 'You'll definitely bring them back?' he asked, talking to Millie.

'Promise,' she replied.

He was still tense, his arms close to his body, his breathing shallow and hoarse. It was like she'd asked for a kidney.

'Just this once,' he said. 'So you can make copies. But I want them back. I know how many are there. They're important, you see. They're mine.' He stopped and then repeated: 'You'll definitely bring them back?'

'Of course,' Millie replied, knowing there was no way Augustus would ever get the photos returned.

FOURTEEN

Queen Victoria Park, Whitecliff

I'm allergic to certain types of grass and, after unsuccessfully trying to find out what sort of grass they have at the park, my boyfriend and I decided to go anyway. There were NO SIGNS mentioning allergies to grass, so I assumed I was fine. After sunbathing for around 40 minutes, I noticed a rash on my leg, which got so big it covered my whole body. I ended up missing a day of work. After messaging to ask the council about compensation, they said I wasn't eligible. Terrible park and terrible service.

One star

Millie read the Google review twice. She never ceased to be amazed by the things people would put online, while putting their real names underneath. And if they put their names to things like that, it was no wonder they really would lose their minds when anonymous.

The review was something upon which Millie had stumbled while googling the park. She wasn't sure what she'd find and, though it was nothing that could relate to their youth, the review did at least provide a snigger.

When she looked up from her phone, Millie realised Guy had pulled up a few car lengths ahead. She looked out towards the surrounding houses of the street in which she used to live, knowing the old Volvo would be getting some curtain twitches in the coming hour or so. If she was really lucky, for pure entertainment purposes, someone would post a picture on the neighbourhood Facebook page and ask if something could be done about it.

Millie got out of her car, stretched to grab Eric's present from the passenger seat, and headed along the street towards Guy's vehicle. He was scribbling in a notebook as she tapped on his window. It was more of his squiggly shorthand and he finished his line, before stopping and opening the door to get out.

'Nice area,' he said, as he stood.

'They won't like you dragging down the house prices.'

Guy chuckled as he nodded across to the house with the balloons tied to the gate. 'This is where you used to live...?'

Millie suddenly felt a wave of self-consciousness, almost like she'd had the night before when looking at the photographs. It was that sense of seeing a different version of herself.

Every time Millie visited the street to pick up, or drop off, Eric, she was struck by an aching sense of longing. She'd worried about the mortgage for the four-bedroom, two-bathroom place they'd chosen. It had been Alex who had assured her, saying his own lawyer's salary could cover it, regardless of what happened with her work. And so they'd bought the place for the future, with dreams of filling it with children and pets and...

It wasn't her house any longer. She was off the deed, despite the hours she'd invested in painting rooms with her own hands. Despite the grouting she'd fixed in the bathroom, the curtains she'd hung, the tiles she'd chosen and the furniture she bought. It was all Alex's now... Rachel's, too.

And so was Eric.

Guy had reached back into the car and taken out an envelope that had something which probably read 'Eric' scrawled on the front.

'Twenty quid,' Guy said. 'I don't know what boys today are into.'

'Boys are *always* into money,' Millie replied. 'Girls, too, for that matter.'

He closed the door and stepped around it, ready to head towards the house.

'Thanks for coming,' Millie said.

'I feel like I owe you one after meeting Augustus...'

'Has he always been so... messy?'

'It's definitely got worse. I've asked him about it once or twice, the hoarding, but it's a mental illness. That's an issue that would take more than me to solve. I think you can guess what might happen if I were to ever bring it up...'

Millie could – and, considering Augustus's obsession with young people, noise, and collecting things, giving him one more thing over which to obsess didn't feel like a sensible idea.

'Did you mean it last night?' she asked. 'When you said you'd make sure I gave back the photos?'

They were in front of Millie's old house but stopped next to the balloons and the gate.

'Sometimes you tell people what they want to hear,' Guy said.

He took a step towards the path but Millie didn't move.

'But were you telling *him* what he wanted to hear? Or are you telling me now?'

That got a sorry-looking smile. 'I think you know the answer to that.'

He took another step away and Millie wanted to say that

she didn't – except there was a question of trust. If she didn't trust him, then why did she bring problems like this to him? Why did she invite him to her son's birthday party?

Guy was already at the front door when Millie caught him. 'Is Barry going to be OK by himself?' she asked.

'I think Barry enjoys having the run of the house when I'm out,' Guy replied. 'Although he would have enjoyed all the begging for food had he been allowed to come.'

A sign was pinned to the front door, with an arrow pointing to the path at the side of the house. 'Round the back' was written in swirly letters, with the 'o' of 'round' turned into a heart. It was, unquestionably, Rachel's handiwork. Even though there was nothing specifically wrong with it, Millie knew she was going to have to keep a lid on her annoyance through the afternoon.

She unlatched the gate at the side of the house – the gate she'd had replaced as the old one was rotting – and they continued around to where the screams of delighted children were mingling with some sort of Adele ambience. Rachel's choice, no doubt.

There was a large table off to the side, covered with a plastic cartoony tablecloth. Platters of crisps and biscuits were layered on top. Next to that was a second table, piled with brightly coloured presents.

At the end of the garden, a course of inflatables had been set up. Kids were throwing themselves over the obstacles, howling with laughter as they ricocheted off each other, before reaching the mini bouncy castle at the end.

Nearer the house, adults were gathering in small groups, clutching bottles of beer, or champagne flutes. Many of the men were wearing suits. Though they were tieless, their inability to dress down – even on a warm Saturday at a child's birthday party – made it clear they were Alex's lawyery friends.

Millie was looking for Eric but spotted Alex first, who

was in his own suit. He was in a small huddle of other men each clutching bottles of Peroni. Alex caught her eye momentarily but then turned back to his friends. Before Millie could head towards him, something collided with her hip, almost spinning her off her feet. She grabbed onto Guy for support, before turning to see that it was Eric who had almost bulldozed her.

'You're here!'

Millie straightened herself and didn't have the heart to tell him off for the low-level assault. He was more interested in what she was holding.

'Is that for me?' he asked.

Millie cradled the gift under her arm. 'No, there's another kid down the road having a birthday,' she replied.

Eric looked up to her suspiciously. 'It's for me,' he decided. 'What is it?'

'If I wanted you to see what it was, I wouldn't have wrapped it.'

Her son pouted his bottom lip as he looked towards the table of presents. It was like at a wedding. 'Dad said I have to wait to open everything.'

Millie handed him the gift. 'Happy birthday! You can open it when Dad and Rachel say it's OK,' she replied.

'I want to open it now...'

He gave her that sideways look he always did when he knew he was playing his mum and dad off against each other.

'On the table,' Millie said.

Eric scuffed his feet as he walked the few steps to place the gift with the rest. When he turned, he made such a show of huffing a sigh and scuffing his feet that Millie had to suppress a smile. He could be an actor one day, although he might have to work on the believability.

'Do you want to play?' he asked.

Millie had another look at the inflatable obstacle course and, though the teeniest part of her was up for it, reality was a stronger pull.

'I think I'd put my back out if I jumped over that,' she said.

'You could try...?'

'Why don't you show me how it's done and I'll think about trying later?'

Eric was happy enough with this. He hadn't yet caught onto the fact that adults saying they'd 'think' about trying something were actually saying there was no chance they'd ever do such a thing.

He took half a step away, before Millie stopped him. 'Before you go, I want you to meet someone,' she said.

Eric looked up to Guy and his eyes widened at the man towering over him. Guy was significantly taller than Alex – and probably most men her son had ever seen.

'This is Guy,' Millie said. 'He was friends with your granddad when they were both your age.'

Eric reeled away a fraction, suddenly shy. 'Hi...?'

'Hello,' Guy said.

With a flicker into his inside pocket, Guy handed Eric the envelope he'd shown Millie outside. 'Some money for you,' he said.

Eric eyed the envelope, then Guy, then Millie. 'Ooooh...'

'On the table,' Millie repeated, with a smile.

Eric turned between his mum and the stranger. 'Is his name Guy because he's a guy...?'

'You don't have to ask me.'

Eric shrank further, using Millie's leg as a barrier. 'Can I go play?' he asked instead.

'Sure.'

He didn't need telling twice. He slipped out from behind Millie, risked a quick glance at Guy, dropped the envelope onto the table with the rest of the gifts, and then bounded back to the inflatables. Moments later he was with a girl Millie didn't know.

She had long blonde hair and was wearing shorts with a football shirt. As she barrelled over the first of the obstacles, Eric followed in quick succession.

Millie was lost in watching her son when she realised someone was waving in her direction. When she turned to follow the movement, it was an older woman she didn't recognise, perhaps a grandparent. As she considered waving back, she stopped herself just in time as she realised the person wasn't trying to get her attention, they were trying to get Guy's.

He was smiling amiably back but muttered quietly under his breath, so only Millie could hear. 'Mary Marsh,' he said. 'She's on the council. Total nuisance.'

'Hi, Mary!' he said, waving back.

She was beckoning him across and he uttered an even quieter apology to Millie before glad-handing his way across the garden towards a small welcoming crowd. Millie watched him handshake his way around the circle, like some sort of celebrity. Somehow, a champagne flute was in his hand as he laughed along to something Millie hadn't heard but knew for a fact hadn't been funny.

Alex's parents were in the general vicinity, too. They were watching Millie in a not watching her kind of way. His mum muttered something, to which her husband gave a short nod. This would be all over their Facebook feeds later, along with memes from five years before that were full of spelling mistakes.

Avoiding them, Millie turned to watch Eric – who was now on the bouncy castle with the same girl. It was his first crush, she thought – if it could be called that when they were so young. His first crush – and she hadn't known about it until now.

Not that she could dwell on that too long because Alex was suddenly at her side. Perhaps it was his presence but she eyed the bouncy castle, remembering they had once talked about planting strawberries in that exact patch.

'Thanks for coming,' he said.

He sounded happy, though she suspected it was more to do with the fizz going around, as opposed to the day itself.

'Where else would I be?' Millie replied.

They made small talk about the inflatables and how Eric had wanted a full-size bouncy castle. He'd had to settle for the course and a smaller castle because there wasn't enough room to get a bigger one into the back. Rachel had organised it all, apparently. It had been a surprise that morning and they hadn't told Millie in case she'd accidentally let on.

Millie could have let that annoy her, and she suspected he'd said it to test whether she'd get angry, but she was more interested in Eric himself.

'Who's the girl?' Millie asked. She nodded towards Eric and his friend, who were now holding hands as they bounced in unison on the castle.

Alex made a show of turning to look, as if he didn't know what she was talking about. 'Chloe,' he said. 'They're in the same class. Her mum does the books for our firm and her dad's president of the rugby club.'

It was a feature of Alex that he always described people by what they did. Millie hadn't noticed it until after they separated but she supposed it had always been there. His first question to someone he didn't know was always, 'what do you do?' – as if he couldn't make a judgement on them until he knew the answer. That was how he judged their worth. It had been so much later that Millie wondered if he'd always judged her on the fact her dad was the local TV newsreader. He was a celebrity in the town and, without wanting to be, Millie was *somebody*. If Alex really was all about the what, not the who, then there was a time in which Millie was almost at the top of the pile.

Not any longer.

Millie blinked the thoughts away as she watched Eric and Chloe play together for a while longer. It was hard to force away the ache of somehow missing out on this. She wondered how many more friends there would be who she didn't know. How many more things she'd find out by accident, because she wasn't in Eric's day-to-day life.

'How are things with you...?'

Alex took another sip from his glass. He'd asked the question with the airy sense of someone who didn't really want to know but didn't know what else to say.

'Y'know...' Millie replied, with equal airiness. 'The same.' A pause. 'I've been back in touch with Nicola.'

'Oh...' Alex had been about to take another drink from his glass but he stopped and turned to her. 'Any reason...?'

Alex was one of the few people who knew about Nicola's affair with Millie's father. As her boyfriend, then fiancé, then husband, it would have been impossible not to tell him why she and her best friend had stopped talking.

'I figured it was time to forgive,' Millie replied.

'Are you talking about just her, or...?'

Millie sighed. 'I don't know. I've been thinking about the past a lot recently. I found a few photographs of us all. Those times we'd hang out in the park, or in town. D'you remember?'

'I guess... I don't really think about it, though.'

That was how Alex had always been. He wasn't one for nostalgia and definitely wasn't the sort to have pinboards of photos up on walls, like those at Nicola's house. The only part of the past he seemed determined to hold on to, not that she could blame him, was the events that led to their divorce.

Some of the events. Not the ones for which he was responsible, of course.

They stood together, mother and father, watching their son and his friend run in a bounding circle around the bouncy castle. They were taking big, leaping steps – as if they were on the moon – giggling the entire time. That was until Eric tripped over his own feet and took down Chloe with him. After a moment of shock, they were giggling once more.

'Do you remember the battle of the bands?' Millie asked. She'd not planned to bring it up but here they were.

Alex let out a low whistle. 'That's going back a bit. Didn't Matty's band play? I remember them being awful.'

'They *were* awful.'

'Wasn't that the night you and Nic got so drunk that you cut her hair? She ended up having it all chopped short?'

'Right...'

Alex was laughing gently: 'We all wondered how drunk you had to be to think that was a good idea. We'd laugh about it and—'

'Who'd laugh?'

Alex straightened himself, not used to being picked up on something. 'Everyone. Me, Charlie and Matty. Will, I guess. It was one of those things, wasn't it? One of those crazy things you do. Don't you remember Matty jumping off the pier because Charlie dared him to?'

He laughed but Millie didn't. She didn't remember it and wasn't sure she'd have found it funny even if she did. There were rocks underneath the pier.

Perhaps it was because she didn't join in with the enjoyment but, as Alex shifted his weight from one foot to the other, it was as if something else was shifting between them. She felt the mood alter, the darker clouds descend.

'I was being serious the other night,' Alex said, quieter now, not wanting anyone else to hear. 'The calls every evening have got to stop. Eric's seen you today, so it won't be an issue tonight. I'll tell him tomorrow.'

Millie was quiet. It wasn't as if she didn't have prior warning but it still sounded brutal. The custody agreement had been clear enough in that she had access every other weekend, but there had been nothing about phone calls. Somehow, organically, the nightly calls had evolved over the past few months and she'd not thought far enough ahead to think they might stop. It had become the highlight of her day.

'He's still my son,' Millie replied.

'And you know what the court said. I can get the papers if you want to read them again.'

He was so patronising sometimes and Millie couldn't remember if he'd always been like that, or if it was a new thing he did specifically to wind her up. As she was trying to think of how to respond, she suddenly realised Rachel had sidled into the conversation. She was standing next to Alex, a possessive arm around his waist.

'There's something else,' Alex said – and, this time, there was a nervousness to his voice. It was going to be something bad.

So bad, in fact, that he couldn't get it out. It was Rachel who finished the sentence. 'We're going to ask Eric to start calling me Mum,' she said.

FIFTEEN

The rage was boiling and instant. This was something they could have told Millie when it was just them. Instead, they'd waited until there was an audience. Millie could sense the merest hint of an upturn to Rachel's lips: that goading, daring look of hers. *Go on, say something.*

Millie dug her nails into her palms to stop the fury erupting. She focused on that sharp, stabbing pain because, if she didn't, the other pain would explode.

Rachel was still speaking, in her chirpy voice. From somewhere, she'd developed the habit of ending every sentence with an uptick, as if asking a question. 'We figured we'd try to get ahead of it before the wedding,' she said. 'For a bit of uniformity. We think it's better if a child has a specific dad *and* mum at the school pick-up. Not to mention all the forms and letters and so on.'

Millie barely opened her mouth as she replied. 'He *has* a mum.'

The smile was fully fixed on Rachel's stupid face now as Alex stumbled over a reply. 'There's no reason he can't call you *both* "Mum",' he said. 'He had two grandmas for a while. We just thought—'

'*She* thought,' Millie interrupted, unable to stop herself.

Rachel's smirk widened a tiny amount.

'*We* thought it would make it easier for him around the house,' Alex replied. 'There's already confusion around "Auntie" Rachel – and we're going to be married soon, so it'll be better for everyone if that's sorted out.'

'Isn't it *more* confusing if he calls two different people "Mum"?' Millie said.

'We're certain he'll get used to it,' Rachel replied, dismissively. She sounded like a primary school teacher at parents' evening, scolding a parent because their kid taught some of the others a swear word.

'Why don't we let him choose what he wants to calls us all?' Millie replied. 'He's old enough to—'

'He's seven,' Rachel interrupted.

'*Eight*,' Millie replied. 'And that's old enough to make a decision about this sort of thing. If he wants to call two people "Mum", then fine. If he prefers "Auntie", that should be up to him.'

Rachel's smile had slipped a fraction at being corrected on Eric's age but it was still there.

'We've already made the decision,' Alex said.

Millie breathed in, then out. Counted to five in her head, realised it wasn't enough, and then continued onto ten. It probably was a good job other people were around.

The tension was impossible to miss and it was Alex who made something of an attempt to break it. 'Mill was saying she saw Nic the other day,' he chirped, talking to Rachel. 'We should have some sort of reunion soon. Christmas maybe? Get the gang back together – or maybe try to do a whole school year thing?'

Rachel mumbled a 'yeah' that sounded as enthusiastic about

the prospect as Millie felt. Millie figured that would be it, except Rachel was bobbing on her heels.

'Actually, no,' Rachel said, louder now. She leaned in and poked a finger towards Millie. 'Why would I want to see *you lot* again? You and Nicola were only ever interested in yourselves. You were always such *bitches* to me and Jenny.' She poked that finger at Alex, too. '*You* might have all had fun back then but I didn't. I was always left at the back, hoping you'd invite me in. Well, forget it.' Back to Millie: 'And you can go on all you like about Eric-this, or my son-that, but if you cared about him, maybe you should've kept your legs closed.'

She finished with a breathless flourish, spinning and stomping off to the tables. She refilled her glass with the sparkling wine and then stormed off to the far side of the garden.

Not for the first time since arriving, Millie was speechless. For a short while, Alex was too. He watched Rachel open-mouthed. She had stopped among a small group of grown-ups, where she downed her wine in one while keeping her back to them.

'That was, uh...' he started. 'She's got a lot on with work and the wedding planning...'

Millie let that fester for a couple of seconds. It wasn't quite a criticism of Rachel but it was about the closest Alex had ever come to it. She pushed away her own anger. There were too many people around.

'When is the wedding?' she managed.

'We don't have a date yet. I mean the early planning. It's probably still a year or two away. There's so much to do...'

There was something unconvincing about the way he said it – but that was the least of Millie's concerns. 'He's still my son,' she said quietly.

'I know.' He stopped for a second, perhaps also aware of

how many people were around them. 'We're not trying to elbow you out.'

Millie didn't trust herself to reply to that. As she stewed silently, she realised there was a man next to the food staring at Alex. He wasn't one of the tieless, lawyerly types. He was in short shorts that would be an obscene publication from the wrong angle. His shirt was loose and linen, the sort of thing a surf instructor might wear. He was around their age, or perhaps a couple of years younger, and standing by himself.

Alex straightened when he noticed they were being watched.

'I think someone wants you,' Millie said.

Alex flattened his hair, while likely not realising he was doing it. 'That's, um...'

'You don't need to tell me who your friends are.'

'Right. I need to, er...'

Alex moved across to the tables, where he mumbled something to the man – and then they both turned and headed towards the bouncy castle.

Millie stood by herself for a while – first watching Alex and his friend, as they turned their backs to everyone else – then taking in the rest of the parents. The lawyer lot were obvious no-goes but there were other people in the garden. Millie recognised a few from the old days when it was her dropping off and picking up Eric from school. Nobody seemed particularly interested in either coming across, or inviting her into their circle.

The next-door neighbour whose husband died of cancer, and whose two sons were at university, was busy chatting with someone Millie didn't know. Her gaze slipped across Millie momentarily but shifted away as quickly as it arrived. That tiny frown of disapproval was something Millie knew only too well.

Alex and the man had twisted back to face the rest of the garden but not for long. They moved quickly, Alex at the front as they strode around the back of the tables and then disappeared into the house, apparently unnoticed by anyone else. When they'd gone, Millie felt the weight of being watched but, as soon as she realised it was Rachel, the other woman quickly turned away and continued her conversation with one of the other mums. It might have been ego but Millie was sure they were talking about her.

At the other end of the garden Eric was still playing with Chloe. They'd straddled one of the inflatable hurdles and were trying to bounce the other off. The other children raced around them, all content in their own small groups.

Millie was alone.

And then Guy was at her side. 'I didn't want to interrupt you,' he said. 'Didn't know if you wanted me to.'

'How was Mary Marsh?' Millie asked, relieved he was back.

'She was wondering if I knew who was going to be judging the vegetable competition at this year's Whitecliff Show.'

Millie looked up to him, wondering if he was joking. 'Do you?'

A laugh: 'I do actually. Not that I told her. She was telling me about her parsnips – and, no, that isn't a euphemism.'

Millie smiled at that – but only until she remembered that Rachel wanted her son to call her 'Mum'.

'I noticed Alex...'

Guy didn't need to say more than that. He was the only person in whom she'd confided about finding her former husband having an affair with a man. Everybody knew about *her* affair, only Guy knew about the why. Millie had kept Alex's affair to herself, not wanting Eric to be *that kid* at school. Then *she'd* ended up getting caught with Peter Lewis, MP, and he was *that kid* anyway. Meanwhile, Alex had a new fiancée and was continuing as if he was the only wronged party. She hated it but it was too late to tell anyone else now. Too late to be believed.

Millie didn't know how to reply and didn't get a chance

anyway because Rachel had started clapping. She was side by side with Alex near the patio doors. His friend had disappeared off to stand with one of the mothers.

At the sound of the clapping, the children had started to gather away from the play equipment.

Rachel waited until everyone was paying attention and then started to talk.

'I think it's time for the birthday boy to open his presents,' she said, although it still sounded a bit like a question.

That got a cheer, predominantly from Eric, who darted across to the table on which all the gifts sat. Parents were taking out their phones to record the action, while Alex's mum was filming vertically on her iPad. Of course she was.

Rachel picked up the first present from the table, read the name from the label – and then the child who'd brought it came to the front to hand it to Eric. There was the ritual opening, a mini round of applause, and then Eric said 'thank you', before moving onto the next.

It was all very formal. Very Facebookable, as the parent of each present-offering child shot their own video, ready to throw onto the internet.

Millie knew she would never have allowed this sort of thing had she been in charge. She'd not posted anything online with Eric's face until he was old enough to go to school and, even then, her privacy settings were at their maximum.

Too late now, of course.

There was unquestionably a hierarchy to the gifts. Three years ago, when he'd been five, they'd played pass the parcel and musical chairs. In Millie's day, she'd have been lucky to get anything that cost more than a fiver from a friend's parent – but now there was the show-off factor. One of the children of the lawyer lot had bought Eric a Nintendo game that must've been fifty pounds minimum. Someone else had bought him a foot-ball shirt from the local team, even though he wasn't particularly into football. That would have been another forty or fifty quid.

None of it felt quite right, especially when one of the children Millie recognised handed her son a card containing a ten-pound Amazon voucher. It was put to the side almost instantly and Millie almost stepped in.

Almost.

She wanted to tell Eric to have more respect for the things he was given, and the people offering them, but it was too late. Rachel had already called forward the next child and on they went.

Millie was quietly wondering if there was anything she could do about all the videos that would be out there, while knowing there wasn't, when she realised people were looking to her.

'Mill,' Rachel said in a tone that made Millie realise she was repeating herself.

'Right.'

Millie didn't have time to seethe at Rachel, of all people, calling her 'Mill', as if they were still friends. She stepped forward and picked up the present she'd brought for Eric, then passed it down to him.

'Happy birthday, love,' she said quietly, wishing it was a moment only for them.

'It's heavy,' he said.

Millie dug a nail into the tape to set him going, and then he tore through the paper to reveal a full box of stickers.

'I ordered it off the internet,' Millie told him. 'There are forty-eight packets inside.'

He gasped in wonder. 'How many stickers is that?'

'I think it's five in a packet, so...'

'A million!'

'Not quite a million... but lots.'

He held up the box, showing his friends – who seemed far more in awe than any of the parents.

'I think it's time for—'

Rachel was cut off because Eric had opened the box and was already tearing into the first packet of stickers. He called across Chloe and showed her the shiny he'd picked out and they huddled together, discussing what to do with it.

'You should open the card, too,' Millie told him.

Eric handed the box of stickers to Chloe and then picked up the card that had been on top of the present. He tore apart the envelope, and then opened the card. He read the message first, then held up the print-out from the inside.

'What is it?' Eric asked.

'It's a voucher for a dog-rescue experience,' Millie replied. 'You can go and play with the dogs for a whole afternoon. It's a bit like a farm – but only for dogs.'

Eric's grin took up his entire face. 'Wow...'

'You can bring a friend,' Millie said.

'Can we go tomorrow?'

Millie risked a small glance to Rachel, whose eyes were narrow and lips were tight. She was holding Alex's hand, *squeezing* his hand.

'Not tomorrow,' Alex said.

'We'll go next time you're with me,' Millie said. 'Hopefully a week today, if it's dry.'

'Can Chloe come?'

The girl gave a high-pitched 'please, please, please'.

'If it's all right with Chloe's parents,' Millie replied.

Chloe looked across to a woman who had half a sandwich in her mouth. She swirled her hand, swallowed, coughed, and then patted her chest. 'I think that's OK...' she said.

That was taken as an unequivocal 'yes' by both Chloe and Eric, who immediately started talking about the breeds of dog they hoped to see.

Millie could feel the daggers being stared from both Rachel and Alex. If there was a point at which she would have cared, it was gone when he told her she'd have to stop speaking to her son on the phone each night. That was before the talk about Eric calling Rachel 'Mum'.

'It's time for our present,' Rachel said, with a forced upbeat tone. She took the box of stickers from Chloe and put them on the table. Then she took the card and voucher from Eric, placing them underneath the box.

'Can I open the stickers first?' Eric asked.

'Later. It's time for our present.'

Rachel looked to Alex, who picked up a large box wrapped in gold paper and handed it to his son. Alex's mum stepped closer, attempting to kneel, giving up, and then crouching like a chicken about to lay an egg. She held up her iPad, still vertical, to film the moment.

'Happy birthday, son,' Alex said.

Millie couldn't ever remember him using the word 'son' like that before.

Eric returned the gift to the table and then pulled apart the paper. When he'd finished unwrapping, he spun the book around, then looked up to his dad curiously.

'What's a junior law... law...?' he stumbled.

'Your dad is a lawyer,' Rachel said, enthusiastically. 'You know that. We found this book that helps teach kids about laws, and how they work, and...'

She tailed off as Eric, understandably, pushed the book away a fraction. Millie couldn't begin to think of where they'd found such an awful gift, and why anyone in their sane mind thought it would interest an eight-year-old.

Nudging it away was exactly what Eric had done with the ten-pound Amazon voucher barely minutes before. This action got a completely different reaction.

'It's rude not to say thank you,' Alex said sharply. 'It's not *only* for the book. It's the party, the inflatables, the castle. Your cake.'

Eric dipped his head from the scolding. His grandmother was still there, iPad at arm's length, recording the lot. Eric never took being told off too well. He'd always been a bit more carrot than stick – and Millie thought the inconsistency probably didn't help. He'd not been picked up on the disrespect when it had been someone else's gift, only this one. Millie wanted to say something but knew she couldn't, not with Rachel there and everyone else watching.

'Thanks,' Eric said, deadpan.

'Say it properly,' his dad replied.

Eric looked up but didn't bother to hide the annoyance of embarrassment in his tone. All his friends were there after all. It was being recorded by his grandmother, so it could be played back who knew when.

'Thank. You,' he said, forcing each word and then holding up a hand to block the iPad that was barely a metre from him.

Rachel was on the brink of a flounce. Millie had known her long enough to see it coming. She huffed herself up, said the word, 'well...' and then spun to walk away. Unfortunately for her, she misjudged the distance of her hip to the table, clipped the edge, and sent a glass of wine spiralling off the edge, directly onto Eric's front.

Everyone froze as it happened in slow motion. The liquid splashed up and onto Eric's face and then down his top. The glass fell to the ground and smashed with a splintering crash.

It was Millie who reacted first. Eric was wide-eyed with shock as he'd not been watching and didn't quite know what had happened. 'It was an accident,' Millie assured him as she checked he wasn't cut.

Rachel was there and so was Alex, both apologising and asking if he was OK – but it was only Millie he wanted. He reached up, wanting his mum, even in front of his friends – and Millie clasped him back. His chin was sticky, his top wet.

'You should probably get changed,' Millie whispered. 'Maybe wash your face, too...?'

He angled away and gave a predictable face pull. Asking a boy to wash any part of his body voluntarily was like asking lorry drivers to stop overtaking each other on the motorway. It wasn't going to happen.

'Do you want me to help?' Millie asked.

He shook his head and squirmed away from Rachel, who suddenly seemed like she had six arms. She was possibly trying to hug him, or semaphore an apology, or something else that Millie wasn't sure about. Like a touchy-feely octopus.

Eric headed inside by himself, closing the patio door behind him. Alex's mum finally put down the damned iPad as Alex raised his arms and forced a smile.

'We'll start the buffet properly when Eric's back downstairs,' he said, talking to everyone. 'Go back to enjoying yourselves!'

It was a lofty ask, given that the birthday boy's stepmother-to-be had apparently lobbed a glass of wine over him.

The children milled in one large group that slowly made their way back towards the inflatables, even though nobody seemed particularly interested in playing any longer. As for the adults, the conversation was more of a hummed mumble than the tipsy jollity of moments before.

Rachel had disappeared somewhere and Alex was on his way across to his lawyer friends, leaving Millie momentarily alone near the patio doors.

It wasn't for long.

Alex's mother had finally wrestled the iPad back into its case, the hinge being close to the limits of her technical capabilities, and now she had eyes only for Millie. Alex's father was a couple of paces behind, watching on uselessly. Only one set of trousers was worn in their relationship.

'You didn't have to upstage Rachel like that,' she hissed.

'Like what?' Millie replied, failing to hide the spite that was overdue.

'They're trying to educate Eric. To buy him things that will broaden his interests... and you're buying him *stickers*.'

'There's no reason he can't enjoy both.'

Millie said it knowing full well her son would barely even look at the junior lawyer book, let alone open it.

'You know what you were doing. You embarrassed her.'

Millie had her hands behind her back and she interlocked her fingers and squeezed, forcing out the tension. 'I didn't know what *they'd* bought him. All I did was buy him something he wanted. Something he can share with his friends.'

Alex's mum huffed as if this was unbelievable and unfathomable.

'He's my son,' Millie said.

'Maybe you should've thought of that before you went sleeping around?'

It was the expected reply and not the first time Millie had been told such a thing. The reply was so close to her lips – that perhaps this woman should know what her own son had done. Perhaps ask him about the man in the shorts who was hanging around.

She didn't do any of that, not because she didn't want to – but because Guy appeared at her shoulder.

'Didn't your parents divorce?' he asked. Guy had a whimsical tone, as if he couldn't quite remember.

For a moment, Millie thought he was talking to her – except he was facing Alex's mum. She rocked back a fraction, neck craning away, but Guy wasn't done.

'Now I remember,' he added. 'It was a bit of a scandal at the time because they were both big churchgoers. They ended up separating because of an affair with the organist, if I remember rightly…'

Alex's mother was aghast. She tried to reply but it was more a succession of breaths than anything else. She turned and took a couple of steps away, then twisted back to Millie, her voice a hissed whisper. 'Your parents would be ashamed of you,' she said.

'Good,' Millie replied.

Guy took a smaller step towards Millie and she somehow knew that, behind him, someone was trying to film on their phone.

'I know plenty about her,' Guy whispered to her – and there was a protective menace in his voice that Millie had never heard before. He was sticking up *for her*. Telling her he had more dirt on Alex's mother if the old windbag opened her stupid gob again.

It felt so good to have somebody take her side.

There was a short pause and then he spoke again. This time there was a controlled alarm to his voice. A warning, perhaps.

'Millie…'

Millie had been staring at the floor but realised Guy was looking at the patio doors, where her son was now standing.

It took Millie a moment to notice why there had been a degree of urgency in the way Guy said her name. Gasps rippled around the groups of adults as they all realised, apparently in unison, that Eric was wearing a dress.

SIXTEEN

Nobody spoke at first. Eric was standing innocently by himself, looking towards the other end of the garden, probably for Chloe.

The dress was shapeless and yellow, down to his knees, with thin straps across his shoulders. Other parents were beginning to talk quietly among themselves as Alex stepped forward. He put his body between Eric and the rest of the garden, though Millie shuffled to the side so she could still see.

'What are you wearing?' Alex asked.

'What do you mean?' Eric replied.

Alex laughed as if it was a joke. He started to say something then stopped himself and Millie knew he was trying not to say that only girls wear dresses.

'You have your own clothes,' he said instead. 'Where did you get it?'

'Swapped it with Chloe the other day.'

Alex looked across to Chloe's mum, who was doing a terrible job of pretending she wasn't listening in. All the parents were.

'I didn't know,' she replied blankly.

The murmuring undercurrent was impossible to miss. A group of people desperate to be modern enough to say that clothes should be genderless, while quietly being horrified when it was in front of them.

Millie didn't know how she felt. Her son had never said anything about wanting to wear anything other than the clothes he already owned. In fact, she wasn't sure he'd ever particularly noticed what he had to wear. She didn't know if this would have any greater meaning when he was older, or if it mattered. He'd only been eight for a few hours. It was all a bit confusing – for her, if not him. She could see in his bemused expression that he didn't understand why everyone was now looking at him.

'Maybe you should go and change...?' Alex said.

'Why?'

Millie would be a liar if she pretended not to take some enjoyment from the way her former husband was trying not to say the thing he definitely would have said, had he not been surrounded by people.

So she said it for him: 'Your dad's saying that only girls wear dresses.'

Alex jumped up straighter, as if he'd stepped on a piece of Lego. 'I'm *not* saying that.'

'What are you saying then?'

He was stuck, with no option other than to back down. Except Rachel had appeared from nowhere – and she had some ideas.

'You got that nice new T-shirt earlier,' she said, looking through the pile of presents, until she pulled out something with a cartoon character on the front. She handed it to him. 'Why don't you put this on?'

Eric looked between the adults who were crowding him and frowned in the way he sometimes did when there was home-work he couldn't figure out. 'I like this,' he said. 'Can we eat cake now? You said after presents...'

Rachel looked to Alex, who looked to his mum, who ignored his useless, gawping dad. All had the general sense that they'd just been asked to explain atomic theory in Latin. None of them were moving, so Millie picked up the wand lighter from the table and lit the candles on the cake. Eric counted them up to eight and then Millie turned to tell everyone they should sing. She didn't fancy starting everyone off – and, luckily, she didn't have to. It was Guy who launched into an off-key 'Happy Birthday' and, by the time he'd hit the second line, everyone had joined in.

Eric conducted his crowd and, when it was over, he took a deep breath and blew out all eight in one go. Millie started to cut and, without prompting, Eric began shovelling squares onto paper plates. He handed the first to Guy, who was closest, then more to whoever appeared at the table. By the time Millie and Eric had finished cutting and serving, she looked up to see Alex on the far side of the garden, next to the fence, having a hushed argument with his parents.

Millie told her son to eat slower – which had become something of a catchphrase as he grew. She then left him to mingle with the rest of his friends near the inflatables. The mix of cake, buffet and jumping was unlikely to end well, though Millie told herself it was one mess she wouldn't have to clean up.

Rachel had been hovering near the buffet table the whole time, not eating, not drinking, just staring.

Millie had been ignoring her but, when they were alone, finally acknowledged the daggers. 'You all right?' she asked.

'Did you know about this?' Rachel replied.

'Know about what?'

'Don't give me that,' she hissed. 'About the dress. It seems like the sort of *stunt* you'd pull.'

Millie was surprised by her own calm. She'd been so angry when Alex had said they wanted Eric to call Rachel 'Mum', but that had evaporated.

'What stunt?' Millie said. 'He liked his friend's clothes and they swapped. We used to do that all the time when we were young. There was a time when half the stuff in my wardrobe was Nicola's – and vice-versa.'

That got a harumph. 'You know this is going to get him bullied at school.'

As Rachel said that, Millie was watching Eric and his friends finish off their cake as they readied themselves for another go on the obstacle course and bouncy castle.

'It doesn't look like they're bullying him now,' she replied. 'Maybe kids today aren't the same as we were? The only people who seem bothered are the adults.'

Rachel seethed until she managed a final-sounding 'Fine!', which didn't make it seem very fine at all. 'I'm not surprised you and Nicola are friends again,' she added. 'It's always drama with you two. If it's not you cheating on your husband, then it's her cheating on hers.'

Millie had expected a dig but it took her a moment to realise what had been said about Nicola.

'What do you mean?' she asked.

'You tell me. I saw her in the lobby of the Grand Royal a couple of weeks back with some guy. Tall, dark hair, in a suit. Definitely not Charlie.'

The Grand Royal was the biggest and, well, grandest hotel in town. It was an old Victorian building that had been reno-vated over and over. When Millie was a child, she'd had the chance to stay a night when a new owner had invited her dad and his family to experience the upgraded rooms. Her father was at the peak of his newsreading fame at the time, while Millie had been a young girl marvelling at the height of the ceil-ings and the size of the beds.

'It doesn't sound like that's any of your business,' Millie replied.

'You'd like that, wouldn't you?' Rachel sneered. 'When we

were young, there was nothing you two liked more than lording it over us. Then Nic got her comeuppance.'

She spat the word and the spite singed the air between them.

'What do you mean by that?' Millie asked.

Rachel pressed away. 'When you got so drunk, she ended up having her hair cut. She looked so stupid – and nobody ever quite looked at her the same after that. Not so perfect, after all, was she?'

For a moment, Millie thought Rachel was going to say something about Nicola ending up in the woods. Was there *really* comeuppance in having shorter hair? Was it *really* deserved?

Both Genevieve and Rachel had said similar things about being left out of the group and Millie wondered if she'd truly been that blind to it all. None of it had been intentional. She had been friends with Nicola before either of the other two.

'We never meant to leave you out,' Millie said. 'I don't think we lorded it over anyone.'

That got a dismissive shake of the head and a sharp 'Whatever', before Rachel headed off to talk to Alex's mum.

Guy was still nearby, carefully picking at his square of cake with a plastic fork. He waited his moment, although the hint of a smile was impossible to miss. 'Don't take this the wrong way,' he said. 'But are all your parties like this?'

Millie snorted a laugh. 'This is one of the quieter ones.'

Guy scooped the final piece of cake into his mouth. 'It might not be the time to ask but I was wondering if you could do something for me tomorrow...?'

'I'm not baking you a cake.'

He didn't smile, instead he stared into nothingness in a way she didn't think she'd seen in the past. 'It's just... tomorrow would've been our forty-fifth wedding anniversary...'

SEVENTEEN

It was well into the evening when Millie knocked on the door of the squat. She hadn't been able to get Will out of her mind since they'd spoken, especially after Genevieve had pointed out how much he hated Nicola.

The music was gone from the last time she visited. As she waited for the door to be answered, Millie turned to take in the view of the town and the bay deep down in the valley. She could see why someone wanted to buy the place, whether or not they lived in the area. The sense of power, of wonder, from being so high up, with such a beautiful sight beyond, would be appealing to anyone.

It was Hannah who opened the door. She held it wide and said, 'I'm surprised you came back,' even though she didn't remotely sound shocked by it. 'Will said you weren't going to help.'

'I figured I'd hear you out properly.'

It was a lie but gave her a reason to be there.

Millie was nodded inside and followed Hannah through to the living room. It was bright outside but the sun must be in a different position than the last time she'd visited, because it was gloomy inside. Half a dozen candles were placed on various surfaces and a lamp was plugged into a power cord that trailed into the hall, where it was plugged into a separate cable that ran upstairs. Mismatched furniture was dotted around as Will sat in the windowsill and smoked.

'I had a feeling you might be back,' he said. Something passed between him and Hannah, as if he'd shared with her the importance of mentioning Pidge. It was his way of assuring Hannah that Millie would be back sooner rather than later.

Three other people were in the living room but they left almost as soon as Millie arrived, leaving Hannah, Will and Millie alone.

As well as the dark, the room was cool, perhaps cold. Blankets were draped across chairs, or piled on the floor. Millie picked one up as she sat in one of the camping chairs, before placing it across her knees.

'What did you do in the winter?' she asked.

'Extra layers and blankets,' Hannah replied. 'Like the old days. If more people did that, perhaps the planet wouldn't be on fire.'

It sounded like she was angling for an argument but Millie had had enough of that through the day. By the end of the party, it had felt as if everyone was quietly whispering to everyone else about the drama.

Hannah was in a plastic garden chair as Will stubbed out the remains of his cigarette and pulled the window closed. He crossed and sat next to Hannah, pulling a blanket across the pair of them. They seemed an awkward couple, if that's what they were. Will was leaning in one direction, Hannah the other. More like a couple who'd been married for forty years and were sick of the sight of each other. Not quite two people in the throes of passion.

'Has your friend decided to write something for us?' Will asked.

'The opposite. He definitely won't... but maybe I will.'

Millie wasn't sure if it was true. Hannah and Will shared a sideways glance and there was an unseen movement from under the blanket, as if they were holding hands.

'The thing is,' Millie added, 'I'm still not sure I know what you actually want. Is it just about staying in this house...?'

She'd figured this might be something of a trigger – and Hannah didn't need asking twice. 'We want people to finally stand up for themselves,' she said. 'We want a massive turnout to send the bailiffs, the lawyers, and anyone else packing.'

Hannah nudged Will and he almost jumped off the seat. 'We want it to start here,' he said.

'You want *what* to start here?' Millie replied.

It was Hannah who replied, giving a fairly clear indication of who had the slogans and who had the ideas. 'It's like we're back to being landowners and peasants,' Hannah said. 'We're the serfs who work all day to pay *their* mortgages.'

'What do you do for work?' Millie asked.

It was a genuine question, which was answered flatly and almost sarcastically. 'I'm talking generally.'

'Right...'

'In 1980, an average house cost roughly three times the annual salary. It's now ten to twelve times that – and I'm talking nationwide. In popular areas, like Whitecliff, it's fifteen to eighteen times – and we're still talking about the national average salary. In Whitecliff, the salaries are lower because we have so many people working in cafés, restaurants and hotels. How are young people expected to live?'

She waited for an answer that Millie didn't have.

'Wages aren't rising but prices are,' Hannah added. 'All we can do is rent, which pays off the homeowner's mortgage, allowing them to take on more debt to buy more places. If *we* want a mortgage, the bank wants endless proof of funds to show we can pay five-hundred quid a month – even though we've been paying more than that in rent for the past decade. It's rigged – and it's a circle that no one's doing anything to break. The people in power are the people who own all these places. They're the ones profiting, so they don't want anything to change.'

Hannah's voice rose as she spoke but it never felt out of control.

In the space of a minute or so, Millie suddenly had an idea of what they were annoyed about. It was something that was easy for her to skip over. She'd grown up in a town in which her father was a local celebrity on a good salary. Millie had never been hungry and never feared having a roof over her head. She fell into a job for which she wasn't qualified because her parents knew people at the council. She bought a house with Alex and had no issues getting a mortgage as he'd inherited money to cover the deposit. When their marriage fell apart, she moved in with her parents – and, months after, when they died, she inherited her childhood home. After losing her career, she started her dog-grooming business knowing it wouldn't cover much more than her general spending. She could only afford to do that – let alone volunteer at the nursing home and spend days chasing facts from twenty years before – because she had no mortgage, or rent.

She'd seen headlines and sound bites about the cost of living and the increased cost of housing... but it had never affected her. She was privileged and hadn't particularly realised it until recently.

Hannah must have seen the shift.

'Bear in mind,' Hannah said. 'We're still paying rent on this house. This is only because they're trying to throw us out to knock it down. This isn't the only place we're occupying. We're in contact with groups around the country who are refusing to move. We have friends who know the law and check every piece of paperwork. You wouldn't believe what a shady bunch landlords are and the stunts they try to pull.'

'Stunts like refusing to move out…?'

Millie said it with a smile that was reciprocated. It felt less dangerous than it had when she'd been in the house with Guy. The talk of war seemed more metaphorical than actual.

'There was an article the other week about how young people are hoping for inheritances to get on the housing ladder – but do you know the average age of inheritance?' Hannah didn't wait for an answer. 'Sixty-two. They're telling us to wait for our inheritances, even though many of us won't have one – and even though those who do will have to wait until they're *sixty-two*. We're a forgotten generation – or we will be if we don't do something.'

Millie had come to the house more to talk to Will than anything else. She'd not expected a debate, let alone something so one-sided that she had no idea how to reply. She wondered if she should ask Guy about talking to Hannah properly, away from talk about 'war'. Perhaps she had a point? Using Guy and his website to spread a message to a different age group might be a good thing?

'I suppose I'm wondering what you hope to achieve on Tuesday when the bailiffs come,' Millie said. 'Even if everything else you say is true and unarguable, that's not going to stop them coming to take back this place, not now they have the court order.'

The row of papers was still proudly displayed on the wall, though there were more than Millie had previously realised.

Unlike before, Hannah didn't answer immediately – which Will apparently took as a cue. 'We're hoping everyone gets to see what it's like for our generation and those after us,' he said.

Perhaps it was because she'd known him before but there was something about the way Will said it that almost made

Millie want to laugh. Rightly or wrongly, Hannah had passion in her voice. Will sounded rehearsed.

'We're going to live-stream everything,' he added. 'We want it all to be documented. If they want to start dragging us away, they're going to have to do it knowing it will all be seen. That's why we want as much coverage as we can get. That's why we've invited everyone we can think of.'

'Whatever happens, happens,' Hannah said coldly.

She was staring as she spoke and chills rattled through Millie, so much so that she realised she had pulled the blanket up past her chest. The clarity of the argument from moments before was gone, and instead it felt as if they were back to talking about war.

'Can I use your toilet?' Millie asked. She didn't particularly need to go – but she wanted out of the room.

'Top of the stairs,' Will replied. 'Second door on the left.'

Millie hurried out of the living room, into the hall. It was lighter there, mainly because of the hotch-potch fairy lights that were taped to the ceiling. Millie followed the power cord up the creaky stairs and onto a landing, where the dying sun was gleaming through a skylight across the bare floorboards. The walls were patchy, with a mix of ripped paper and peeling paint. There were dots of mould across the ceiling, with more spidery black spots around the window.

The door directly across from the stairs was open and, with nobody else around, Millie poked her head inside. The floor was bare, though the walls had been painted far more recently than any other part of the house. They were a light pink, though whoever had painted had left drips on the floor that had dried. A double bed was against the far wall, with messy covers on top and a spaghettied mangle of wires and cables stretching from the only plug socket. On the ceiling, exposed wires hung where there should have been a light fitting.

There was a creak from somewhere on the stairs below, so

Millie quickly turned to the left and opened the door. She was expecting a toilet and hopefully a sink – except she hadn't opened the second door on the left, she'd opened the first.

And inside, stacked against the wall in a small cupboard, was a pile of thick club-like sticks.

EIGHTEEN

It might have been strange to keep twenty to thirty sticks in a cupboard – but, the more Millie scanned the collection, the more they didn't seem like *only* sticks. There were four broom handles, with ends that had been filed down to points. With the more obvious pieces that had come from the woods, bark had been sanded away to create something handle-like – and with them being thinner at one end, while flat at the other, they were more like bats or paddles.

She picked one up and almost dropped it immediately, as the unexpected weight at the wide end pulled her down. They were the sort of clubs that might be seen in crude images of cavemen, hunting with rocks and sticks. Easy to pick up, as long as you knew it was going to be heavy, easy to swing – and devastating if it connected with something, or someone.

Millie leant the club back with the others and then noticed the pair of supermarket carrier bags almost hidden in the shadows. There was something soft inside and, when she crouched to look more closely, Millie realised that what she thought was a pile of scarves was actually balaclavas and cable-knit beanie hats.

The creak from the stairs had Millie moving as quickly as she ever had. She closed the door and almost dived through the next one, where there was a toilet and sink. There was also an olive green bath crusted with limescale and a shower curtain stapled to the ceiling. Millie locked the door and sat on the toilet, with the seat down, as she listened for if someone had followed her up the stairs.

There was momentary silence and then another squeak before the sound of footsteps. Someone walked along the landing and opened a door, before closing it behind them.

Millie was holding her breath as the silence hit once more. She waited and listened until she had convinced herself the footsteps was someone returning to their room. It wasn't only Hannah and Will who lived in the house.

Millie considered calling the police. It was never her first choice and, after an experience of being arrested a few months before, her scepticism of them was higher than ever. Except Hannah had talked of war, they wanted reinforcements – and here was a hidden weapon stash.

Or was it?

Millie wondered what would happen if the police did show up, only to find what could easily be called a pile of sticks. That's what she thought they were at first. The pointed mop handles could be some sort of temporary fence posts to spike into the ground, while Millie was sure there was some sport that used clubs like the ones she'd discovered. She'd definitely seen it somewhere: curling, or hurling, or something like that.

Then she wondered if it was actually the perfect weapon store. If they had knives or machetes, it would be hard to pretend they were anything else – whereas these *could* be explained away as sticks.

But there was also the fact that Will and Hannah wanted coverage under their own names, while their faces were known. They could hardly put on a balaclava and pretend to be someone else. Millie had never seen anyone wear a balaclava – but it was cool in the house, despite the heat outside. It would be even worse through a winter.

Millie had no idea what to do. She was convinced there was a weapon stash ahead of a war as much as she was that it was nothing.

Either way, she couldn't stay in the toilet much longer. She flushed it, let the taps run for thirty seconds, noted there was no towel, and then headed onto the deserted landing.

Downstairs, the living room was empty, except for Will. He was back in the windowsill, fingering himself a roll-up on the sill. When Millie entered, he didn't look up at first, instead continuing with what he was doing until the joint was ready.

'Want to share?' he asked, finally taking in Millie.

'Not my thing.'

'Don't drink, don't smoke. That's not the Millicent West-lake I used to know.'

She almost winced at the use of her full name. Nobody called her that in her real life. The last person to do so was prob-ably her mum.

'Maybe you never knew me properly?' Millie replied.

That got a laugh. 'True.'

He stretched into his pocket for a lighter and then lit the joint. The smell took seconds to cross the room, even though Will was making a half-hearted effort to smoke it out the window.

'Where did Hannah go?' Millie asked.

'For a walk with some of the others.' He clucked his tongue, then switched into some sort of showman's voice. 'It's just you and me!'

Millie considered leaving, even though it was Will she'd come to see. She barely knew her but Millie felt safer with Hannah in the room.

'What is it you want?' Millie asked. 'Specifically. I know

you said you want coverage – but, if you're going to live-stream things, you know what you're doing online. You can recruit people far more easily yourself than asking some bloke who's nearly seventy and who was made redundant over a year ago. It's not like his website has an audience of millions.'

Will sucked on the joint and held the smoke for what felt like too long before letting it out.

'I know you've always been into protesting—' Millie added – but she didn't get to finish the sentence.

'I stand up for things, for *people*. Are you against that?'

'No, it's just—'

'What have you ever stood up for, Mill? What causes? What people?'

Millie tried to think of something, anything, but the only thing that stuck in her mind was something from primary school when she'd help run a bring-and-buy sale for Comic Relief. Was that standing up for something? Probably not. And it hadn't been her idea anyway, it had been Nicola's.

There must be something. There definitely would be if he'd given her twenty-four hours' notice. She'd stood up for Ingrid six or so months before, when the older woman said she'd seen someone fall from a roof and nobody seemed to believe her. Did that count? Did it count that her son had put on a dress and she'd refused to let it be weird?

Millie had already taken too long in giving an answer, which Will took as a reply in itself. He was looking at her smugly, argument won – and he allowed himself a puff of the joint in celebration.

'I just don't want anyone to get hurt on Tuesday,' Millie said. 'You said you want lots of people to be here but they'll all be people worried about where they can live and affording houses. They won't be coming here thinking there might be trouble.'

'Who said there will be?'

'Hannah said this is a war you didn't start.'

That got a shrug and a deliberate roll of the eyes before Will pushed himself off the ledge. He nodded his head for Millie to follow as he passed her and strode through the house. They were soon at the back, where any sign of a party from the previous days had been replaced by washing lines that zigzagged across the lawn. Towels and clothes had been dried stiff from the heat and breeze.

'What am I looking at?' Millie asked.

'Hannah says a lot of things,' Will replied. 'She spent all morning washing this lot in the sink. Do you really think she's some sort of revolutionary?'

Millie assumed revolutionaries still washed their clothes at some point, so didn't really get the point. She considered mentioning the clubs she'd seen in the cupboard upstairs – except she couldn't see any way he'd either tell her the truth, or that she wouldn't end up feeling silly. Or, worse, she'd find out at close quarters that they were something dangerous.

'Say you get a big crowd,' Millie began, 'and say you turn around the bailiffs and you get to end up living here for longer. Maybe the buyer gives up and sells to someone who doesn't mind you being here? There's some big segment on the news and you go viral on Twitter. Everyone thinks you're brilliant. Even if you get everything you want, it's not going to stop other people from outside the town buying houses here. Look at the view from the front: that's why they want to buy here. It won't stop that and it won't stop developers building places that locals can't afford. You can't control any of that.'

Will took a long breath on his joint, held it and then blew it towards the newly clean towels. He crouched and stubbed out the remains on the patchy, dry lawn.

'You don't get it,' he said.

'So help me get it. You wanted Guy to write something for

you but he won't do it. I'm the one here asking you to help me understand.'

A cloud drifted overhead, leaving them in temporary shadow. There was a bang from the house behind, somewhere upstairs, as Millie wondered if Hannah and the rest of the housemates had truly gone for a walk. It would be a strange lie – but the only place to walk from the house was down the hill towards town, plus Millie had heard someone enter a room upstairs when she'd been in the toilet.

'Shall we sit at the front?' Will asked.

'The living room?'

'The *actual* front.'

Millie looked up and realised it wasn't a cloud that had left them in shadow. The sun had dipped, leaving it close to night-fall. The story of the other housemates being out for a walk felt even less likely.

Before Millie could reply, Will was off for a second time in as many minutes. He bounded through the house, through the front door and into the overgrown garden. Millie was a few steps behind as he grabbed a couple of folded deckchairs that had been hidden among the weeds. He fought until they were both on the path facing the town.

The view was an unquestionable pull. The sun was begin-ning to dip and the lights of the pier were starting to sear into the gloom.

'Best spot in the town,' Will said.

They sat quietly for a few moments and it was hard not to agree.

'It was amazing at Christmas,' he added. 'You could see the outline of the tree at the end of the pier, plus everything strung along the prom. We'd spend hours just sitting here with a fire and watching.'

'What did the neighbours say?'

A snigger – but he didn't reply to that specific question. Instead, he answered the one that had gone before. 'It was Hannah who wanted more coverage,' he said. 'She manages the social media stuff and uploads our videos to YouTube. The groups around the country she talked about are contacts she's made. She's the one who said we should get a local paper here on Tuesday. We looked into it but couldn't find anyone. Then she saw your friend's news site and thought he'd be perfect. I think some of the other groups have contacts on their local papers, or TV stations. That's why she thought it would be good.' A pause. 'I didn't expect *you* to turn up...'

Millie wasn't sure how to reply, though he wasn't quite done as he added: 'Why don't we talk about what's going on with you...?'

Millie knew it was trouble but she wanted to hear about Pidge. The name had been hanging since she'd last seen Will.

'In what way?' Millie replied.

'I always wondered what happened with you and Nic,' Will said. 'You were such good friends. Inseparable. Matty and I used to talk about whether you were *more* than friends.' She felt him glance sideways to her, as if this might get a fervent denial. When it got nothing, he continued: 'Then it was like you were dead to each other. We were at that wedding a few years ago and you were on different sides of the room. I had to come over to one side to talk to Alex, then over to the other to say hello to Nic.'

'I don't want to talk about what it was like back then.'

There was glee in Will's voice. 'Something changed, didn't it? It was never quite the same after the night you cut her hair – or that's what you *said* happened.'

Millie shivered and perhaps it was the oncoming chill, but perhaps it wasn't. The light seemed to be slipping fast now that it had started. The town below was a web of cream and orange street lights, plus red and white headlights and tail lights.

Beyond that, the ocean was barely moving as the crisp white of the moon licked across the tips of the gentle waves.

'Are you saying that's not what happened?' Millie replied.

It felt a dangerous question.

'I'm saying it's a strange story,' Will replied. 'I've been drunk before. Everyone has. I've never heard of someone being *so drunk* they want to cut their hair, much less have their best friend go along with it. It never made sense. I might've believed it if one of you got drunk and cut your own hair – but how can you *both* be in such a state that one of you does it to the other...?'

He had a point and yet it was impossible not to wonder whether he was saying this as speculation, or if he knew the actual reason why Nicola's hair had gone.

'I thought you didn't remember much about that night...?' Millie replied.

'You brought it up the other day and it got a few cogs turning.'

He tapped his temple, although it was hard to see at first because he was barely a shape in the night.

'I saw Jenny yesterday,' Millie said. 'We had lunch together.'

He turned in his seat, surprise: 'Did you? What did you talk about?'

'Being young in general, I suppose. Lots of things. We swapped numbers.'

'Did you tell her you're friends with Nic again?'

'Why wouldn't I?'

'Because she *hated* Nicola. She always did, even when we hung around together all those times. Even when Matty and Charlie were each other's best men – and it meant Nic and Genevieve were sort of family.'

Millie was momentarily confused: 'They're not related.'

'No... but you know what I mean. Their husbands were best

friends. They were each other's best men. They must have seen each other loads – even though Genevieve couldn't stand Nic.'

Millie had somehow missed that they had to have seen each other a lot. Genevieve had said that she'd hated Nicola when they were teenagers – but their connection had lasted much longer.

'Funny. Jenny said that *you* couldn't stand me and Nic...'

Will didn't reply to that, not properly. He said something about it being a long time ago – but the past few days had left Millie wondering how much her memories of her teenage years were actually real. Any group would have their own mini rivalries and friendships and yet it was increasingly feeling as if theirs involved a series of feuds that Millie had somehow missed. Could it have been that bad? Six of the eight married each other – and the seventh, Rachel, was now in a relationship with one of those six. It was only Will who'd stayed apart from it all.

It had gone from the final dregs of daylight to dusk to dark. There was a glow of upstairs lights from the house behind and the vague sound of someone shuffling around. Millie knew Will had lied about the others going for a walk, although it was impossible to know why. Perhaps he was one of those who lied about everything. Maybe not big lies but stupid little ones for the sake of telling them. She didn't think he used to be like that but then she was wondering whether she ever really knew the people who used to be her friends. She'd felt let down, to say the least, by Nicola when she slept with her dad; then Alex – before she had her own affair. Their silly little group had spent all these years letting each other down.

'I think I should go,' Millie said. She couldn't bring herself to talk about the real reason she'd come – but Will knew anyway.

'Are you not going to ask about Pidge?' he said.

'Why would I?'

'I assumed that's why you'd come.'

She couldn't see him but Millie could hear the smirk in his voice.

'I'm going to go.'

'Pidge told me what you bought the week before your mum and dad died...'

The deckchair was low and Millie was struggling to heave herself out of it. She couldn't quite push herself forward and up at the same time.

Will laughed and then he was in front of her, offering a hand that she had little choice but to take. He pulled her up and then she was standing, so close to him that she could feel his breath flitting across the top of her head.

'You can't believe a word Pidge says,' Millie replied. 'He got done for selling ecstasy near the school three or four years ago. I'm surprised he's out.'

'Got an interesting story about you, though...'

Millie moved away, sashaying around Will and ending up in the long grass.

'Like I said, he's a liar. They had him on camera dealing to those kids and he still denied it...'

Millie stepped back onto the path.

'I believed what he had to say.'

Will wanted her to ask what had been said, like those Facebook attention seekers and their cryptic posts wanting others to ask how they were. She wouldn't do it.

'I'm gonna go,' Millie said, taking another step away. There were a few metres between them now, with Will silhouetted by the upstairs lights of the house behind him.

'Didn't your parents OD on Vicodin?' Will said. 'Both of them? On the same night? I'm sure I remember hearing that, or reading it. Someone said it was a joint suicide...'

'You seem to know the answer already.'

Millie had known what was coming two days before when

Will had fallen into her life again and mentioned Pidge. There was only one thing he could have been talking about.

'I thought I did,' Will replied. 'I heard what people were saying about you, that you killed your mum and dad and all that – but I thought it was nonsense. Old people with too much time on their hands and too much Facebook. Then I got talking to Pidge – and he told me you bought a mountain of Vicodin from him not long before they died.'

NINETEEN

The golf ball zipped across the smooth green, swooped down the curve of the course, clipped the edge of the spinning windmill blade – and dropped neatly into the water with a not-so-satisfying *plop*.

Guy was studiously avoiding Millie's glare as she stepped away from the start of the hole, allowing him to place his ball on the tee-off mat.

'Does that go in your little book?' Millie said.

'It's not that sort of book.'

Guy reached into his back pocket and passed across a palm-sized leather-covered pad. She'd seen many of his notebooks in the past and they were all seemingly filled with endless short-hand squiggles. As far as she could tell, they were indecipherable to anyone but him.

This small book *was* different, mainly because Millie could read it. The first page had a year written at the top and then a table of numbers, with a small write-up at the bottom.

Carol wins 4&3 with holes-in-one at the eighth, ninth and fifteenth.

The next page had another year at the top and a similar report at the bottom.

Carol wins 2&1 with a hole-in-one at the eighth.

Millie continued flipping through the pages as Guy waited and watched.

'You played crazy golf every year on the same day?'

'It was our wedding anniversary tradition. We played every year, rain or shine.'

'And you kept all the scores...?'

That got a nod and a gulp as Guy crouched and re-placed the ball that was already in the correct position. When they'd arrived at the course, he'd told Millie that he kept a crazy golf book. She thought it was a joke until it was in her hands.

Millie gulped too and had to breathe it away as she and Guy avoided looking at each other. Eye contact would make it too real.

There were more than forty years of little write-ups in Guy's meticulous books. Scores for every hole he and his wife had ever played, plus a record of every hole in one.

Millie flicked to the most recent page, the one from the year before, where there was a single column of numbers against the hole.

Guy finished the course with a hole-in-one at the second

'You played by yourself?' Millie said, knowing the answer.

Guy turned and settled himself for the shot. He clipped the ball gently and it slipped to the right of the green, swished down the slope towards the centre, darted through the slot underneath the windmill with perfect timing, and then emerged on the other side, a foot or so from the hole.

He motioned to step after it but Millie reached for him,

taking his hand and squeezing. He gripped her fingers too, not for long but for enough, and then accepted the book back.

Suddenly, this wasn't an eccentric Sunday-morning quirk – as she'd thought when they'd ended up at the entrance to the crazy golf course. It was something important.

The poor sod.

Millie retrieved her ball from the water and tried again. It took her four attempts to get the ball through the windmill and five more to get it in the hole. Guy putted from his original position – and she watched as he wrote the scores in his book.

There was an ache in Millie's stomach for the sort of trust and love that came with something that had endured for so long. It wasn't about the golf, not really. More that two people had done the same thing, on the same day, for more than forty years until one of them had died.

'That puts me one-up,' Guy said.

'Did you usually win?'

They carried their balls and clubs across a dinky bridge to the second hole. There was no obstacle as such but, instead, there was a series of triangles jutting out from the sides. The ball could only reach the hole in one if it was hit at the perfect angle to ricochet through.

'Not for years,' Guy replied.

He'd won the first hole, so had first go at the second. He dropped his ball and then edged it onto the tee-off mat with his toe.

'Carol won for the first fourteen years. In the tenth year, I was leading up to the final hole, then I lost my bottle and accidentally chipped the ball off the ramp into the pond. I took nine shots to finish and she did it in two. She won by a single hole.'

Millie wasn't entirely sure of what he'd said but she had enough of a gist.

'But you finally won in the fifteenth year...?'

He grinned. 'I practised. I came here once a week or so

without telling her. I got so much better. I still only won by two holes.'

'Did you tell her?'

A laugh: 'She'd already figured it out. Not many people got one over on Carol – and certainly not me.'

He lined up his next shot, cannoning the ball around two thirds of the zigzags before it ended up resting in a corner, next to one of the triangles.

'What was the final score in years?' Millie asked.

'Thirty-one–twelve to Carol.'

'That must've been the longest-running rivalry in sport...'

Guy laughed: 'I'd never thought of it like that... but yes. I think Carol would've found that funny, too.'

The continued around the holes as Guy explained how the course had changed over the decades. There had been different owners and different layouts. After the great storm of October 1987, three trees had come down and hole eleven had been redesigned around a fake tree to symbolise it. Millie was surprised the course had lasted so long – but then Guy pointed out that many things around the bay were the same. The pier had been in place for over a century, with the arcade on the same spot at the front for almost as long. There were fishmongers on the front that dated to the 1920s. Things changed... but perhaps they didn't.

Guy won the first nine holes but Millie had her moment on the tenth. Her ball drifted down the slope and then rolled perfectly up to the top of a small hill. It skirted around the cup, appeared to pause in mid-air, and then dropped neatly into the hole with a plop.

'Total skill,' Millie assured him when Guy asked playfully if she meant it.

That claim of talent was somewhat undermined on the next hole, when her shot bounced off the fake tree that had survived from the eighties, rebounded off her heel, and ended up in a bush.

The conversation about Guy's anniversary and the golf had run out of steam, not that it was a problem. There was an unquestionable calm about ambling around an almost empty mini golf course on a Sunday morning.

Bells rang in the distance and Guy told her how someone from the caravan park next to the church had once stormed in on a Sunday morning and demanded they turn the volume down. He'd written a story about it but couldn't remember how long ago. There was also something comforting about being with a person like Guy who had genuine knowledge of what they were talking about, along with seemingly no agenda.

It was also good for Millie to forget about the other things for a short while. About Will and what he knew, or what he *thought* he knew. She'd realised after leaving the squat the night before that he didn't particularly want anything from her. When he'd said in the first place he wanted Guy to write something for them, he wasn't overly bothered. It was more for Hannah. He hadn't made any demands when they spoke in the front garden – but he wanted Millie to know that he was holding what Pidge had said over her. It was the power that was important to him.

Back on the course, Guy had won the eleventh, twelfth and thirteenth holes. He noted each of the scores in his book, even though the element of competition was long gone. Millie wondered if this was a new tradition. Perhaps they'd be back in another twelve months for another round to mark what would have been his forty-sixth anniversary? She thought she'd probably like that.

Millie and Guy were in no rush, so they stood to the side, allowing a group of four boys to overtake them. They were twelve or thirteen, full of boisterousness and bluster as they smashed the golf balls too hard and then tried to trip one another up on their way to the next hole.

She knew she wouldn't ask about it but Millie wondered whether Guy and Carol had ever tried for children. They would have been married at a time in which most brides were pregnant within a year – a little like Ingrid had said. She figured if he ever wanted to talk about it, he'd say. Millie had had enough of people asking her about children when she'd first married Alex – and that had been decades after Guy.

They finished the course and handed back the clubs and balls, then Guy asked if she wanted ice cream. It wasn't even noon and Millie didn't really – but she said 'yes' anyway. Guy treated himself to a double ninety-nine. He'd pushed one of the flakes down into the cone and was using the second as a spoon to scoop up the ice cream. Millie had gone with a standard soft serve, which had started to run almost instantly.

They sat on a bench, facing the ocean as the sun climbed higher. The streets were starting to fill with holidaymakers as the tinkling din from the arcade on the pier skimmed the warm breeze. Millie wondered if this was another ritual for Guy and Carol's anniversary. Crazy golf and an ice cream wasn't a bad way to start a summer's day. Not a bad way to remember a wedding.

Below them, the ocean was beginning to creep across the beach. A handful of people had set up towels on the sand but Millie knew they'd have an hour at most until the ocean would send them back to shore.

'How was Eric after yesterday?' Guy asked.

'I've not heard. Alex said no phone call last night and I don't usually text first, unless there's something important.'

'Is that through choice...?'

'After the custody hearing, my solicitor asked if I was happy with the outcome,' Millie said. 'I wasn't, obviously. I went from seeing Eric every day to every other weekend. She said that if I ever wanted it to be re-examined in future, the best thing I could do was stick rigidly to every part of the decision. She said it's double standards. If you get bad faith from the other side – if they want to swap days, or times, or holidays, that sort of thing – that you should try to accept it. But you do that while knowing the same leniency won't be given the other way.'

'That must be hard for you.'

'It was worse when it first happened. She said to get everything on the record. Try to avoid in-person talks and do it via text, or email. Something that can be reproduced as proof if it's ever needed. She said there's not a lot of point in trying to force a re-examination. That I should try to give Eric the best times I possibly can when he's with me. If he talks about seeing me more, or wanting to live with me – I've got his opinion, plus years of proof that I've done everything I can to obey the court.'

It all sounded so unemotional, but that's what courts dealt with. There was no other choice.

Guy was almost done with his ice cream and so Millie handed him the rest of hers. He asked if she was sure but didn't need telling twice as he polished off both. Millie was reminded of being with Eric, when she'd buy him McDonald's fries as a treat, as well as getting the same for herself. She'd know full well he'd end up eating most of hers.

Guy wiped his fingers dry and then pressed back into the bench. 'Did you know anything about Eric's choice of outfit yesterday?' he asked.

'No... when I told him I was leaving, he asked if I liked it and I told him that what mattered was whether he did. He said it was comfy. I don't think he'd really noticed much more than that.'

'I'm not sure everyone saw it that way yesterday...'

It didn't sound like a criticism. Millie wondered whether Alex had made him take it off once everyone had gone. Whether Eric had been made to feel that he'd done something wrong. She wanted to call or, better yet, visit – but that would only cause more problems.

As she finished speaking, a seagull the size of a medium dog swooped down and landed on the bench a few metres along the prom. It grabbed a discarded chip wrapper and began pecking at the potatoey mess it had created.

'I went to see Will last night,' Millie said. 'I met Hannah again.'

'How's her little war going?'

Millie couldn't work out if he was teasing.

'I keep feeling like I'm missing something,' she said. 'It's like Will has his own idea of what's going on, while Hannah's not too bothered about the house itself and wants a bigger, ideological fight. I don't know if they're a couple, or just living together. I don't know if any of that matters.' She stopped and then: 'What do you think?'

'I think they're going to be evicted this week, whether they like it or not.'

Millie thought about that for a moment. Guy was probably right.

'I went upstairs,' she said. 'There was something in a cupboard up there. Bats, or sticks, or... it's difficult to say. I thought they might be weapons but maybe it's firewood? Maybe it's some sort of decoration? There were a few balaclavas there, too. I wondered if I should call the police – but it's not as if owning bits of wood is illegal.'

Guy took a few seconds, as she'd hoped he would. He wasn't the instinctive sort and that felt like a good thing. The legality of the wood didn't matter. There was something that felt like a problem. 'I think you're right,' he said. 'I know someone I could talk to but the whole point of court orders is that the police can't simply enter a property. If you'd seen guns, or evidence of something like widescale drug dealing, that would be different. But they'd be very reluctant to do anything when there's already a bailiff removal date set for Tuesday.'

On the other bench, the seagull had finished the chips it had dumped on the pavement and had its head in the bin once more.

'Are you going to witness things on Tuesday?' Millie asked. 'It's definitely a news story...'

'I've not decided. I don't cover *everything* in this town. The *Journal* still exists and they have a reporter – even though she doesn't live here.'

The hint of bitterness at his former employer was impossible to miss, although Millie let it go without comment.

As she wondered if he was going to say anything else, Guy stood abruptly. 'I'm going to pop to the car,' he said. 'I'll be right back.'

Millie watched him cross the road and then she turned back to the path, where a second gull had joined the first. It was busy pecking at the empty chip wrapper as the bigger bird continued to delve into the bin.

It wasn't long until Guy was back, with a battered satchel under his arm. It was primarily made of leather but the soft finish had been worn away, leaving something thinner and scratchier. Millie wasn't even sure what colour it had once been.

Guy put the satchel on the bench between them and then flipped the top, before passing her an old six by four photo. The colours were washed out and the image not entirely in focus. When Millie angled in closer, she suddenly realised why he'd handed it to her.

'Is that Mum?' she asked.

There were seven teenagers, each with chains around their legs and wrists, attaching them to a metal fence. On the far right of the photo was a woman with curly dark hair and big hexagonal glasses. She was wearing a white vest that had an anti-nuclear symbol on the front.

'I thought you might be interested in that,' Guy said. 'I knew I had it somewhere. They were protesting the closure of the old factory that Factory Lane is named after. There are houses there now but it used to be a plant that made tyres. There was a time pre-war where around half the men in the town were employed there. By the time it closed, it was nowhere near that.'

Millie pressed a finger to her mother on the photo. 'I remember being in the car and we'd drive along Factory Lane to get to school,' she said. 'They were building the estate and Mum said there used to be a tyre factory there. She never said she chained herself to the gates.'

It felt so strange because Millie struggled to think of her mother in any way other than through the prism of her father. He was the famous one, who dominated the relationship. He earned the bulk of the money and made the decisions. He was responsible for discipline and telling Millie how he thought she should be acting.

Her mother was there and yet... not. She worshipped her husband, which made Millie a daddy's girl by default.

And yet here she was doing something away from Millie's father. There had been a time in which she had her own opinions and ideas.

'My dad used to work there,' Guy said. 'Most dads, I suppose. There were always two industries in Whitecliff – tyres and tourism. Young people, men especially, assumed they'd have a job for life at the factory. When it was announced they were closing, lots of people from the college and polytechnic went and blocked the road.' He pointed to the photo, working his way along the line. 'That's your mum. That's Carol... and that's me.'

Millie gasped as she held the photo closer. Now he'd said it, it was so obvious that the man in the work overalls who had his wrists and ankles chained to the fence was Guy.

'You had a lot of hair in those days,' Millie said.

That got a laugh.

'Was Dad there?' Millie asked.

'I don't remember him being at the factory. He's definitely not in any of the photos.' There was a hint of spikiness. 'It was a bit of a party for a while. Some of the residents brought us drinks and food. There were photographers and reporters. Someone from the county radio station came down with their mics and asked what we were doing and why. I sometimes wonder if that was why I ended up wanting to be a reporter.'

Millie eyed the photo again. She'd never known Carol but her mum and Guy seemed so impossibly young. They'd have been about the same age as Millie when she and Nicola had been hanging around on the bandstand. There was no need to wonder why her father wasn't there. Assuming he was the same person in his youth as he was as an adult, he would have wanted to be loved by everyone. If he'd taken a specific stand against the factory closing, it would have meant potentially annoying those who wanted to close it. He was the ultimate two-sides man in public.

Not so much in private.

'What happened in the end?' Millie asked.

'They waited us out,' Guy said. 'There's only so long you can chain yourself to a fence. That first day was all free drinks, food, radio stations and reporters. Day two was a bit less food and drink. It rained on day three – and that was us done. We ended up unchaining ourselves and going home. The factory shut for good six or seven months later – and then it was knocked down.'

The symbolism and the timing was impossible to miss.

'Is this you saying all protests are futile?' Millie asked.

'Far from it. We'd still have the poll tax if not for protests. Women wouldn't be able to vote. More or less every advancement in human wellbeing has come about through some form of protest – even if it's at a very low level.'

'What *are* you saying?'

'That I'm old and I'm sceptical. I see people wanting to man barricades because they can't afford places to live – and a big part of me agrees. Another part remembers when the rain came on that third day and how the security guards waved us goodbye as we went on our way. Whatever happens on Tuesday – and I'm ninety-five per cent sure they'll be evicted – they'll get waited out regardless.'

Millie couldn't help but feel he was right – and she wasn't sure how she felt about it.

Perhaps it wasn't *only* her father who could two sides an issue.

She handed back Guy the photo and he asked if she wanted to keep it. Millie took a picture of it on her phone and said that would do, before he put it away.

'I found something else,' Guy said.

As he spoke, two more seagulls joined the first pair on the other bench. The original one was out of the bin and the four began squawking an ear-grating symphony at each other.

Guy slipped a folded copy of the *Whitecliff Journal* from his satchel and started to unfold it. It was crumpled and ripped in a few places, with a large advert on the front for the 'summer culture pull-out'.

'How old is that?' Millie asked.

'Twenty years, or so...'

Guy opened out the paper to reveal the eight-page pull-out in the centre. He flipped it over to show the back page and, from nowhere, Millie was seventeen again. The headline read: 'Whitecliff rocks to battle of bands' and, underneath was a collage of grainy black and white photos. Millie already knew that Matty's band hadn't won – but, until she saw the top photo, she'd completely forgotten that the winner was a four-piece boyband in poorly fitting suits. They'd sat on stools and sung Boyzone covers. That meant they were largely singing covers of covers – which was something that had Matty raging at the judges. Matty's band had written their own awful songs, for which he wanted credit. Or, at the very least, a share of the prize money.

'It's so weird to see people smoking indoors,' Millie said as she scanned the photos. She couldn't remember when it had been banned but it felt like forever. She'd first started going to pubs when people would smoke wherever they liked, and a permanent fog seemed to hang.

There were some photos of the bands but plenty more of the crowd and the bar. One of the lead singers was topless and carrying a rubber chicken for some reason, while at least three of the other bands dressed, and had attempted to sing, like Liam Gallagher.

The line at the bottom said there were more photos inside, so Millie turned the page, which is where she saw the large picture of Matty clasping the microphone and bellowing to the audience. They'd been woeful but had finished in the top three or four largely by default. All the Oasis copycats cancelled each other out – and by the time the lunatics with things like rubber chickens had been discounted, there wasn't a lot left.

'I did spot one familiar face,' Guy said. He pointed to the opposite page, where a photo of the battle of the bands crowd had been put in a collage with crowd pictures from other 'cultural' events around the city.

And there they were. The old gang. It must have been after Matty's band had finished because he was on the end, his hair greasy and clinging to his face as he saluted the camera with a bottle of beer. He'd have been underage but they all were. Matty had a hand on Nicola's shoulder, with Genevieve on his other side, looking up to him. Millie was in the middle, next to

Rachel – and then there was Alex, with Will on the end. There was no Charlie, but he'd have been working.

They were all grinning but there was an exhaustion about them too. It was hard to hide the bleary eyes of a whole day in the sun, followed by a night of drinking, plus nowhere near enough food or water. Nobody ever talked about drinking enough water in those days anyway. It felt like someone had invented it in around 2010. Sparkling water had come even later.

Millie was about to turn the page to see if there were more pictures – but then she saw it. Will was on the end of the row, leaning at an angle that almost took him out of frame. He had one arm around Alex's shoulders, the other raised high. And there, attached to his wrist and hanging free, was a pair of fluffy handcuffs.

TWENTY

The photo was so grainy that Millie was almost touching the paper with her nose before she lowered it and showed it to Guy.

'Are those handcuffs on Will's wrist?' Millie asked.

It was Guy's turn to bring the paper closer to his face and then further away. 'Looks like it.'

'When I found Nicola, she was cuffed to the tree with handcuffs exactly like these. They were pink and a bit muddy. The keys had been left on the ground a few metres away from her. I found them next to a clump of her hair.'

Guy put down the paper on the bench and Millie had another look. It was hard to see any sort of chain given the quality of the photo – plus she couldn't know if they were pink because it was black and white. But whatever was attached to his wrist was definitely light and fluffy.

'Why would Will be wearing handcuffs?' Millie asked, talking to herself. 'We were there for hours because it took ages to get the bands on and off. Where would he have got handcuffs?'

Guy turned to look over his shoulder, across the road towards the shops on the far side. The pub on the corner had not long opened but there was already a mass of people in the beer garden. The smell of Sunday roast was creeping over the street. Further along was a chip shop, then two competing tat stores with displays of tea towels, actual towels, and cheap buckets and spades.

'Maybe one of the novelty stores...?' Guy replied.

As he spoke a topless man sunburned red trotted out from one of the tat shops with a blow-up doll under his arm. His mates gave a 'wa-hey!' as he hooked the doll around his neck and started to conga towards the pub.

It wasn't even noon.

Those sorts of stalls all sold arrays of disposable rubbish for stag and hen parties. If anything, the market for that stuff would have been higher twenty years before. There was a very good chance one of those places sold fluffy pink handcuffs back then – and probably now. Will could have easily bought, found, or stolen a pair.

When Millie turned back to the beach, more memories swirled. They'd been sitting underneath the pier one time when Matty had found a sand-covered dildo half-buried in the sand. It had washed in on the tide and the boys had a competition to see who could throw it the furthest. They slung it around as if it was a javelin.

Millie glanced to the photo once more and then closed the paper.

'Don't tell Nicola,' she said. 'Not yet. I'm going to think about what to do. One of our other friends told me that Will always hated Nicola and me because Nic didn't give him the attention she gave other boys. That other photo, from Augustus, made it look like he was the last to leave the park, so maybe he could've run into Nic when she was on her way back...?'

It could be that simple. Will was the last to leave, he'd bumped into the returning Nicola when it was only them, he had apparent motive – and the handcuffs. It was hard to know what he could have done that would have made Nicola forget it was him but perhaps it could be explained through her drunkenness? Unless he knocked her out somehow? Or perhaps they'd shared a drink and he'd spiked her with something?

Either way, it felt like a very large accusation to make against someone based entirely on a couple of photographs.

'Thank you for playing golf,' Guy said.

'Same time next year?'

He smiled kindly at her. 'Perhaps best not to make too many commitments...? I don't want you to feel pressured.'

That sounded fair.

'Thanks for coming to Eric's party.'

Guy stood and picked up his satchel. Over by the bins the four seagulls decided they'd had enough. There was a mass flap of wings and then the four of them soared off towards the pier, leaving a mess of paper and crusty ketchup on the ground.

'I've got a few things to do this afternoon, plus I have to get back to Barry,' Guy said. 'I'll keep digging to see if I have any other papers or notes from that week. It feels like this is something that's going to be hard to figure out. I didn't want to say when I was in your friend's kitchen. I know someone left her those shoes – but, if they're not going to identify themselves, and there's no footage of them being at the house, this might remain a mystery.'

Millie knew he was right. She'd known all along, really, but it was hard to tell that to Nicola. Especially when she'd called so out of the blue.

'Perhaps if it brought you and your friend back together, it's a success...?'

Millie hadn't thought of it like that, and she wasn't yet sure they were back together – but maybe Guy had a point.

'Don't take this the wrong way,' he added, 'but from everything that happened at Eric's party, if doesn't seem as if you have a whole lot of people looking out for you.'

Millie took that in the spirit she assumed it was meant – but it was still hard to hear. She had Jack and Rishi in her life and then... who? Only Guy – and he was more of a father figure than a friend. Or perhaps both. She didn't want to think about it too much. She'd had friends in her office, or thought she did. Once she became front-page news and then the centre of gossip after her parents died, there wasn't a line of people getting in contact to check on her.

Guy had taken a step away when Millie spoke impulsively.

'I never wanted to go to university,' she said. 'Dad wanted me to but I knew it wouldn't be my thing. I left college and bummed around doing a few things here and there. I worked in the college bar and did some promo for their events. I had no idea what I wanted to do – then Dad got me a part-time job as a runner for the TV channel where he worked.'

Guy slipped back onto the bench and lowered his satchel.

'I was twenty-three, twenty-four,' Millie added. 'This was a bit before Alex and I got together. I was seeing this other guy who Mum and Dad didn't approve of. Dad, especially.' She pointed along the prom, out towards the centre of town. 'He was a tattoo artist. Worked in a studio over there. I think I was only seeing him to annoy them. They didn't want me working in a bar, so we'd argue about that. Then we'd argue about my boyfriend and my lack of a career. Dad was the big TV personality, so couldn't have his daughter serving drinks to drunk tourists.'

'I can imagine it wasn't the sort of thing to go down well with your father...'

Millie laughed. Guy and her dad had been very good friends until Guy refused to do a favour that would've created ethical issues.

'Mum was trying to work her way up to head at her primary school around then,' Millie added. 'I used to go over for tea on a

Sunday and she'd tell me she couldn't be a headteacher if her own daughter was such a screw-up.'

'Why did you keep going round?'

'Because she was still a good cook...'

It was Guy's turn to laugh. 'I see.'

'Anyway, Dad got me this shift where I was supposed to be running errands for a producer on this game show. It was being filmed at the same studio where Dad's news show was put together. This giant warehouse place out near the motorway.'

'I know it.'

'I had to get this guy drinks and food – or run off to find the contestants and get them on set. That type of thing. Terrible job but better money than working in a bar and I wasn't working lates. I'd brought this presenter a sandwich or something – and he leant in, patted my arse and said "thanks love".'

Millie stopped momentarily as a couple walked past, sharing a packet of chips. The word 'arse' had come as they'd drawn level and there had been a definite hesitation in their pace. When they were gone, Millie continued.

'I walked out,' she said. 'Didn't say anything to anyone. Just drove back to Mum and Dad's house. I think it was a Tuesday afternoon, sometime during the week. I wasn't living there but I still had a key. I let myself in and went through to the living room – where Nicola was on her knees in front of Dad.'

There was a long, long pause. 'Oh.'

Millie didn't know what else she expected Guy to say. She turned to look over the beach, where the tide was now almost the whole way in. The sunbathers' towels had disappeared but there were a dozen or so paddleboarders in various stages of accomplishment. One woman was standing as if she was on level ground, while effortlessly paddling across the water. More than one of the others was straddling their board while wobbling precariously from side to side.

'I think I took it out on the wrong person,' Millie said. 'It should've been Dad, obviously. He was twice her age and more. Married. She was his daughter's best friend. It's not like I said nothing to him – but it was Nicola I stopped talking to.'

'Sometimes it's hard to get past an initial shock. Harder to say sorry later.'

'Nic and Charlie used to break up and make up all the time. They'd be on and off, sometimes for months at a time. They'd broken up that morning and Nic had gone to the house looking for me. Dad took advantage of her – and I didn't know then but it wasn't the first time. Either way, I didn't see it like that then. It's easier now I'm older, and I think about being twenty-three, twenty-four. You're an adult but it's not like there's a guide. You learn as you go. I thought it was all her fault – but... it was his.'

Below them, one of the straddling paddleboarders was now in the water. A cord was linking him to the board and he was using it like a float aid at the swimming pool, holding on with his hands and kicking with his legs.

'I know I said I was going out with the tattoo guy to annoy him,' Millie said, 'but I think I still wanted Dad's approval. It was complicated. But because of that, I told Nic I never wanted to see her again – and that was fifteen years ago or so. She married Charlie and I never went to the wedding. Then I married Alex and she never came to mine. Over time, I realised Dad wasn't...'

Millie left it there, before she said too much. Except she'd already said too much.

'What did you realise?' Guy asked.

Millie ignored the question. Instead she watched as the paddleboarder crawled back onto his board, tried to stand, and immediately toppled into the water. The woman nearby who was straddling hers pointed, laughed and then pulled a phone out of her swimsuit and started recording.

'Can I take photos of all the pictures from the battle of the bands?' Millie asked.

'I assumed you'd take the paper. It's yours if you want it?'

'I don't want to mess up your archives. Anyway, it's easier to have on my phone.'

Guy offered her the paper back and Millie opened the pull-out, where she took close-ups of everything – especially the handcuff on Will's wrist.

Once she'd done that, she put her phone back in her bag and removed the transparent packet of pictures she'd taken from Augustus's house. She could have taken phone photos of them, of course – but both she and Guy knew that wasn't why she'd taken them.

'Augustus called last night,' Guy said. 'Five times in a row until I picked up.'

'What did you tell him?'

'That I hadn't seen you.'

'I'm not giving these back.'

Guy was silent at that, although he must have already known this was going to happen.

'He stole these,' Millie added. 'The memories, I mean. He stole all these memories from all these kids and he keeps them in biscuit tins.'

Guy touched her knee momentarily and then took away his hand. It was all it needed. All she wanted. She didn't crave grand gestures – all she wanted was what Guy was offering.

Someone who actually acted like a father.

TWENTY-ONE

Millie spent a large part of the afternoon hate-scrolling her own name on the internet. The only time he'd caught her doing it, Jack had threatened to cut the phone lines to her house and steal her phone. Millie told him she'd stop, though she never had.

Since all the rumours had gone around that she'd killed her parents to inherit the house, the reviews for her dog-grooming business had been getting one-star hits a couple of times a week. They were always from someone she'd never met, let alone worked for. She'd been accused of losing dogs and killing dogs – and the process for getting things removed was only partially successful.

Millie would read back all the old, false, reviews of herself and everything she'd apparently done, with no real explanation for why she was doing it. She could block the people who sent her abusive messages through her business's Facebook page – but that meant they would disappear. That meant she wouldn't be able to read them when she wanted to feel bad about herself.

Which happened too often.

The only positive was that all those messages and reviews

had begun to tail off. At one stage, it had been a fake review or an abusive message every day. Now it was one or maybe two a week.

Millie was only distracted when her phone began to buzz, with Alex's name on the screen. It was later than Millie thought, after half-past seven, and she hadn't eaten since the ice cream on the prom.

'You'll have to talk to him.'

Alex was furious as he spoke, with no hint of a 'hello', or anything close.

'Talk to who?' Millie asked.

'Who d'you think? He's been screaming for over an hour. He kicked a hole in his bedroom door and slapped Rach on the arm.'

There was a rustle and then a croaky sob. 'Mum...?'

'What's wrong?' Millie asked.

Eric spoke through a series of gasps and cries, needing close to a minute to compose himself. He'd been told by Auntie Rachel that he wasn't allowed to call his mum in the evenings any longer – which is when all hell had apparently broken loose.

There was the sound of something slamming in the background, then a woman – presumably Rachel – shouting.

Millie eyed her car keys and a part of her was already on her way over to Alex's house. Except she knew she couldn't. Her solicitor's voice was never far from her thoughts when Eric was involved. If she wanted increased access, or future custody changes, she had to play exactly by the rules and never stray. Unsolicited visits were something that would almost certainly be used against her – and, indirectly, Eric – if it came down to it.

'I think they're trying to get you into a routine,' Millie found herself saying. It was definitely her voice but not what she wanted to say. 'You'll need a routine when you go back to school in September.'

Eric's voice was still a series of breathy sobs. 'I only wanted to say 'night...'

'I know, love. I know...'

Millie listened as her son blubbed to himself. She eyed those car keys again though, really, it was Alex at whom she was furious. It wasn't that big a deal to have Eric call her to say goodnight. She was fairly certain the real reason to stop him doing so was more about Rachel wanting to be 'Mum', as opposed to creating a routine.

'I want to stay with you,' Eric said.

Millie didn't reply at first, she couldn't. It was the first time he'd ever said such a thing. When custody was being decided, Eric didn't particularly get a say as he was too young. It was assumed he'd stay with Alex – because Alex was the respectable lawyer who'd not had an affair publicly exposed.

They were only six words but Millie felt as if she'd been waiting her whole life to hear them. Certainly *Eric's* whole life.

'It's not up to me,' Millie replied, as pragmatic as ever – even though she hated being that person. She wasn't allowed to be emotional. An emotional woman was *too* emotional to make any sort of judgement, or hold any responsibility. An emotional man was bravely baring his soul. Everything Millie did in relation to Eric felt judged. 'We'll have fun next weekend,' Millie added. 'We'll visit that dog shelter if it's dry.'

Eric gasped an 'OK' as he started to calm down. None of this was his fault.

'Did you open all your stickers?' Millie asked.

He told her that he only needed seven to complete his book and that one of his friends had two of those to swap. He was hoping to get them on Monday and then he'd be on the hunt for the final five. His voice had stopped quivering and he sounded almost settled.

'What else did you get up to today?' Millie asked.

Eric didn't mention much but he did say his dad had told him that the dress he'd been wearing the day before needed a wash, so he couldn't wear it again.

'It probably *was* dirty,' Millie said. 'You were on the bouncy castle with it yesterday…'

'He said my friends won't want to be my friends if they see me in it again.'

There was a heartbreaking wobble to his voice.

Millie realised she was pulling at her hair. She'd twirled a thread around her fingers, like wool around a knitting needle. It felt as if it was about to pop from her head until she released it.

'I'll talk to him,' Millie said, knowing it would be an awkward conversation to say the least.

Whenever something day-to-day came up about Eric, Alex would always say that he had to make the decisions because she wasn't there. Of course, if she tried to impose her will on anything such as this, she'd be accused of overstepping boundaries. That double standard once more.

'Auntie Rachel threw it out,' Eric said.

'The dress?'

'Dad said they were going to wash it but I saw her throwing it in the big bin.'

That meant the large wheelie bin at the back of the house. Millie always called it that and at least Eric had taken one thing from her, even if it was naming a trash receptacle.

'Is your dad there?' Millie asked. A conversation was going to have to be had and it wouldn't go well.

'He's in the bedroom with Auntie Rachel.'

'Can you get him? I promise to say goodnight to you after.'

Millie took a breath, listened to the rustling, and then a door opening. Eric said, 'Mum wants to talk to you' and then there was more rustling until Alex spoke.

'Have you sorted it?' he said.

'Sorted what?'

'Your son was throwing a right tantrum.'

Millie almost laughed at the predictability of it all. When Eric did well at school, he was Alex's son. If he was ever naughty, Eric was hers. It was so hard to hold back her fury.

'Have you been listening in?' Millie asked.

'What? No.'

'Why did Rachel throw out the clothes Eric wanted to wear?'

There was a momentary pause and Millie could sense the pieces slotting together for her former husband. He knew Rachel had thrown out the dress but he didn't know Eric had seen, nor that he'd told Millie. The hesitation only lasted a moment – and then he went on the aggressive.

'Why do you think?! He's only eight. He's not old enough to be making these decisions.'

'*What* decisions? He's been choosing what to wear for years. It was only last year you bought him an England rugby top. He doesn't play rugby and he's never shown any interest in it. Why is that OK and this isn't?'

Alex's moment was gone as he stumbled to defend the hypocrisy. 'Look, he's not with you day to day. You don't have to deal with it if kids bully him. It'll be Rach and me.'

'Rachel's not his mum, despite what she wants him to call her.'

There was a large huff from the other end of the phone that made Millie angle it away from her ear. 'I'm not going through this again,' Alex replied. 'If you want things to change, take it to court – otherwise it's none of your business.'

Now it was Millie's turn to be speechless. She knew he thought it but he'd never said it quite so brutally. The idea that her son was none of her business left Millie gasping.

'Of course it's my business,' she managed eventually.

'What's your business, Mum?'

Eric was back on the line, unannounced, and without Alex bothering to answer any of her actual concerns. It was so typical.

'Dad says I can't be long,' Eric added.

It took Millie a moment to readjust. She didn't want Eric to hear the anger in her voice. 'Is there anything else you want to do next weekend?' she asked.

Millie got herself together as Eric told her about the big plan he'd come up with. It involved Millie taking him and Chloe to the dog shelter. They'd get KFC for tea but with McDonald's fries, as they were better. He wanted ice cream after that but he couldn't decide on whether he wanted a McFlurry, or if he preferred something from the ice cream van that was permanently parked at the end of the prom during the summer.

Millie didn't have the heart to tell him that there was no chance he was going to get all that junk food. Her phone buzzed from a text but she ignored that as she continued to listen.

'Does that sound OK?' he asked at the end. His plans seemed to involve a thirty-hour day, no sleep, and somewhere in the region of forty-thousand calories.

'We'll see,' Millie said. 'We've got to say goodnight now. It's past your bedtime.'

There was a low whine. 'Can't we talk longer?'

'Sorry, you know the rules, you should be in bed. We'll talk again soon.'

'Tomorrow?'

Millie knew she should say no but, this time, she couldn't force out the word. 'Tomorrow,' she confirmed.

At that, Eric gave a chirpy 'night' – and then he was gone.

Millie put down her phone and did a good bit of staring at the wall for a couple of minutes. Some genuinely world-class staring. Alex had told her to take it to court knowing full well she wouldn't. Or, if she did, that he and his lawyer friends would do everything they could to keep things as they were. Or, worse, to *reduce* her access. It was hard not to feel defeated.

Millie picked up her phone, where a text from Nicola was waiting.

Can u come over?

Millie replied to ask what was wrong – and she got something back almost immediately. It was a photo of one phone, taken with another. A Nokia 3210, with a scuffed pink case that suddenly seemed so familiar that Millie realised she was touching her own phone's screen. Nicola had bought the pink Nokia case from Whitecliff's Saturday-morning market at the same time that Millie had bought a yellow one. On a market of barely twenty stalls, there had been at least four selling nothing but Nokia and Motorola cases, cables and chargers. Each had a plastic rainbow wall, featuring hundreds of cases.

The pink Nokia was the phone that had been taken from Nicola on the night she was left in the woods. The same one used to send Millie the message telling her where to find her friend.

The next part of Nicola's message arrived as Millie was still staring at the photo.

Someone put this thru my door

TWENTY-TWO

Millie got out of her car and turned to take in the organised chaos of the construction yard. On one side, a bloke in a forklift was busy moving pallets from one place to another, for no apparent reason. Across the other side was an enormous warehouse with 'lumber' in huge letters across the entrance. Someone was reversing a flatbed lorry towards a sign marked 'pick up', as a man backed him in with the classic spinning motion of the arm. It was a very blokey environment and Millie couldn't see a single woman until the door of the office opened behind her. Nicola was standing in a smart suit that was at odds with the jeans and scruffy T-shirts everyone else appeared to be wearing.

Nicola nodded Millie into the reception area of Grants, then swiped a pass against a scanner and led her along a corridor into a small staffroom. The walls, the carpets, probably everything, smelled of cheap instant coffee. Half-a-dozen mugs stained with brown streaks were upside-down on the draining board as a white plastic kettle fizzed on the counter.

'My boss doesn't work Mondays,' Nicola said, as she nodded Millie towards the table. 'Do you want a coffee?'

'I'm good.'

Nicola scooped three teaspoons of freeze-dried granules from a massive tub into one of the not-quite-clean mugs. She flicked off the kettle and then filled the cup before sloshing a generous amount of skimmed milk on top.

When she sat opposite Millie, she picked up her bag from the back of the chair and removed an envelope that she slid across the table with a sigh. Millie knew what was inside but it was still a shock to actually hold the phone. Part of it was what it represented. As far as she knew, the final time it had been used was to send her a message, letting her know where Nicola had been left.

Then there was the nostalgia. Millie was so used to smart-phones that were all broadly the same that she'd forgotten things like buttons and a screen which did nothing when it was touched. It was a slice of her life that was somehow relatively recent, yet ancient.

The pink cover was sleek and slippery – although, from what Millie remembered, this type of Nokia was close to bombproof. Dropping it would be more likely to dent the floor. There were scratches on the back and more on the side around the seams of the case from where it had been put on and off.

'Did you try to turn it on?' Millie asked.

'I think it's fully charged but I turned it off because I don't have a charger.'

Millie pressed the buttons on the front but couldn't figure out what to do. Eventually, Nicola pointed out the nodule on top, which Millie held down. The result was almost instant. Four bars appeared along the right side of the tiny monochrome screen, above a small image of a battery. The word 'Menu' popped up at the bottom, with a triangle on the left side, plus an empty reception meter above.

'Someone kept it all this time,' Millie said.

'Like my shoes.'

Millie pressed a couple of buttons but couldn't remember what to do. She had the urge to tap the screen, even though she knew it wouldn't do anything.

'Did Charlie see it?' Millie asked.

'No. We were in the living room, watching TV. I was on my way upstairs and it was on the welcome mat in that envelope. There was no name and, at first, I wondered if Charlie had dropped it. I almost called him through but it wasn't sealed, so I looked inside – and that's when I saw the phone.'

It was still in Millie's hand and she finally realised the word 'menu' was telling her that the button directly below would bring up the menu. Millie pressed it and then used the left and right buttons to scroll through the options. The first was 'phone book'. Millie clicked into that and then scanned through Nicola's two-decade old list of contacts. The first name was Charlie and Millie's first thought was that it was top because he was her husband. It was only as she saw 'Dad' and 'Gen' as the next two names that Millie realised it was in alphabetical order. Millie scrolled and everyone was there. She was under 'Mill' and she clicked into the entry, which listed her old o7 number. Her *first* mobile number. She'd taught it to herself one evening by repeating it over and over in the same way she'd learn Blur lyrics. She'd lost the number a few years on, when she'd changed phone companies and it had been too complicated to swap. Millie surprised herself by being able to recite the number as if she'd learned it that morning.

'I didn't know what to do,' Nicola said. 'I messaged you but Charlie was home last night.' She paused to sip her coffee. 'I don't understand why now?'

Millie looked away from the phone. 'Was there any note?'

'Nothing.'

'Was there anything more after the shoes?'

A shake of the head.

Millie couldn't figure it out. Someone wanted Nicola to

know that *they* knew what had happened two decades before. Or, more likely, that they'd tied Nicola to that tree – and yet they didn't want anything. They didn't even want to reveal themselves. There was no ransom, no blackmail. Nothing.

'I just want it to go away,' Nicola said. She was cradling the mug between her fingers, as if holding it for comfort. 'Who knows what's next? Did they keep some of my hair?'

Millie pressed back in her chair and picked up the phone again. The most recent messages in the inbox were from Millie herself. It took her a short while to figure out how to read them as there was no back-and-forth narrative. The top message simply said 'where ru?', then the one before that said 'huh?' Millie had to move between the outbox and the inbox to realise that she'd sent those two replies in response to the message 'Past the Kissing Tree. Before the feild'.

Apart from the typo, it was almost as she'd remembered. She'd woken up to see the message about the Kissing Tree and had replied with 'huh?' Later, when she couldn't find Nicola, she'd sent 'where ru?' It was only then she had followed the instruction out to the woods, where she found Nicola. She would have found her hours before if she'd realised what the first message meant.

Millie passed the phone and the envelope back across the table. Nicola picked up the device and turned it off, then slipped it into the envelope. She cradled her coffee, sipped it, then yawned.

'Did your friend find out anything?' she asked.

Millie thought of the photos from the paper, with those handcuffs on Will's wrist. 'Not yet,' she said. 'He's working on it.'

She wanted to talk to Will before passing on anything to Nicola. It didn't look good – but it wasn't proof of anything.

'Did you ask your neighbours about cameras?' Millie asked.

Nicola replied quickly: 'I went up and down the other

evening but nobody had anything facing the right way.' She licked her lips and then continued: 'I wanted to ask you something.' She was staring into the bottom of her mug. 'Will you come up to the woods with me? I was thinking of going on my lunch...'

That could only mean one thing. They weren't about to go hiking.

'The Kissing Tree...?'

A nod. 'I've never been back. I thought maybe you and me could...?'

She didn't need to finish the question because Millie knew what she meant.

'Let me go get someone first,' Millie said.

TWENTY-THREE

Millie leant on the stile as the warmth of the early afternoon sun prickled her skin. Barry paced around her feet, eager to shoot around the stile and head off to chase squirrels and decide which stick was the best.

Tyres scratched on gravel and Millie looked up from her phone to watch an SUV pull into one of the empty spaces. A man in shorts and a vest opened the back doors and a trio of German shepherds leapt out. They bounced excitedly as the man led them towards the stile. He nodded a 'hi' to Millie as the dogs gave Barry a sniff and then dashed away to follow the man into the trees. Barry watched them go and then looked sideways up to Millie as if to ask why she was being so cruel in making him wait.

She told him 'sorry' and then looked back to her phone.

Clifftop Forest Trail, Whitecliff

If you get excited about trees and enjoy walking for no reason, you'll love this. There are NO TOILETS in the woods and I had to wee behind a bush. There was no toilet paper anywhere. Where does all my tax go????!!!!!

One star

Millie didn't think there was ever a time when she'd get tired of reading the one-star reviews people left for the town's various attractions. With most tourists arriving in the summer, it was prime time for nutters.

This time, the car crunching across the gravel belonged to Nicola. She was still in her work clothes, though she'd swapped her low heels for a pair of white pumps. If it wasn't summer, they would be coated with mud before they'd even crossed the stile.

Nicola locked her car and hurried across the car park. 'Have you been waiting long?' she asked.

'Five minutes.' Millie crouched and ruffled Barry's fur. 'But if you ask him, he'd say five hours.'

Nicola crouched and said hello to Barry, even though he was more interested in cracking on with things. When Millie ushered him ahead, he didn't wait to be told twice. He slipped around the stile and darted towards the nearest pile of wood. When he emerged seconds later, he was clasping a stick twice as big as he was.

Millie and Nicola were a little slower in getting over the stile.

'Do you ever come here?' Nicola asked.

'I walk Barry a couple of times a week with my friend, Jack. He's into ghosts, so he's brought me out to see something he calls a "ghost tree".'

'What's a ghost tree?'

'To be honest, I'm still not sure. He read something about a woman being hung as a witch centuries ago. Someone on one of his ghost forums reckoned they'd identified the tree, so he's dragged me there to look for ghosts. He's too scared to go on his own and his boyfriend's having none of it.'

They continued along the path for a few paces. 'The Kissing Tree sounds much more fun...'

That was true enough.

They didn't talk much as they ventured further along the trail. The ground was hard and dry, with cracks creeping almost the entire way across. The trees towered high, leaving them in shade for much of the walk. Barry dropped his stick the first time he saw a squirrel, instead trying – and failing – to chase the creature up a tree. He looked at Millie, apparently offended at his lack of opposable thumbs.

It took Millie and Nicola a little over five minutes to reach the first junction. There was a map and signs for the rest of the trail system – but they ignored that as they stepped off the trail and trampled around the various downed trees and bushes. They walked on autopilot, even though neither of them had visited the tree in years. It was on no maps, with the knowledge of its existence passed anecdotally from one generation of horny teenagers to the next. It was a couple more minutes until the undergrowth thinned to a natural clearing where, on the other side, stood the Kissing Tree.

It was more of a trunk than an actual tree. People said it had been hit by lightning, which is why the entire top half had split away, leaving a hollow pyramid. Some of the bark at the bottom had crumbled away, creating something that looked like an open door.

Their pace slowed as they neared the tree.

'Did you ever come here with someone?' Nicola asked.

Millie laughed. 'All my teenage fumbling was strictly in private.' As she replied, Millie suddenly realised why Nicola had asked. 'Did you?'

'Once. Me and Matty were out here one time. He said he had something he wanted to show me.'

'Never trust a teenage boy who says that.'

Nicola sniggered. 'True – but he wanted to show me the

tree. Asked if I'd ever been out to it, which I hadn't. It's not quite something a girl dreams of, is it?'

They were at the tree now. The bark was crispy and dry, with hearts and initials etched on almost every available space. It had filled in over the years.

'That was before I got together with Charlie,' Nicola added, as if Millie had thought any differently.

'What was it like?' Millie asked.

'It was a kiss in a tree. How good could it be?'

Millie stepped into the tree itself. The floor was a mess of cigarette ends and chocolate wrappers, with a tunnel of light spiralling down from above. It was tighter than Millie would have guessed from the outside, with barely enough room for two people to stand. That was likely the appeal. When Millie stepped back outside, Nicola had crouched and was wrestling Barry for the stick he was carrying. He snarled playfully and, when Nicola let it go, he burst off in the other direction.

'How many couples that came here do you think are still together?' Millie asked.

'It's hardly one for the grandkids, is it?' Nicola replied. 'When they ask how you met and you say there was a tree in the woods...'

Millie couldn't quite laugh at that – though Nicola had a point. She wondered if every town had this sort of place. Probably not a tree but a tunnel, or a spot under a bridge. She wondered how many girls had first been felt up by handsy young lads in places they regretted. Far too many, probably.

They continued past the tree and around a rotting log, deeper into the woods. The mood felt darker as the pattern of the trees grew denser. Barry followed, not charging ahead any longer now they were so far away from the trail. There were goosebumps on Millie's arm as she remembered following the exact route herself. It was two decades before. So much had changed but, as they walked, it felt like so little. Trees, downed logs and bushes were all in the same place.

They walked slowly, sometimes barely at all, knowing what was to come.

'It was Eric's birthday on Saturday,' Millie said.

'How old is he?'

'Eight.'

Nicola let out a low breath. 'Eight... Wow. You'll have to introduce me one day. I'd love to meet him.'

It felt like a natural suggestion, especially as they were sharing this moment as if they'd never fallen out. And yet Millie still wasn't quite sure that they were there. That conversation hadn't been had.

'Rachel was there,' Millie added. 'I told her we were back in contact.'

'How'd she take that?'

'Not well. Said she'd never liked either of us. She said we were only bothered about each other. I saw Jenny a few days ago and she said the same.'

Nicola didn't reply at first. They'd stopped walking and were standing next to a tree that had fallen and was covered with a mangled web of vines and thorns.

'I don't remember it like that,' Nicola said.

'Neither do I.'

'We were friends first anyway. Then we started hanging around with Matty and Charlie. They knew Alex and he knew Will. Will had some connection to Genevieve, who was friends with Rachel. Of course we were going to be better mates than everyone else.'

Millie had forgotten almost all those connections – but Nicola was right. They'd known each other since primary school and it was only over time, much later, that they'd ended up part of a wider group. It was a strange grudge to hold that they had a stronger relationship with each other than to any of the others. She wondered why it hadn't fully occurred to her before.

'Rachel said she saw you in the lobby of the Grand Royal a couple of weeks ago,' Millie said. 'She reckoned you were with some guy in a suit who wasn't Charlie. She told me she thought you were having an affair – so perhaps she's telling other people?' Nicola didn't reply immediately, so Millie added: 'I thought you should know...'

'Do you know if she told anyone else?'

'Not that I heard – but I hardly ever see her. We're not exactly on the best of terms. We weren't anyway – and that was before she moved in with Alex.'

Nicola didn't deny the affair, not that she had to.

They'd properly stopped and were now sitting on the end of the downed tree that wasn't covered with leaves and thorns. Barry was milling at their feet, unsure if he should carry on without them.

'I nearly called you when I saw you on the front page with that MP,' Nicola said. 'I couldn't believe it was you at first. I still can't believe they showed your face.'

Millie hadn't talked properly about her affair with anyone. She had told Guy about Alex's own indiscretion as some sort of reasoning, even though two wrongs didn't make a right. Sometimes it felt like a distant dream in which she couldn't quite believe she'd done it.

'He came by a few months ago,' Millie said. The first time she'd told anyone that.

'The MP?'

'He drove up to the house as if nothing had changed, even though he hadn't contacted me since that front page.'

'What did he want?'

'I don't know, really. He brought a dog for me to bath – one of his neighbours'. He said he wanted to see how I was...'

'Do you think he wants to start up again...?'

Millie almost winced at 'start up'. It felt like something they might have talked about a long time ago, when they shared everything.

'I don't think so,' she replied. 'I would've said no.'

'I suppose I wondered...?' Nicola didn't quite ask the question but she was close enough – and Millie realised she'd been wanting to talk about things for a long time. Since before the affair had started, let alone when the details had come out.

'I thought I was in love,' Millie said. 'He said he was going to leave his wife. Then, when it came to it, he ghosted me. I don't blame him really. He has kids. I have Eric. It should never have happened.'

'Were you and Alex having problems...? I know he told Charlie he had no idea what was happening, or why...'

Millie hadn't known that. It wasn't really a surprise that Charlie and Alex were in contact, even if Millie and Nicola had fallen out. As far as she knew, they weren't sharing regular pints – but a quick WhatsApp message wasn't hard to send.

'Problems is one way to put it,' she replied. She did want to talk – but it was going to take a while before she was comfortable to tell the rest of it. It had taken enough for her to tell Guy that Alex was having an affair with a man.

Alex didn't even know that she knew. He still didn't.

Perhaps sensing that, it was Nicola who spoke next. 'I'm not having an affair,' she said. 'That guy in the suit was my boss from the yard. We were scouting locations for the Christmas party. If you want the Royal, you've got to book this far ahead.' She stopped to see if Millie would reply and, when she didn't, Nicola added: 'Rachel should mind her own business.'

'That's what I told her.'

Barry was sitting, staring up at Millie with confused eyes, wondering why she'd brought him all the way out to his favourite place, only to sit and do nothing. The woods was for running and chasing, not sitting and chatting.

Millie took a long, deep breath and decided it was time. 'I've been thinking about this a lot,' she said. 'Probably since before you called – but definitely in the last few days. I wanted to say... ... ... *sorry.*'

A lump had appeared in her throat and Millie tried to swallow it away. Nicola was squeezing the bridge of her nose with her thumb and finger, half-looking away.

'With you and Dad, I blamed you when I should have blamed him. I was too proud to ever contact you and say that afterwards. He was so much older and I know he took advantage. We live ten minutes' away and could have been friends all these years – but I think I was too stupid...'

Nicola wasn't moving, not at first. Then, slowly she began to bob up and down. Millie reached across and took her friend's hand, holding it as Nicola sobbed quietly to herself.

It felt like such a waste. That if Nicola had been in Millie's life, she'd have had someone to talk to about Alex. She'd have never fallen into that destructive affair with Peter. She wouldn't have had her life pulled apart and lost access to Eric.

'I'm sorry, too,' Nicola said.

'You didn't—'

'I knew what I was doing. It's not like I was fifteen, or something. I just...'

She sighed a breathy gasp and Millie felt it too. There were no words they could say to each other. They'd wasted so many years for so little reason.

They sat for a few minutes more, not talking because they didn't need to. These were the moments they used to share, sitting in each other's bedroom with a magazine, not talking. Or on the phone, watching TV together, still not saying much.

Time passed and then Millie realised Barry was no longer at their feet. She stood and turned, looking deeper into the woods. There was a rustle from the bushes as Barry darted after another squirrel. Millie called his name but he'd been sitting still for too long. Nicola took the hint and, together, they quick-stepped their way after him. It was only another minute or two until they stopped once more. They were in another clearing, this one smaller than the last. They still didn't speak – but it was for a different reason this time.

Sitting across from them, isolated from the other trees, was the one that Millie still sometimes saw in her dreams.

'That's where you found me,' Nicola said.

TWENTY-FOUR

The tree wasn't quite as obvious a landmark as the Kissing Tree a few minutes behind them. Although it was off the trail, it wasn't by far. Unlike much of the other areas through which they'd walked, there was almost no shade. The soil was scorched almost grey through a lack of water and there was a scratchy tennis ball off to the side. It looked like someone had been in the area recently to either play with a dog, or perhaps have an impromptu game of something like cricket. If they were to continue on for another few minutes, they'd hit the trail again – and then the field with all the hay. The field from the text message Millie had received.

It felt as if Nicola was reading Millie's thoughts. 'I did shout for help,' she said. 'It seemed like hours but I think I was also asleep for some of it. Or out of it. I don't remember very well. Nobody came until you. Do you remember how croaky my voice was?'

Millie didn't remember – but it's not as if that was the first thing she'd thought about when she'd stumbled across her friend tied to a tree in the woods.

'I had these visions of being found by wolves,' Nicola added.

'I don't think we have wolves here.'

'I didn't know that. I think there'd been something on TV that week, or a film. I was convinced they were going to come for me.'

'I wasn't completely sure where I was going,' Millie replied. 'I knew how to get to the Kissing Tree, just because everyone knew where it was. I knew roughly where that field was – so I kept walking. I think I was calling your name but I don't really remember. I thought I was going to get lost, then I saw this flash of pink and I clocked it was someone's top. I thought it had been left, or lost. Then I realised it was attached to someone. Then I realised it was you...'

It still felt like a dream, even though they were now back in the place it had happened. An impossibility that was somehow possible. Being young was like that sometimes. Something would happen that was taken in a person's stride and then, years later, they would realise how unique or bizarre it was.

When they'd been in primary school, someone in their class had meningitis and had never gone back to school. Millie had been so young, that she'd assumed it was something normal. In the many years since, she'd often wondered if that person had died. Or whether they'd got better but moved house. So many things felt different with age.

'I didn't know where I was,' Nicola said. 'The woods, obviously, but I didn't even know it was *this part*. It could have been the other side of the valley, or further along, out towards the cliffs. It might not even have been around Whitecliff. And then, suddenly, when I'd almost given up, you were there.'

They were still standing and staring at the tree. It was only a few metres away and yet Millie didn't want to get any nearer. Nicola seemingly felt the same.

Millie wasn't sure why they'd come. There was no specific benefit, other than that something about being here on this day, in this moment, felt right. Perhaps this was part of healing their friendship? Regardless of what had happened later between Nicola and Millie's dad, they were always bonded by this spot.

'Do you know who did it?' Millie asked.

She wasn't sure why she'd said it.

Nicola replied with a quick: 'What do you mean?'

'I don't think I ever asked you. Or maybe I did? I was thinking about it and I always assumed it was some sort of stranger. But I guess I wonder if you've ever had an idea since. If you were drunk, or drugged, perhaps you've had dreams or something like that...?'

Millie didn't know how else to put it. They hadn't talked about things too much in the immediate aftermath. It had been a long time in which Nicola might have remembered something new.

'I suppose...' Nicola stopped and then started again. 'I used to have these sorts of flashbacks,' she said. 'I don't know if they were real or my imagination. I'd wake up at two or three in the morning and it felt like I'd had a dream. I didn't know what was real.'

Millie waited.

'I always thought it was someone from school,' Nicola added. 'Maybe someone in the year above who recognised me? Some boy messing around?'

'Why would someone who didn't know you just leave you?'

'I don't know.'

'Why would they return your things after all these years? Especially if they're not asking for anything?'

'I don't know, Mill.' Nicola gathered herself and then added: 'I don't think I want to talk about this any more.'

Millie cringed at having asked. If Nicola had some idea who'd done it, there'd have been no need for her to call Millie.

They stood for a while longer, neither of them apparently quite ready to say they should leave. Barry was sniffing the tree and then set off in a wide circle, his nose to the ground.

'Do you want to come back to mine?' Nicola asked.

'Don't you have work?'

'I'm going to phone in sick. My boss is off anyway, so nobody's going to care. I don't think I can face any more today.'

'I'll have to drop off Barry – but it would be good to spend a bit more time together.'

Nicola let out a relieved breath. 'I was worried you'd say "no".'

'How come?'

'I guess I thought this would come to nothing and that would be that. We'd end up not talking again.'

It would have been a lie for Millie to say anything different. Until they'd been sitting on the log together and she'd apologised, she wasn't sure they'd ever be friends again either. She'd not planned to say sorry but it had come out and she'd meant it.

Millie doubted Guy would find out anything more about Nicola's abduction and it was perhaps silly to ask him in the first place. That night felt like some sort of fairy tale. Something incredible that had become normal.

'I'll cook,' Nicola said out of the blue. 'Charlie will be hungry after work, so I'll make enough for him too. You can either stay, or head off before he gets in.'

From nowhere, Millie wanted nothing more than to sit at Nicola's table. She'd eat her cooking and tell her about Eric and his dress. About Rachel being such a bitch and wanting *her son* to call her 'Mum'. And maybe she would tell her oldest friend about the reason why she'd had the affair. She had told Jack some things and she'd told Guy others. There was much more she'd kept to herself and, just for once, it would be nice to tell someone *everything*.

She might even tell Nicola the truth about her parents.

They weren't even out of the woods and Millie was excited about the prospect. They had fifteen years of news on which to catch up.

They walked back the way they'd come to the trail and then took a slightly longer route back to the car park, allowing Barry to get a little more exercise. They talked but Millie couldn't remember too much of what about, even as they were having the conversation. It was the nothing sort of small talk that keeps a friendship sustained. Nicola said they had waited too long to book a place for her work's Christmas party the previous year. That meant they'd ended up hosting the event in the yard itself. There was a giant marquee and patio heaters – but it was difficult to have fun and get a party atmosphere going when one of the walls was taken up by circular saws. Millie talked about volunteering at the nursing home and about taking Barry out for walks a couple of times a week.

Millie was disappointed when they arrived back at the cars. She could've talked all day – and then she realised they still could.

It really *did* feel as if something was different when she walked into Nicola's kitchen after dropping Barry back at Guy's. The previous times she'd been there, the returned shoes had loomed over them. She'd thought the Nokia's reappearance might do the same – and yet being in the woods with Nicola had somehow changed things for both of them.

Someone was obviously trying to play games but if they wanted to intimidate Nicola, or blackmail her, they could handle it together.

Nicola almost danced around her kitchen as she moved from cupboard to fridge to freezer, listing what she had in – and what she could cook.

They were busy reminiscing about the fish finger sandwiches they used to cook for themselves as teenagers when there was a bang from the front of the house. Millie had been mid-word but stopped herself as they both turned towards the source of the sound.

The front door slammed closed and there was a scuff of shoes being removed before the kitchen door opened. The man took a step inside and then jumped back at the sight of two people in a place he clearly didn't expect them.

Charlie turned between his wife and Millie as a curious, confused expression enveloped his face.

'What are you doing here?' he asked.

TWENTY-FIVE

He was talking to Nicola, who took a moment to close the fridge door. 'I could ask you the same thing,' she replied.

Charlie pointed across to the counter, where a laptop sleeve was tucked in next to the microwave. 'Forgot my laptop,' he said.

'I didn't put it there,' Nicola said, with a definite edge.

'I never said you did.'

'That's not what you were saying last night when you couldn't find your phone charger.'

'Because it didn't grow legs and walk away! I left it on the arm of the sofa and then it turned up in a drawer.'

'Maybe you left it in the drawer and forgot?'

The argument rat-a-tat-tatted between them, almost as if it was rehearsed. The familiarity was almost painful for Millie as she remembered those nights with Alex towards the end. They'd argue about who'd forgotten to fill up the car, or who'd eaten the last of the lasagne leftovers.

Or who'd moved a charging cable.

The last time Millie had seen Charlie was a couple of years back, when they'd noticed one another in the Tesco bakery section. There had been a couple of seconds of eye contact, a brief nod and mutual 'all right?' – and then they'd gone on their way. He'd put on a bit of weight since and was slightly puffier in the cheeks. There was something more that was harder to define. Perhaps a weariness in his face? As if he'd not had a full night's sleep in a long, long while.

For a moment, it felt as if Charlie was going to fire something back at his wife. Millie had no doubt he would have done if it wasn't for her presence. Instead, he sighed, puffed himself up, and then focused on Millie, who was sitting at the table.

'I've not seen you since you were in the papers,' he said.

'I—'

Millie didn't get a chance to finish because Nicola was in first. 'You don't have to be so snidey all the time.'

'What are you on about?'

'You could just say you haven't seen her in a while. Why'd you bring up the papers?'

'I didn't mean—'

'It's OK,' Millie said, holding up her hands, trying to separate the warring parties, even though they were on opposite sides of the kitchen. She turned to Charlie. 'I know what you meant and it's fine.'

It felt like the moment that something important was dropped and the millisecond before it hit the ground. That sense of something awful being in the process of happening, even though nothing could be done to stop it.

Except, it wasn't a millisecond. Whatever was going wrong in Charlie and Nicola's marriage felt like it had been happening for a long, long time.

Charlie snatched his laptop from the counter and stuffed it under his arm, glaring at his wife as he moved. 'See ya later, I guess,' he said. He spun and bounded out of the kitchen, into the hall. The slammed door was delayed, primarily because he had to put his shoes back on. But it came in the end – and Millie jumped as the boom rattled through the house.

Neither of them said anything for a few seconds. Millie was still at the table, Nicola by the fridge. It didn't need words, really – but they came anyway after a while.

'Charlie's had it hard since Matty died,' Nicola said. She sounded haunted. 'You know what they were like. We were best friends – but so were they. Except they'd been best friends all this time. It was almost thirty years. Then Genevieve called one morning and said there'd been a crash. It was the first we knew – but Matty was already gone. He died on the spot. He and Charlie were supposed to be going golfing a couple of days later. Then they had tickets for the football after that. Then the four of us were off to the Foo Fighters later in the month...'

Millie realised what she'd seen in Charlie that she'd been unable to identify. It wasn't *only* tiredness – although that was part of it. It was loss. He'd lost something that he'd never get back. It was so much worse because there'd been no warning, no actual goodbye. All those plans, all that *life*... and then nothing.

'He wouldn't talk about it,' Nicola added. 'You know what men are like. Don't want to talk about their feelings and all that. He started taking on more hours at work. He's in property management. His company bought a different company and Charlie apparently volunteered to absorb their workload. Sometimes I'd go days and barely see him. I don't think he cried about Matty – or, if he did, it was when I wasn't there. He read that poem at the funeral and then acted like it hadn't happened.'

Millie remembered that the funeral was the last time she'd seen Charlie, not the supermarket. Somehow it had slipped her memory.

'He's been like this ever since... but maybe it's me as well? I do think about that – but it's hard not to get drawn in. Like that stupid charging cable last night. I don't think I tidied it away but, if I did, I didn't remember. He might have put it away himself but, if he did, he didn't remember. And it's this stupid, nothing thing. It doesn't mean anything – and yet, somehow, we argued about it for an hour and then didn't talk for the rest of the night...'

Millie ached with the familiarity. Those long, ridiculous arguments she'd had with Alex over whose turn it was to empty the dishwasher. Eric would be upstairs, so they'd go at it in hushed, hissed whispers – and then barely talk for days afterwards. Of course she shouldn't have had the affair. Of course she wished it hadn't come out. Of course she wished she had custody of Eric. But something had had to change – because she doubted she'd have lasted another eighteen months or so with Alex if things had stayed as they were.

And here was Nicola in a similar place.

'I wonder if there's something *I* should do,' Nicola said. 'Maybe *I* should talk to someone, or go to the doctor. But then I figure it's not me who needs that, is it? Or it's not *only* me. I can't be fixed if he won't be...'

Millie stood, crossed the kitchen and then pulled her oldest friend into her. She sensed the wetness on her shoulder, through her top, as Nicola let out something that felt as if she'd been holding on to for a long, long time. They were there for a few minutes, perhaps lots of minutes. Nobody was counting.

When Nicola pulled away, she reached for the tissues on the counter and blew her nose long and loud. She apologised, then did it again, before opening the cupboard under the sink and dropping the two tissues into the bin. She filled a glass with water and gulped at it, before leaning on the sink. Her gaze flickered momentarily towards the back of the door and then away again.

There was a second picture board there that Millie had missed when it had been wedged open. She crossed to it and took in the photos, that had a similar look to the larger board in the hall. There was a photo of Charlie and Nicola puffed up in thick coats, holding onto a pair of poles. 'Skiing,' read the caption. Another had them at a table with a sunset in the background. 'Eating,' was written underneath.

'The captions are very informative,' Millie said.

Nicola coughed a laugh. 'Charlie's idea. He thought it was funny because Genevieve used to write these really detailed descriptions for the photos she and Matty had. Have you ever seen her Facebook albums? Every picture has a couple of hundred words and Charlie used to go on about how nobody was ever going to read all that.'

There was a hint of a smile and Millie could see why. These silly one-word captions were the sort of private jokes that only couples understood. The sort of thing that could last years. Decades. Millie thought of Guy and his little book of crazy golf scores. Not just decades: lifetimes.

She looked at the photos and there were easily identifiable landmarks in some, but generic backgrounds of grass or snow in others. There were oceans and the blazing orange of a sunrise or sunset. What they all had in common was the smiles and thumbs-ups of the two people in the centre.

It felt like something a long time past, given what Nicola had described. Perhaps even the idea of a photo collage was quaint, given how everything was online.

'Do you still want to stay for tea?' Nicola asked.

'Yes,' Millie replied. 'I'd really like that.'

TWENTY-SIX

It had been a strange day for Millie. She'd received the photo of the Nokia the night before and had expected a day full of anger, confusion and perhaps something a lot more sinister. Instead, she was sitting in Jack and Rishi's flat with a growing sense of appreciation for the people in her life.

Rishi was fussing around her, first straightening pillows and then hurrying into the kitchen and reappearing with a duster. He rushed to the window, pulled across a chair to stand on, then started wiping across the bracket at the very top. The place that was always coated with years of dust, that nobody ever had the heart to clean.

'I think he's lost it,' Millie said, looking across to Jack, who was on the sofa.

Jack risked a glance to Rishi, who was on the chair, facing away from them. His lips said nothing, his eyes said 'not now'.

Rishi ignored her as he finished what he was doing. He returned the chair to underneath the table, then spent two minutes trying to get the dust off his top, before deciding to change.

Millie didn't move from her spot in the armchair – and neither did Jack on the sofa.

'Do you reckon he'll clean my house for mates' rates?' Millie asked.

Jack angled a look towards the open door of bedroom on the other side of the living room. 'Shh.'

'What's he going to do? Feather-dust me to death?'

Jack didn't smile and it wasn't long until Rishi breezed back in. He scanned the room, looking for anything out of place, like a hovering eagle eyeing the ground for prey.

'You know where the glasses are, don't you?' he asked Millie.

'Cupboard over the sink.'

'Maybe I should get some out, just in case.'

He made a movement towards the kitchen.

'In case of what?' Millie said. 'In case I forget somehow? In case I go into the kitchen to get them, trip, and hit my head on the sink?'

Rishi glanced to Jack: 'She's right. Why do we keep them over the sink? It's an accident waiting to happen!'

He took a quickstep towards the kitchen and Millie had no doubt he was about to start rearranging the entire room.

'I'm joking,' she said quickly. 'I know where the glasses are. I know what's in the fridge. I know where the cleaning stuff is in case there's a spill. I know where the spare toilet rolls are kept – even though there's a brand-new one on the holder in the bathroom. I don't know what you think's going to happen that'll need a full roll to clean up – but, if it *does* happen, I will jump into action with a new one.'

Rishi had frozen mid-pose and there was still a sense that he wasn't getting the joke. Millie realised this was precisely why Jack had told her to shush.

'I've been here hundreds of times,' Millie said. 'I've literally slept on your floor because Jack had too much to drink and was sleeping on the toilet.'

That got a horrified look from Rishi. 'You're not going to tell her *that* are you?'

'Which bit? The toilet or the floor?'

Jack had clearly had enough. He leapt up from the sofa and put himself between Millie and Rishi. 'She's *joking*,' he said firmly. 'This is Mill, yeah? We know her. She's going to be fine.'

'I just—'

Jack ushered Rishi towards the front door. 'We'll go and leave her. She can—' He didn't finish because the bell sounded, which momentarily made everyone freeze.

Rishi looked to Jack, who looked to Millie, who looked to Rishi, as if they'd all forgotten what to do.

It was Jack who finally remembered. 'We'll be at the pub,' he told Millie. 'Call when you're done – or come find us. Whatever you want.'

He grabbed his keys from the hook next to the door and then opened it wide. The woman from the adoption agency was on the other side. She was roughly the same age as all of them and already knew Jack and Rishi. There were *hellos*, *how are yous*, and *how nice to see yous* all around – and then Rishi gave Millie the grandest of introductions. She was 'one of our best friends', a 'really great person' and they'd 'known each other forever'.

The woman already knew who Millie was, of course, given Millie had been one of the references on their form. There was a shorter hello and then Rishi stood in the doorframe for a moment. He was likely fretting about something like whether the curtains were open equal amounts, but Jack dragged him away and the door was closed.

'I don't think anyone's ever talked me up like that before,' Millie said.

The woman laughed and introduced herself properly as

Angela. She said there was no need to be nervous and then set herself up on the sofa.

Millie had expected forms and perhaps to be recorded – but it was nothing like that. Instead, they sat across from each other and talked. They went into more details about many of the things Millie had covered in her supporting letter for the adoption application. She'd known Jack for almost eleven years and had met him through work. He was working as a temp and she was supposed to be his supervisor. They'd ended up chatting most break times and then, when he'd moved onto his next job, they'd stayed in contact. She now volunteered at the nursing home where he worked. As for Rishi, she'd known him for seven or eight years and had met him when he'd started seeing Jack.

It was hard not to think about the bonds made with friends as a young person versus those as an adult. Was her friendship with Nicola worth more, simply because they'd known one another so long? Millie had felt a kinship in Nicola's kitchen that she didn't think she'd ever feel again. But then, in recent years, Jack had been there for everything.

Angela was continuing through her questions. She asked how often Millie saw Jack and Rishi, with Millie replying that she saw Jack every other day. With Rishi it was more like once a week. Angela wanted to know what they did in their leisure time, which had Millie momentarily stumped. She couldn't come up with much other than 'sit around and watch TV', which felt like the sort of thing everyone did. Or maybe it was just the people *she* knew. It was certainly how many of her evenings were spent.

Millie had been answering the questions almost without thinking. There didn't seem to be anything to trip her up and it was more a general knowledge quiz about her friends. It was probably that sense of comfort that left her blank.

'Do you think they both want to be parents?' Angela asked.

Millie had been anticipating something else and she

realised she was doing the fish bob with her mouth. 'Sorry... I didn't catch that,' she said.

Angela repeated the question but the extra couple of seconds hadn't given time for Millie to form an answer. She should say 'yes', of course, except the word felt stuck.

Perhaps Angela sensed that as she continued: 'I suppose what I'm getting at is that parenting is a joint thing,' she said. 'Both people in a relationship have to want to bring a child into their lives. That's what I'm asking you about Jack and Rishi. Do you think they're both happy to become parents?'

She was blowing it for them in a way that couldn't be forgiven. Millie knew that, even as she didn't reply. The little voice at the back of her mind, the one that forced her to read the negative reviews about herself, wouldn't stop talking. It was telling her that her own parents never particularly wanted children. Millie only existed because, almost four decades back, it was expected that a married couple would have a child. It had taken her a long, long time to realise that she didn't need their approval. There was some poor child out there, looking for new parents. Rishi was desperate to offer every part of himself. To offer a safe, loving space for that child to grow into an adult. Was Jack offering that, too?

Millie realised she hadn't spoken in a while. The room swirled slightly at the edge of her vision. Angela was watching her with a kindly smile.

'Sorry,' Millie replied. 'It's a deep question, I think.'

'I appreciate the thought you're putting into it.'

It could have been a sarcastic reply but it felt genuine to Millie. The woman was a professional after all.

'I suppose I'm wondering about the exact definition,' Millie said. 'Say one person is really, *really* happy to do something but the other person is only really happy. They both want the same thing but one person's a bit more into it than the other. I'm not saying that's what it's like with this. It's more theoretical. I just mean...'

Millie stopped herself. She was making such a mess of what should have been such a simple thing.

'I guess what I'm saying,' Millie concluded, 'is whether two people have to be *equally* interested in the same thing...?'

Angela thought for a second. There was a contented sort of confusion on her face that made it clear she'd never been asked this before. It almost certainly meant anyone else who'd ever been asked it had simply said 'yes'.

'That's quite the question,' she replied.

'Am I overthinking it?'

That got a small laugh which gave Millie some comfort. 'I guess what I'm asking,' Angela said, 'is whether you think this is something both Jack and Rishi want. If one of them is ten out of ten into it, and the other is nine, that means they both still want it.'

Millie took another second to think. She could feel the weight of whatever she said. If she said 'no', it could, probably would, be the end of a friendship. If she said 'yes', she could never forgive herself if things ended badly.

She had one further second, one short breath, and then gave her answer.

TWENTY-SEVEN

It was early. Too early. Whoever it was that invented five in the evening couldn't leave it there, could he? Oh no. Little ol' David Time, or whatever he was called, decided there had to be a five in the morning as well.

Millie yawned as she got out of the car and headed over the road towards the squat. It was almost six but she'd been up for the best part of an hour already. Someone who might have been Hannah had said something about bailiffs not being able to appear before 6 a.m. if they were enforcing court orders. As Millie walked, she wondered if that's what had *actually* been said, or if she was misremembering due to the time of day.

She could feel eyes on her as she approached the house. It wasn't only Will and Hannah standing outside, nor even some of the faces Millie had seen at the garden party. There were people of all ages lined across the front of the house, holding hands and forming a human chain.

As Millie got closer, she realised they weren't holding hands, everyone was cuffed together. The line of people at the front was only the start. A full ring stretched around the sides of the house and presumably all the way around the back. There would have to be seventy or eighty people for that, plus more hanging around at the front.

The cuffs were a mix of standard-looking metal ones, or interlinking cable ties. Millie even saw at least three pairs of fluffy hen-do types like those someone had used to tie up Nicola years ago. The kind Will had been wearing in the photo.

Hannah and Will were in the centre of it all, outside the front door – although they weren't tied into the rest of the group. Hannah was pacing, while Will was joking with someone in the chain.

There was no sign of bats, sticks, or any other sort of weapon. The most offensive thing was a woman's T-shirt that had 'Twerk if you love Jesus' on the front. It seemed like it was a slogan designed to annoy more or less everyone. She was next to another who had *Coffee. Kids. Husband. In That Order* on hers.

Hannah had a wallet of papers in her hand and, when she spotted Millie, she nodded her across.

'We've got extra cuffs if you want in,' she said.

'I'm more here to observe,' Millie replied. 'These are impressive numbers, though. I don't think I was expecting this.'

Luckily, Hannah took it in the spirit intended. 'I tried to tell you we're a movement. Maybe you believe me now?' She checked her phone and then turned to the crowd. 'It's six o'clock!'

The shout brought about a rippled cheer that wrapped its way through the people on the far side of the house and back again. By the time Millie looked back to Hannah, she'd hooked a larger lens onto her phone and was holding it sideways to film the crowd.

'What do we want?'

'Houses!'

'When do we want 'em?'

'Now!'

Will had drifted away, closer to the front of the garden

where it was easier to see approaching traffic. Millie trailed him along the path until she was at his side. The view across the town and bay was as stunning as ever. An orange wash swam across the horizon, doubly thick with the reflection in the ocean. Above it, a brilliant, perfect blue stretched high and wide.

As he noticed she was there, Will mumbled a quiet 'hi' and then they stood for a short while, listening to the noise from behind. The chants had moved onto songs and a modified version of 'Hey Jude'. Instead of 'Jude', they sang 'Dude'. Instead of 'a-fraid', they sang 'a' – and then something that Millie first thought was 'runt'.

'That is one potty-mouthed songbook,' Millie said, after realising the initial mistake.

'You should've heard the other versions.'

'How much worse could it be?'

'In one line—'

'That was rhetorical.'

Will snorted and left the sentence unfinished. The road below was clear with no sign of the bailiffs and he turned to look back towards the house and everyone in front.

'I really didn't expect this many people,' Millie said.

'Thanks,' he said it with a laugh, as if he didn't believe she meant it.

'How long are you going to wait?' Millie asked.

'What do you mean?'

'The bailiffs might not come until much later. People will need to eat and drink. To pee...'

'Hannah's got a giant bunch of keys for the handcuffs and everything's numbered. We can tag in and out if people need a break.'

Millie was about to congratulate him on the organisation when he spoiled it.

'My idea was to superglue everyone together but that got voted down.'

'You needed a *vote* on whether seventy or so people should be superglued?'

A shrug. 'I figured they can cut through handcuffs. Nobody's cutting through arms, are they?'

Millie wanted to argue with the logic but there was at least some degree of thought there. She almost dreaded to ask what the vote count had been but it would've almost certainly been 52–48.

'How come you and Hannah aren't cuffed?' Millie asked.

'Someone has to deal with the bailiffs when they get here.'

Millie pictured the bats or sticks she'd found upstairs. 'What do you mean by "deal with"?'

'Someone needs to check their paperwork. Hannah's lawyer friend sent her a checklist of everything to look for. If anything's missing, they have to leave.'

'What if everything's in order?'

Will didn't answer that.

Half a dozen sleepy-looking teenagers had emerged over the brow of the hill and were scuffing their way towards the house. Millie could see herself and her friends in them. If this had been twenty years before, in the summer they'd spent drinking and smoking and doing little else, perhaps she, Nicola, Alex, Charlie and the rest would have made a detour up the hill. In a town where it often felt as if nothing was happening, this would have been something.

A girl drifted to the front of the group and asked Will if this was the house that needed 'defending'. He pointed them up the hill, saying there were more than enough handcuffs to go around. Given his age, and given *their* age, it would not have sounded good out of context.

The group carried on along the path, where they were met by a resounding chorus of 'Don't Look Back In Anger', in which 'Sally' had been substituted for 'the bailiffs'.

'I'm not convinced that scans,' Millie said.

'You should hear their cover of "Imagine".'

There was a sense of déjà vu as they waited together, looking over the town. It was a little over a couple of days before they'd sat in the garden together as the sun set.

'Where did all the handcuffs come from?' Millie asked.

'Hannah knows people – we told you that. Someone from one of the other sites turned up yesterday with a box they'd collected from other protests.'

It sounded genuine and probably true but, as Millie looked back to the house, there was a flash of something pink and fluffy from one of the chained wrists.

'I found a picture,' she said.

'What kind of picture are we talking?' He smirked. 'Dick pic? Because it's not mine and nobody can prove otherwise.'

'It's from the battle of the bands night.'

She felt Will turn and stare at her. 'Why are you still going on about that? It was years ago.'

Millie could hardly let on what had happened to Nicola. It still wasn't her story to tell.

'Everyone except Charlie's in the photo.'

'OK...'

'You're wearing handcuffs on one of your wrists. A pink, fluffy pair.'

Will didn't reply, instead waiting for Millie to look away from the view and turn to him. His face was blank and confused.

'Are you having a breakdown?' he asked. 'I know you've been through a lot, or whatever, but why are you so bothered about some stupid contest from so long ago?'

She couldn't really answer that.

'What did you do with the handcuffs?' she asked.

He shook his head and scrunched up his face. If they had been younger he'd have swirled his finger around his ear to indicate he was talking with a nutjob. 'I don't remember any handcuffs,' he said. 'If I *was* wearing them, which I don't think I was, then I don't know where they came from or where they ended up.' He stopped, then added: 'Can you remember everything you did on some random day when you were seventeen?'

Millie couldn't answer that either. Or she could, with a straightforward 'no'.

'Have you been messing with Nicola?' she asked.

Will didn't react at first and then he simply shook his head once more. 'You really do have problems, don't you? I don't even know the last time I saw Nic. Why? Has she told you I'm messing with her? What am I supposedly doing?'

Millie wasn't quite sure why she'd brought it up, other than that Will had apparently had an issue with Nicola in the past. That, and she had few others ideas about who might have left her friend in the woods. If Millie had considered the conversation at all, she would have realised this was the only way it could have gone. Instead, she'd thought there might be some sort of confession. She'd have been able to tell Will to leave Nicola alone – and that would be that.

It now seemed obvious that was never going to happen.

Will turned and took a couple of steps back to the house. 'Look. I'm sure there's someone you can talk to. Some therapist, or doctor, or something. I don't know if this is all because you fancy me, or—'

'I don't fancy you.'

He smirked and she realised that she'd given him the set-up he wanted. He didn't even bother with a punchline. He nodded up towards the house. 'Are you hanging around?'

'Maybe. I kinda hoped the bailiffs would be here at six. Not worth getting up early if they have a lie-in.'

Will didn't laugh and perhaps didn't realise she was joking. She was trying to do anything to get the conversation away from the way she'd embarrassed herself. Will obviously considered the conversation over. He led her up the path towards the ring of people just as a burger van arrived at the front of the house. A man got out and headed up to the house, asked who was in charge, and then had a private word with Hannah.

'Who wants a bacon roll?!' she shouted, which sent the cheers going round again.

Millie walked around the house a few times, doing her best to avoid Will. She spoke to a couple of people in the chain. With the talk of Hannah being in touch with other groups around the country, she'd half-expected it to be some sort of organised invasion. Instead, everyone was either from White-cliff, or one of the villages along the coastline. Some people knew who Millie was, some didn't. For once, nobody seemed to care.

Seven o'clock passed and there was no sign of the bailiffs. Eight. Nine. It was like a mini festival, with the smell of bacon and burgers in the air. The guy at the van even had a vegan menu.

Will, Hannah, or one of the other housemates would unlock people who would run inside for the toilet. Someone would sub into place and the chain would remain complete.

The songbook had more of a rec centre *Mamma Mia* vibe for a while, before moving onto Bob Dylan. Some bloke with too much body hair had turned up with a guitar – which left Millie asking nobody in particular why *he* couldn't be chained up like everyone else.

The smell of meat was replaced by the smell of marijuana as Millie realised the people in the chain were understandably becoming bored with the whole thing. They'd been told they were going to be part of the resistance and, instead, they were listening to a human carpet sing bad songs badly.

Before long, the chain was broken completely. Some people were milling around with only one cuff on their wrist. Others were sitting and chatting – or on their phones. It was a warm day, with some of the protestors escaping the sun under a couple of beer garden umbrellas that had probably been nicked. More had drifted inside, away from the heat.

Millie was considering whether she should go home. It was ten o'clock and she'd been up for five hours and at the house for four. The only crime she'd witnessed was the butchering of the songs – but nobody went to prison for that.

And then, as she was halfway along the path, there was a growl of engines. The man with the guitar finally stopped playing and something simmered in the air. Everyone felt it as, almost as one, the protestors dashed back into place. Cuffs were re-cuffed, ties were re-tied.

Two dark vans had come to a stop at the end of the path. Nothing happened for a minute, perhaps two, as Hannah and Will stood at the front of the protest. Millie got herself out of the way and watched them talk quietly, hands in front of their mouths.

Another minute and still nothing happened.

The van doors then opened in unison with a solid clunk of metal. The men moved uniformly, too, rehearsed and efficient. They were big and wide, the sort who stood at the front of clubs in bomber jackets and waved anyone inside who was wearing a skirt. The men gathered in a small group next to the vans, in no rush – which left Millie thinking about Guy and his protest at the factory. The one in which they'd been waited out by jeering security officers.

Millie counted eight of the bailiffs – and then, as one, they turned and walked up the path.

TWENTY-EIGHT

It struck Millie that she didn't know what bailiffs actually were. She vaguely remembered something on TV where some big bloke had broken into a house. He'd taken a host of electrical equipment as payback for outstanding debts. There had definitely been crying children and an inconsolable mum – but that was fiction and it would have been years before.

Millie had assumed these bailiffs would turn up with bolt cutters, or perhaps a battering ram. Something that would allow them to smash their way into the house. They'd grab anyone who was inside and then... Millie had no idea. Was that even legal? Surely only the police could arrest people?

The bailiffs continued up the path as, ahead of them, Hannah was shouting to someone that their handcuff hadn't been clipped in properly. The woman behind was panicking because her other hand was cuffed to someone else and she couldn't attach it herself. In the end, Will marched across and snapped the cuff into place.

The festival air had gone and the bloke with the burger van wasn't far behind . He was busy doing a three-point turn, before hurtling down the hill back towards town.

Millie was close enough to hear what was going on, while far enough way to make the point that she wasn't *actually* protesting if it came down to it. She realised it was cowardly but told herself she was covering things for Guy's news site.

The shortest of the bailiffs was still a good five foot and a lot. He separated from the rest of the group and continued until he was a metre or so away from Hannah.

'Are you Hannah Flynn?' he asked.

'That's me,' Hannah replied.

The bailiff listed the address then added: 'You're the primary and sole tenant and you've been served notice to leave.'

It was the first time Millie had thought the main tenant was anyone other than Will. The first time she realised he didn't live at the house in any official capacity. 'Sole' tenant was quite the push, given the number of people Millie knew were living at the house. She wondered about Hannah's motivation. Was it to stop the developer, or landlord? To actually have this as her house to live? Because some people wanted to fight, no matter what? A bit of everything? None of it seemed quite clear.

'That's one way of interpreting things,' Hannah replied.

'Here is a copy of the notice.'

The bailiff passed across an envelope of papers, to which Hannah replied that she needed a few minutes to check over everything. The bailiff agreed and returned to his group.

It was a lot more civilised than Millie thought it would be. With all the talk of 'war', she didn't expect a dignified exchange of paperwork, along with an agreed timescale to check for typos. It was more accountant going about his business than soldiers marching to war.

Hannah and Will sat in front of the protestors who, as far as Millie could tell, looked completely bemused. Hannah was scrolling on her phone, cross-checking it against the documents she'd been handed. Will pointed to something on the first page but she shook her head. Around five minutes passed until they turned their backs, and huddled close, making sure nobody could overhear. When they separated, Hannah's face was stone.

She walked towards the bailiffs, who had stopped chatting among themselves. It was theatre as she stopped within touching distance of the group and offered the papers back to them. When nobody reached for them, Hannah tore them in half.

'We're not leaving,' she said.

A cheer erupted from behind, circling around the house at least twice.

Hannah had her phone out again, with the lens attachment. She swung around to film the house and then back to the bailiffs.

'What are you going to do?' she said. 'Are you the sort of men who get off on hitting women?'

Millie had somehow missed that it was all women at the front. The men must have been sent to the back.

Perhaps it was the mention of hitting that did it. People must have known there was a chance of trouble but, as Millie scanned the faces of the women in the chain, there was fear. The sing-song of moments before seemed a long way away.

The bailiffs had barely moved in the time Hannah had been talking. They'd not reacted to her tearing up the papers, or to her filming them. Instead, the one who'd handed over the papers leant in and said something to one his clones. The guy turned and strolled back towards the vans, as if he was on a casual walk along the prom. When he got there, the sidelights blinked on and off – and then he reached into the boot. When he re-emerged, he was carrying two pairs of bolt cutters.

It wasn't a cheer that rippled around the human chain this time, it was concern. Millie could see those around the edges straining to try to see what was happening. The people at the back would have to rely on those relaying messages around.

Hannah felt it, too. She moved towards the chain and held

her arms wide. 'Nobody's going to hurt anyone,' she shouted – except that made it worse. Someone screamed, which set off another person further around the chain. People were actively pulling in opposite directions to each other, as calls of 'hold the line' sounded.

The bailiff with the bolt cutters was almost back to the main group when Will stepped forward. He was halfway between them and Hannah as he turned between both parties.

'Can we talk about this?' he said. He pointed from his chest towards the bailiffs, as if they wouldn't understand otherwise.

The bailiff handed one of the bolt-cutter sets to the guy who seemed to be the leader. He kept the other to himself and then stood, waiting for an order.

As the leader moved ahead, Will intercepted him. 'Can we have a word? Just you and me, mate. Nobody wants trouble here, do we?'

For the first time, there was a hesitation in the bailiff's step. He looked up past Will towards Hannah with her phone filming them.

'The order's already been issued,' he said.

'Two minutes.'

The bailiff who'd collected the bolt cutters moved ahead and was almost past when his boss held out an arm to stop him.

'Two minutes,' he replied.

Millie had never thought of Will as being the charismatic type – and this sort of intervention seemed so out of character that she couldn't quite believe it was happening. She was hoping to hear what was said but, when Will beckoned the man into the long grass, he followed.

The conversation probably did last around two minutes. Will said something and the man shook his head. Will said something else, so the man took out his phone and tapped something into the screen. Moments later, he held it to his ear and then turned his back.

The only other person who would've been able to hear the call was Will. He stood with his arms folded, studiously refusing to look back towards the house.

And then it was over.

The bailiff walked quickly towards the rest of his group, said something quietly, and they all headed back to the vans as one.

It felt as if everyone was holding their breaths as the bailiffs got inside, slammed the doors – and then did a pair of three-point turns. A moment later and they were over the brow and gone.

Will was on the path, watching them leave but, as soon as they were out of sight, he turned back to the house with his arms high.

'VICTORY!'

The explosion of joy and relief was something that Millie wasn't sure she'd ever seen before. Hannah was looking to him curiously but he said she might as well unlock everyone.

'They're not coming back,' he said.

'I don't understand,' Hannah replied.

'Unlock everyone first. We'll talk later.'

A bemused Hannah did as had been suggested. She flipped through a massive keyring and then approached the line, where she started unlocking people. There were people crying, others laughing. Nobody seemed to know what to make of it all.

Will bowed for his newly adoring audience, which got a fresh cheer. Millie had been watching in disbelief and she approached as Will was onto his third bow.

'Did you tell them they'd have to listen to "Imagine" again if they didn't leave?'

Will ignored the jibe. He was lost in the moment, waving to someone in the crowd.

'I Derren Browned them, didn't I?' He said. 'Gave 'em the

ol' one-two.' He punched the air, *bang-bang*, in the style of a boxer who was about to get his head caved in.

Will waved to someone else and then blew a kiss. He was one step away from giving it the double finger-points.

'What did you really say?' Millie asked.

'What does it matter?'

'You're going to have to answer at some point. People don't ignore a court order just because you ask nicely.'

Will shot a double finger-point at a girl who was probably half his age. If she'd been nine, it might have got a laugh. Instead, the teenager frowned at him as if he was her embarrassing dad. The ridicule apparently brought Will out of his bubble.

'I told them that we weren't going anywhere,' Will said.

'Hannah had already said that.'

'Right but I took him to one side and said that everything was being filmed. I asked him what it would look like if they were on YouTube bolt-cutting their way past women to get into a house.'

'What did he say?'

Will nodded towards the road. 'That was all it took, wasn't it? Ran off with their tails between their legs.'

The woman in the *Coffee. Kids. Husband. In That Order* T-shirt bounded across and gave Will a high-five, like they were on the sort of work training course that only maniacs enjoyed.

'Where am I in your order?' Will asked, pointing at her shirt.

'Top!'

Millie had to stop herself from laughing. She'd never seen anything quite like it. Around them, those who'd been in the chain were settling among the grass. Crates of beer had appeared from somewhere. Despite it still being morning, ring pulls were snapping and the festival feel was back. Unfortunately, the bloke with the guitar had also reappeared. He was strumming something that would have Bob Marley in his grave turning at such a rate that the earth would be in danger of spinning off its axis.

Millie suspected something else entirely had happened between Will and the bailiffs, though it was impossible to know what. She had no intention of spending the afternoon listening to the bloke with the guitar, unless he was being garrotted with it. If nothing else, his screams would likely have a better sense of tone and pitch.

She was halfway along the path when she realised Will was chatting to the teenage girl who had passed them that morning. Despite the heat, she was in a black beanie, with a checked shirt, shorts, and long socks past her knees. The girl was grinning up at him as he gave it the full 'aw shucks'.

And, suddenly, Millie couldn't let it go. She turned and headed across, slotting in next to Will and hooking her arm into his. The girl scowled at her.

'You got a minute, babe?' Millie asked.

Will shook her off but it was too late. The teenager was already backing away. By the time Will called after her, she was already off in the crowd.

'What was *that*?' he demanded.

'I need to show you something.'

'I thought you didn't fancy me?'

Millie ignored the false bravado, instead taking out her phone where she loaded the photo she'd snapped of the image in the *Journal*. The one that showed them at the battle of the bands. She pinched in, until Will was the whole shot – and then just the handcuff on his wrist.

'Why are you showing me this?' he said.

'I want you to try to remember why you were wearing them.'

He threw his hands up. 'Why are you still going on about this? What's wrong with you?'

'If you can remember something, I can leave you alone.'

That got a huff. He was on his tiptoes, looking over the crowd, presumably for the girl young enough to be his daughter.

'I told you: I don't know anything about it.'

What might have been a look of confusion broke into a smirking amusement.

'Why are you asking?'

'That doesn't matter.'

'Tell you what. You tell me what *you* know – and I'll tell you what *I* know.'

It was so direct that Millie needed a moment to process what he'd said. The issue, the *threat*, of Pidge and the Vicodin was hanging silently between them.

'So, you do remember...?'

He laughed at her. 'It's like being fifteen again, Mill. You show me yours and I'll show you mine.'

'Was it you?'

Another laugh. He was taunting her now. 'Was *what* me?'

Millie almost said it. *Almost*. If it had been her secret, she would have already spilled. She couldn't work out if he was toying with her or if he genuinely did know something.

Millie took a step back, her phone clamped tightly with the photo of his hand on the screen.

Will gave another of his smirks and stepped towards her. 'Offer's still there, Mill. You show me yours first.'

TWENTY-NINE

Millie spent the rest of the day stewing over what to do – if she should do anything. She thought about asking Guy, except he was busy working on something for the local food bank and she didn't want to interrupt. Jack would have been an option – but she hadn't told him anything about it so far. That and he was at work. Millie thought that, if she saw him face to face, she might blurt out her hesitation with Angela from the adoption agency the night before.

There was an excitement as she messaged Nicola to ask if she was free after work. Millie didn't know whether she wanted to tell her about Will and the handcuff photo – but she did want to see her friend again. She wanted to hear about Nicola's day, even if it had been uneventful. She'd tell her about her morning at the squat and the miraculous conclusion of the protest.

It didn't take long for a reply to come back. Nicola said she'd be off work at five and that Charlie wouldn't be home until seven. They could have leftover lasagne, that she'd fry to crisp up – and, in a moment, Millie had never wanted anything more.

She sat in her car outside Nicola's house, waiting for her friend to appear. Millie wondered what would happen if she showed her the photo of Will wearing those handcuffs. It was circumstantial at best – and yet perhaps it would offer some degree of closure? He'd messed with her then and he was doing the same now. He'd made no demands – and, if he did, they could face him down as one.

Who else could it be?

If he wanted to make a big deal of whatever Pidge had told him, Millie would deny everything. People would believe what they wanted but, either way, Pidge was a convicted drug dealer, so not exactly a beacon of truth.

It almost felt like the spark before a first date as Nicola pulled onto her drive. Regardless of what else they talked about, Millie was going to tell Nicola about the problems she'd had with custody and Eric. If there was time, she'd also tell her about Jack and how Millie wasn't sure he wanted to adopt. How she felt caught in the middle of not wanting to let him down but also not wanting to put a child in a situation that didn't work. She could explain about finding out Guy was her godfather and that he'd turned into something of a father figure.

Finally, *finally*, she had someone to whom she could tell everything.

The garage door slipped open and Nicola pulled into the space before exiting onto the drive. She removed her sunglasses and waved at Millie, who was halfway towards the house.

'It was so good to get your text,' she said.

'Thanks for inviting me over.'

'Thanks for coming!'

They were teenagers again, calling round each other's house before or after school.

Nicola unlocked the front door and led the way inside.

'Charlie won't be back 'til after nine now,' she said as they entered. 'He said he's going to play squash with someone from work.'

'Isn't that a bit late for squash?'

'That's what I thought – but I didn't think it was worth asking.'

Nicola kicked her shoes off onto the rack and squished her feet into a pair of Scooby-Doo slippers.

'It's the best feeling, isn't it?' she said.

'Scooby-Doo slippers?'

A laugh: 'Taking your heels off after work... but the Scooby slippers are good, too.'

She headed along the hall towards the kitchen as Millie took off her own shoes. She was a few paces away when one of the coats on the hooks near the door slipped and fell to the floor. Millie picked it up and returned it to the hook then, as she turned, she found herself face to face with the picture board.

'Do you want to eat right away?' Nicola shouted through. 'I usually eat about six, 'cos I don't sleep well on a full stomach.'

Millie found herself drawn to the photo in the top right. Nicola and Charlie were at some sort of music festival. They were both wearing bucket hats, one arm around each other's shoulders, the other raised. There were wristbands on each of their arms, with a stage in the distance. They had to be a long way away because, behind them, instead of a crowd was a long stretch of grass.

Millie almost moved on.

Almost.

Except there was something about the caption below the photo. A typo she'd seen before. One she'd seen recently.

IN A FEILD!

THIRTY

'Mill? Are you there? Do you want to eat now?'

Millie turned from the photo to the kitchen. There was a clatter of frying pan and then the sound of the fridge door opening and closing. Millie couldn't move. She leaned in, closed one eye, then the other – except the typo didn't correct itself. I before E, except after C. It didn't explain neighbour, or weigh, or seize, or forfeit, or weird.

But it did explain field.

Millie drifted through to the kitchen and clasped the back of the chair that was sitting half-under the dining table.

'Are you all right?' Nicola asked.

Millie shuffled onto the seat and pressed her temples. 'A little headache,' she said.

'I've got some paracetamol in the cupboard upstairs, if you want one?'

Millie said no and then sat quietly for a moment.

I before E.

'Do you still have the Nokia?' Millie asked.

Nicola was busy scooping a lump of lasagne from a plastic

tub into a frying pan. It landed with a meaty *thunk* and then she flipped it over. She replied without turning: 'Why?'

'I just wanted to check something.'

Nicola stopped for a moment but then spun. 'Will you keep an eye on that?' she asked, nodding towards the oven. 'I'll go get it.'

Millie crossed to the oven and used the wooden spoon to slide the slab around the pan, before realising that the heat wasn't even turned on. Through the ceiling, there was the sound of some banging and shuffling and then, a minute or two later, a breathless Nicola bounced back into the kitchen. The pink phone was in her hand and she passed it across to Millie.

'It was under the bed,' she said. 'I didn't want Charlie finding it.' A pause. 'What are you looking for?'

Millie held the button at the top and didn't reply.

'I was thinking of getting rid of it,' Nicola added. 'And the shoes. No point in keeping any of it, is there?'

She probably had a point. If someone was trying to torment her, what better way to handle it than to simply throw away what they'd left?

What *they'd* left.

A horrible thought was beginning to creep through Millie.

'I don't think the hob's turned on,' Millie said.

Nicola spun, muttered 'silly me', and then twisted the knob, before sliding the frying pan into place.

Millie pressed the menu button on the phone, then scrolled down to messages. She clicked into the inbox by mistake, forgetting she was interested in what had been sent by the phone, not what was received.

There was so much déjà vu as her fingers moved. They were the days when each text had to be tapped out by pressing the numbers once, twice, or three times to get each individual letter. Millie had been fast but so was everyone their age. She still knew her sign-off – six once, four three times, five three times twice and then seven four times. 'Mills' was what she called herself, although that soon become 'M'. Then she realised everyone who needed it had her number anyway and sign-offs weren't needed.

She pressed the button for Nicola's outbox and the screen froze. The lasagne had started to sizzle but Millie's heart was beating louder than that. The screen hadn't moved, so she tapped the menu button, then up, then down. Nothing was moving.

And then it appeared as if there had been no delay. She pressed to load the top message and it appeared instantly. It was the one that had been sent to Millie by the person who abducted Nicola. The one telling her where to find her friend. That person must have spiked Nicola's drink, or something like that. Whoever sent it must have known Millie was the right person. A stranger might have guessed based on the number of messages between them but it would still have been a *guess*. A dangerous one, with a young woman left in the middle of the woods.

And there it was.

Past the Kissing Tree. Before the feild

It had been there all this time. A simple misspelling that the sender had never learned to spell correctly. E before I.

Nicola had her back to Millie and was poking at the lasagne with a spoon.

'Nic...'

Nicola turned, to where Millie was now standing next to the picture board. 'Did you say it was your idea for these captions?' she asked.

'No, Charlie's.'

'Was it his idea for the ones in the hall, too?'

Nicola was busy jabbing at the contents of the pan and it took her a moment to reply. 'There's one in the bedroom, too,' she said. There was a pause and then: 'Why?'

'No reason,' Millie said. 'No reason.'

THIRTY-ONE

Millie hadn't slept well. She'd eaten with Nicola and let her friend talk, while not trusting herself to contribute. The truth was in Nicola's old phone and on their wall the whole time. If that relic of a Nokia hadn't been returned to Nicola, Millie wouldn't have seen it and the chances were it would have gone unnoticed forever.

She'd been trying to figure out why Charlie had done it so many years ago. He had been working and not at the park with everyone else. Presumably, he'd gone looking for them after his shift had ended. He'd run into Nicola, who was searching for everyone else and... what? He'd bought her a drink and spiked it? She was already out of it?

Later, much later, they were married and he'd held onto that knowledge the whole time. Could a marriage really be in such a bad state that he'd return her trainers and phone? What was he hoping to achieve? Was it simply about being cruel?

It felt unbelievable and yet horrifyingly possible. And if it *was* possible, then Millie probably needed something more than a typo. Nicola had been handcuffed to a tree – and those cuffs had come from somewhere.

It was early, too early, and Millie was driving across the largely deserted town. There was none of the orangey haze of the day before. Instead a fluffy gloom clung to the horizon. Grey and black swirled overhead and a cool wind fizzed from the ocean. The poor sods on clean-up duty were busy hosing down the pavements after a usual summer night of drunken overindulgence. Hundreds of plastic pint glasses had been swept into a mound near the end of the pier and, even with her windows closed, it was impossible for Millie to miss the undercurrent stench of spilled lager and dried urine.

She continued through and then up on the hill towards the squat.

In the previous days, Will had told her about his memory being jogged by her bringing up the battle of the bands. Perhaps, in the twenty-four hours since she'd showed him the photo, he'd remember something more about why those cuffs were on his wrist? More importantly, where they'd ended up. Had he given them to Charlie? Could Charlie have been cleaning up after the event and found them?

On their way down the hill was a pair of lads in three-quarter shorts and polo shirts. They had the vacant gaze from the morning after the night before. The angle of the slope meant they were speeding up as they walked – and it was almost inevitable as one of them missed his step, slipped off the kerb, and bounced into the road. Millie was on the other side of the road but she slowed anyway. She considered buzzing down her window to check they were OK. There was no need as, almost as soon as he'd hit the road, the man popped back up and straightened his top as if nothing had happened. His mate was doubled over, laughing, while the one who'd tripped flicked Millie the Vs.

She continued on but, as she did, the sight of the two men had given Millie another idea. She remembered being drunk with Nicola at various times after what happened in the woods.

They'd stumble home and make sure each other was safe. They'd help one another through doors and work as a duo to ward off unwelcome advances. Through that, what she'd learned was that people are heavy. *Really* heavy. Dead weight was called that for a reason. If people were unable to support themselves, it was hard to manoeuvre them.

For whatever reason, Millie had always assumed it was one person who had left Nicola in the woods. But what if it was two? Will given away by a throwaway photo of him in handcuffs; Charlie by his inability to spell.

Will had been the last to leave the park, Charlie could have been the last to arrive. Both might have been there at the time Nicola came stumbling back. Millie wondered if it made more sense, or if it created more problems because it was one more person to keep a secret?

She was so engulfed in those thoughts that, as she crested the hill near the squat, she almost drove into the back of the parked van. The surrounding houses all had wide driveways, usually behind big gates. People didn't really park on the road – especially not in a van so early.

Millie swerved and then straightened the car, before pulling into a spot a little past what turned out to be two very familiar vans.

They were the same pair that had arrived filled with bailiffs the day before. The last time Millie had seen them, they'd been turning in the road and heading back towards the town.

Now, it was one minute to six and they were back.

Millie didn't need to get out of her car to see what was happening. Will was standing in the front door of the house. One of the bailiffs handed him something that might have been an envelope. It quickly disappeared into a backpack Will was carrying – and then he was outside, leaving the door wide. The clock in Millie's car flipped to precisely six and then all ten bailiffs strolled purposefully into the house.

Will remained by the front door but it didn't take long. Within a couple of minutes, the bailiffs were marching people out of the house. Hannah was there, in leggings and a giant top. She was struggling but only half-heartedly. There were three or four others but, even from a distance, Millie could see the fight was gone.

Sort of.

Will had transformed. He was shouting at the men for whom he'd stood aside moments before. Millie was out of her car now and his shouts carried across to the road. 'You can't do this!' and 'We're not leaving!' were among the ones she heard clearly.

A couple of the bailiffs stood around, effectively guarding Will, Hannah and the others. Hannah and one of the other women were on their phones, while Will was sitting in the long grass, sulking. The others who'd been escorted out had already walked off, heading in the general direction of town.

While that was happening, the other bailiffs were getting to work. In seemingly no time, they'd replaced the locks on the doors, barred the windows – and were starting to put up a fence.

With no way back into the house, the bailiffs who'd been acting as guards headed across to the others to continue work on the fence.

Only Hannah and Will were left and, as Millie reached them, Hannah lowered her phone. 'Did you know about this?' she asked, accusingly.

Millie shook her head. 'I came to see if Will was up.'

That got a frown from him and something close to puzzlement from Hannah.

'What time did you get here?' she asked.

'About six.'

'Did you see them breaking in? It's illegal if they did. I'm trying to find out if we can get an injunction, or something, but nobody's up.' She looked longingly at her phone. 'It didn't even charge properly last night.'

'I don't think they broke in,' Millie said. She could feel Will watching her carefully, wondering precisely what she'd seen.

Hannah looked down to him, as if remembering he was there. 'What did *you* see?' she asked.

Will blinked at her and then stumbled over a reply. 'I dunno. I was up early and, suddenly they were inside. They told me to get out. There were loads of them.'

'So they broke in...?' Millie said.

'I don't know. I didn't see.' It felt as if he might chuck in a conspiratorial 'maybe...' Probably because he wasn't sure what Millie *had* seen, he didn't.

Hannah looked down to her phone again. 'The library opens at eight on Wednesdays,' she said. 'I'm going to head down, charge this, and see if I can get hold of someone. This isn't over.'

She took a step away and then stopped when she realised Will hadn't moved from the ground.

'You coming?'

'Maybe in a bit.' He nodded towards the bailiffs and the house. 'I'll keep an eye on this lot and catch up with you later. You never know, they might leave a gap in the fence, or something...?'

Hannah eyed him for a second, then Millie, then shrugged a *suit yourself*, before heading off in the direction everyone else had gone.

Grey continued to swirl overhead and the clouds were so low that Millie felt as if she could touch them. Over by the house, a couple of bailiffs had dragged across another set of mesh fence panels from their vans. There was a *burr* of drill and *thunk* of hammer. Regardless of what Hannah was going to do at the library, this resistance was over.

Will picked himself up from the tall grass and brushed

down his arse. There was a large wet patch from the dew that he seemingly hadn't noticed. He grabbed his backpack from the ground and then yawned.

'I'm off to get breakfast,' he said.

He moved a few paces away, almost as if he'd expected Millie to follow.

'How much did they pay you?' she asked.

He stopped with his back to her, then half-turned. 'Huh?'

'I saw you let them in. I saw one of them give you an envelope. So how much did they pay you to open the door?'

Will clucked his tongue and then pursed his lips. 'I never knew you were so nosey,' he replied.

'Is that what you told them yesterday? If they came back early the next day with a few hundred, you'd open the door and that would be it? No need to get recorded bullying young women out the way. No need for all the bad press. Whoever owns this place must be worth millions – so what's a couple of hundred quid to make it nice and easy?'

A goofy, lopsided grin slipped across Will's face. He shrugged, with something that made it seem like he was impressed at her deduction. 'I'm not that cheap.'

'How much?'

'None of your business.'

'Is it Hannah's business?'

A shrug. 'I guess you and me both know things about each other...'

A high-pitched whirr cut through the morning, somewhere from the other side of the house. An angle grinder, or something like that. Will and Millie moved away side by side, hurrying along the path and over the road, until they were near her car.

The noise stopped almost as soon as they were away. Then, probably not coincidentally, one of the bailiffs started dragging fences across to the entrance of the property itself. They weren't simply going to block off the house, but everything around it. That grass was going to get even longer...

'End of an era,' Will said. Millie was unsure if he was talking to her. He didn't sound particularly upset by any of it. After all, it wasn't his name on the lease.

'Where are you going to stay now?' Millie asked.

'There's always somewhere. Like Hannah said, we know people. There's a whole network of us. There's always a floor here, or a pull-out there. If I get really desperate, I'll go back to Mum and Dad's.'

'You sold your friends out...'

Another shrug: 'This lot were going to chuck us out anyway. We'd been on borrowed time for ages. Might as well make something out of it.'

'What would your friends think of that?'

The angle grinder started up again from the distance as lights came on in the house behind. The mist was lower now. It was all around them, like a chilled, unwanted hug.

As they watched, a trailer pulled in with even more fence panels. Within minutes, they were unloaded and in the process of being bolted into a large, steel square.

Millie and Will had been watching it all unfold without saying much. For Millie, there was a morbid curiosity to it all. Perhaps she would write something for Guy's news site after all. She had kept returning to the house, and it felt like there was a story to tell.

'Why did you come?' Will asked. 'You said to see me...' Millie was about to reply but then he answered his own question. 'It's about those handcuffs again, isn't it? About that stupid battle of the bands?'

'Yes...'

'What happened that night?' he said. 'It must be something for you to keep going on about it.'

It was impossible to deny after the number of times she'd returned to ask him about more or less the same thing.

'Can't you just tell me what happened to the handcuffs? I don't have anything else to offer you.'

'I told you I don't remember. I don't even remember *having* them – let alone doing anything with them, or where they might have ended up.'

'Did you give them to Charlie?'

Will sighed and hunched until they were eye to eye. 'I. Don't. *Remember*. If I paid any attention in French lessons, which I didn't, I'd tell you it in French. I don't know what you're talking about. I don't know what's happening in that photo. And I don't know why you keep going on about it.'

He spat the final words, and a wild speck of saliva flew across the gap between them and landed on Millie's chin. She wiped it away and dug out her car keys.

'You've got problems,' Will sneered. '*Real* problems.'

'Tell me something I don't know.'

She unlocked the car and opened the driver's door but Will wasn't about to let her leave. 'Don't forget, I know things about you, Millie.'

'No you don't.'

'I spoke to Pidge and—'

'Pidge is a convicted drug dealer. He sold to kids *outside their school*. You can tell people what you want about me – but the first time anyone asks where you heard it, you're going to have to tell them that you heard it from a *convicted drug dealer*. And then you'll have questions about why *you're* hanging around with a *convicted drug dealer*. Because the only reason anybody spends time with a *convicted drug dealer* is if they're buying drugs themselves.'

Will was shaking his head. 'They won't. I'll—'

'You're not going to say anything. I know it – and so do you.'

Millie climbed into the car but Will grabbed the driver's door and refused to let it be closed.

'Are you going to tell anyone about...?'

He held up the rucksack he was carrying in his spare hand. The one with the cash inside. The bribe.

'Because no one will believe you, either,' he added. 'Everyone knows what you did to your husband. Half this town think you killed your parents for the inheritance anyway.'

Millie started the engine, though Will didn't release the door.

'I know what you did,' he shouted at her, trying to be heard over the engine.

Millie edged forward, slowly at first, not wanting to run him over. As she gathered speed, Will had no option other than to release the door. Millie swiftly slammed it and then continued up the hill until she was far enough away that she could turn without him catching her.

He was still in the road as she drove back the way she'd come. For a moment, she thought he might dive across her in a mad attempt to stop her leaving. Instead, he stood, watching as Millie slowed and buzzed her window down. He didn't bother to approach, he simply hefted his bag onto his shoulder.

'No you don't,' Millie replied – and then she was gone.

THIRTY-TWO

Millie didn't trust Will – but she did finally believe him when he said he didn't remember the handcuffs, or what happened to them. If he'd been the person who had returned Nicola's shoes and phone, there wasn't much point in continuing to deny he was involved when Millie challenged him with evidence. Even if that evidence was circumstantial.

But if it wasn't him, all she had left was Charlie and that single typo. It wasn't much.

Millie couldn't work out what to do. If she told Nicola and was wrong, it would destroy their rekindled friendship. If she told Nicola and was right, it would destroy her marriage. If she *didn't* tell Nicola and she was right, then she was condemning her friend to remain married to a person who'd abducted her years before. A person who was going out of his way to torment her about it.

She drove aimlessly around the town, running through potential scenarios of what might happen if she chose to do a certain thing. Regardless of what she came up with, Millie couldn't think of anything that didn't involve Nicola getting hurt, perhaps badly.

One thing that didn't seem possible was to leave things how they were. If Charlie was that manipulative, his wife surely had to know? She was the one who had to live with him. Their marriage was on the rocks anyway – but Nicola thought it was because of Matty's death. Were the shoes and the phone all a vastly misplaced result of Charlie's grief?

It didn't feel like the sort of thing Millie could reveal at Nicola's work, so she found herself parked outside Nicola's house, without much idea of what to do next.

She had been there less than five minutes, browsing her phone, when there was a tap on her window. Millie jumped and dropped the device into the footwell as she craned up to see… Charlie.

He angled himself down and squinted through the glass, then took half a step back as Millie opened the door.

'Nic's at work,' he said.

Millie was still flapping, trying to find her phone. Charlie moved away a little further, waiting until Millie had scratched the skin on the back of her hand as she dug the phone out from under her own chair. She had no idea how it could have travelled so far.

'I know,' Millie replied eventually.

'What are you doing here?'

'Waiting, I guess.'

'I suppose I'm asking in the wider sense. You've not been in our lives for, what, ten years? Fifteen…? What changed?'

Millie wasn't sure she had a proper answer for that. She certainly didn't have one while she was sitting in a car, wrapped in a twisted seatbelt, while someone stood over her.

'I didn't mean it quite like that,' Charlie added quickly. 'I meant… it was a shock seeing you the other day.' He paused to run his fingers across the sweat on his forehead. 'Do you want to come in? It's cooler in there than it is out here. I'm working in the living room – but you're welcome to wait in the kitchen.'

The day had shifted quickly from hazy morning mist, to searing early-afternoon heat. He was right that Millie couldn't realistically wait in her car – but, for whatever reason, she wasn't keen on returning home.

Was it safe to be alone with Charlie? He was wearing sand-coloured chinos with a black belt and a polo shirt with horizontal stripes. He had that dad-with-grown-up-kids-who's-given-up vibe about him. He worked in property management and didn't *look* remotely intimidating. If anything, he looked slightly desperate for company. Not only that, Millie had known him on and largely off for a long time.

'I should say sorry for the other day,' Charlie added, perhaps seeing her hesitance. 'I was annoyed because I'd forgotten my laptop, then... there are other things going on with me and Nic. She might have told you. I didn't mean you to be caught in the middle.'

Despite everything, he sounded as if he meant it.

Before she'd thought things through, Millie was out of her car and following Charlie along the drive. The front door had been left open and they headed inside. Charlie closed the door and then hovered outside the entrance to the living room. 'I'm working in here,' he said, before pointing along the hall. 'The kitchen's there if that's where you want to wait...?'

There was an implication that she could perhaps keep him company while she waited, though Millie was only half-listening. She was eyeing the picture board as she had the previous evening.

'Nicola said these were your idea,' she said.

Charlie looked at her blankly. 'What?'

'The picture captions.'

He blinked quickly with surprise. 'Oh, right... yeah. Because Jenny's always giving these really long descriptions for everything. Have you seen them? She and Matty would go on holiday somewhere, then she used to get me and Nic over. She'd talk us through everything in the craziest amount of detail. I thought it'd be funny to do the opposite. I told Matty and he...' Charlie bit his lip and glanced away. 'Anyway, if you need something, I'm—'

'He *wrote them*?'

Millie suddenly realised that having the idea of the captions – and *writing* them were two different things. The sentence had gone unfinished at the very moment in which Millie thought she knew where it was going.

'He... what?'

'Were you going to say that *Matty* wrote the captions?'

Charlie shook his head slowly. 'No, he said he thought it would be funny.'

'So you wrote them?'

Charlie's face creased into a confused frown. He'd clearly never been asked such a thing before – but then, why would he?

'Nic wrote them,' he said matter-of-factly. 'It was my idea but she put all that together. There's one in the kitchen and another upstairs. You know what she's like. She was always the artsy one out of us all.'

Everything felt as if it had stopped. There was a ringing in Millie's ears, like an alarm, or... she didn't know.

Of course Nicola was the artsy one.

If Millie had ever forgotten, it had been right in front of her when she unhooked the Converse from the washing line. Nicola was the one who'd drawn a heart on her shoe.

Everything had been in front of her the whole time. All of it.

Millie looked to the picture board and the way the photos had been cut into shapes to fit the space. There were hearts and circles, plus crocodile teeth zigzags along the edges.

It was obvious Charlie hadn't done any of this.

'She's got neater handwriting than me anyway,' Charlie said.

Millie focused in on the caption that revealed everything and it felt as if she was falling. She knew what had happened twenty years before and she knew what had happened a week ago. It was so clear now. It always had been.

Without meaning to, Millie's finger was resting against the word 'feild' and Charlie leaned in.

'Huh...' he said. 'I never noticed that before. I guess we should've spent more time in class and less time bunking off...'

He laughed – but he was being polite anyway. It was never Charlie who did the bunking off.

Millie angled back towards the door. 'I'm gonna go,' she said. 'I'll call Nic instead.' She got to the door and fumbled with the clasp. 'It's been good to see you,' she added.

'You don't have to leave, I—'

'It's not you,' Millie added quickly, as she finally got the door open. She burst through, exploding back into the warmth of the afternoon, her legs unable to move quickly enough to take her. The world was spinning as she struggled with her keys before finally getting herself back into the car.

The truth had been there the entire time – and now Millie had to tell someone what it was.

THIRTY-THREE

Barry couldn't believe his luck.

Millie would take him to the woods once or twice a week, depending on the weather – but here he was getting out twice in three days. He'd lost none of his energy as he hurtled across the path and pounced towards a tree. The squirrel he'd been chasing was already partway up, scurrying in a circle around the trunk. It stopped when it reached the first branch – and Millie was certain it was the same squirrel from the other day. It probably did the same thing to any passing dog.

'Hannah, Will and everyone else are gone from the house,' Millie said.

'I figured that was the most likely outcome,' Guy replied.

'It took an extra day – but there are fences up around the house and the garden now. I was there this morning.'

'I said you're a natural reporter.'

Millie didn't feel comfortable at being called a natural at anything. 'I'm really not.'

'If you want to write something,' Guy said, 'the offer is always there for a place to publish.'

'I can't,' Millie said. 'I was there yesterday, too. There was a chain of people and the bailiffs were about to cut through their cuffs with bolt cutters. Will went and said something to them and they ended up leaving. He told everyone he'd said something about it being a bad look – but, really, he told them to come back this morning. They paid him a few quid and he opened the door for them.'

They continued for a few more paces until Guy replied. 'I suppose that's a better outcome than what might have happened...'

That was true. Millie still didn't know what all the sticks were for. Perhaps they were for some sort of art project? It didn't really matter any longer.

'I bet the owner wishes he threw a little bit extra at the problem a while ago...'

Guy sounded almost amused as he spoke. As pragmatic about the real world as ever

'It was only one person,' Millie replied. 'Hannah and the others didn't know anything about it. They still don't know it was Will who took the money and opened the door.'

They'd reached the crossroads where the trails met. Guy pointed from side to side, asking which way, but Millie stepped away from the path and continued on into the trees.

'This way,' she said.

Guy crunched and wobbled his way across the brittle, dried-out twigs. He said that his knees weren't really in a good state for anything more than a trail – although he continued walking. They could be going anywhere but he trusted her.

'What are you going to do about what you saw?' he asked.

'The bribe?' Millie said. She quite liked the sound of the word.

'The bribe,' Guy confirmed.

Millie had been thinking about it on and off all day – although largely off since visiting Nicola's house. It wouldn't take much to track down Hannah and tell her everything. Perhaps she'd believe it, perhaps not.

'I think I'll leave it,' Millie said.

Guy didn't press her on why and, even if he had, Millie wasn't sure she had an answer. Despite everything she'd told him when he was holding open her car door, it was hard not to forget what Will knew. Or thought he knew. Most people wouldn't believe something a convicted drug dealer was saying – but some would. Some didn't care who the messenger happened to be, as long as they were saying what that person wanted to hear. That was the problem with more or less everything in the modern world.

Barry knew where they were going and led the way into the first clearing. He headed for the hollowed-out tree at the end and began sniffing the ground.

Millie and Guy stopped in the centre of the clearing and Guy wafted his shirt to try to cool himself.

'Is this the famous Kissing Tree?' he asked.

'The one and only.'

Guy walked across to it. He touched the bark when he got there, running his fingers along the grooves of people's initials.

'Funny the things you don't know,' he said. 'I've worked in this town all my life. I've done stories about young people, old people, and everyone in between. I've written about the ocean, the beach, the buildings, the people, the animals, the woods... and I've never once heard of this tree.'

He was looking at it the way a first-time astronaut might stare down upon the earth.

'I like to think there's lots of these little things around,' he said. 'Not trees, as such. Mysteries.' He stopped and then added: 'There are caves underneath the town. I found out three years ago. They were knocking down the old C&A building and they had to do a scan of the ground to check the foundations. Turns out, there's a whole network down there. Nobody knows how far it stretches. It could turn out the entire town is built on a system of caves.'

Millie wondered if she was missing some sort of joke. 'If the whole town is built on top of caves... how come I've never heard about it?'

'Nobody knows whether it is or not. That's the point. There are *definitely* caves below that one building – and it seems very unlikely something like that would be isolated to a relatively small square. The only option would be to go into every private business and perform a similar scan. Except, because not all buildings are the same, nor are the foundations, that would be impossible.'

'Wouldn't people want to know if there's a chance their house, or business, could fall into a sinkhole?'

Guy was now past the Kissing Tree and sitting on the tree where Millie and Nicola had sat barely two days before. For maybe the first time since she'd met him, he seemed like an old man. He struggled with the cap of his bottle and Millie had to help before he could drink.

She asked if he was OK but he waved her away. Barry had returned from his escapade, perhaps remembering the tree and how bored he'd been the last time they'd had a sit-down in the woods.

'We can go back...?' Millie said.

'There's a lot of things people probably don't want to know about this town,' Guy said. 'It was hit during the Blitz and I can guarantee there are unexploded bombs in people's gardens. Maybe there are houses built on a cave system? Nobody has the money to bring in the equipment and do a deep scan on the whole town.' He paused to sip his water, then added. 'I suppose what I'm saying is that I never cease to be amazed by the secrets this place throws at me.'

Millie perched on the trunk at Guy's side and asked him if he was sure he was OK. Perhaps it was his generation of men and the culture of never admitting a weakness – but he insisted he was fine.

'I know who left the shoes on Nicola's line,' Millie said. 'She also said her old Nokia was put through the door a few days ago. I meant to tell you but it's all blurred together.'

Guy was quiet for a moment and she wondered if it was because he was feeling ill.

'I have to say I'm surprised,' Guy replied. 'When I went to her house, I had the sense nothing would come of it all. That is unless the person who left those shoes wanted Nicola to know who it was.'

He didn't ask – and it was probably that which made Millie want to tell him. The worst person to hold power was the one who craved it – and she thought that might be true of knowledge as well.

'Nicola did it to herself,' Millie said.

She spoke softly, quietly. Barely able to believe it, let alone say it. It still boomed through the trees.

'She did it all,' Millie added. 'When we separated and she said she was going back to the park, she either went home or went to the woods. Maybe both. She cut her own hair. She sent me the text to let me know where to find her. She cuffed herself. I think they probably were the ones Will was wearing in the picture. He might've put them down, or maybe there were various pairs at the gig? I've not been able to remember but, sometimes, bands did silly things to promote themselves. There was one band that had a guy giving out carrots to the audience because they had a song that mentioned carrots. Maybe there just happened to be fluffy handcuffs around that night? Maybe there was a hen party or two in?'

Millie tailed off, knowing she'd never have a proper answer. Knowing it didn't really matter where the handcuffs came from.

'That's... a big claim,' Guy said. It didn't sound as if he

believed her. Or, perhaps he simply wanted her to be careful. 'Did she tell you that herself?'

Millie shook her head. 'No... there was something else. Something silly that gave her away.'

He thought on that, even though she hadn't told him what. 'Why would she do that?'

'I don't know for sure. Will said it was the last summer we were all together – and I think he was right. It felt like things were ending. We still had school but people were already talking about gap years and university. About travelling, or getting a job. All that stuff had to be planned ahead. Then we left the park, me and her, and nobody stopped us.'

Millie took a breath and tried to remember the darkness of the evening setting in. The way it felt like an end and how the tipsiness only made it worse.

'I think I felt it that night, too,' Millie added. 'This weird sense of wanting to keep what we had, while also knowing it was over.'

Guy leant forward and had another sip from his bottle. He rubbed his forehead and Millie knew he was thinking of Carol. What was it like to be married to a person for so long and then wake up without them? She couldn't imagine it.

'I was talking to Ingrid at the nursing home,' Millie said. 'She said that sometimes you have to be ruthless in letting go of things – or in trying to keep hold of what you have. And that is ruthless, isn't it? We'd been friends since we were girls but we were going to start thinking about applying to universities, or getting jobs. Maybe I'd have taken a year off and gone travelling? Anything could have happened – but, after I found her in the woods, in that moment, with the secret we had, we were sisters. More than sisters, in some way. There was this bond that neither of us thought would ever be broken.'

Guy was silent but Millie somehow knew what he was thinking – and she had answers for that, too.

'Maybe the two of us are back like that again now – and it was this that got us there.'

Still no response.

'Do you remember last year, when we first met? I told you that Ingrid had seen someone fall from that roof. We didn't know whether it happened but you asked who benefits from one person saying it did and one person saying it didn't. I was thinking about what you said then – and what you said when we were sitting on the bench after playing crazy golf. You said all this might be a success if it brought me and Nicola back together... and it has.'

'I think—'

Millie didn't want him to interrupt. 'The person who benefits from those shoes reappearing – and the phone – is Nicola. I saw her with Charlie, her husband, and the way they argue with each other. His best friend died and he's not been the same. She doesn't know what to do and she probably thinks things are slipping away. And I know it sounds arrogant, like I'm some sort of egomaniac. I'm saying she did all this for me, for us. Like I'm some sort of catch, or prize... but I really think she did. I think she needed someone and I think... maybe I do, too...'

Millie only realised she was crying when the tears hit her bare knees. She wiped them away but they kept coming. That was one of the other problems with summer – no sleeves.

Guy touched her back gently, just enough, as Millie rubbed her thumbs into her eyes, desperately wanting to regain some control.

Guy waited – and so did Barry. When she opened her eyes, the dog was sitting at her feet. He was staring up with those big, brown eyes, asking if there was anything he could do. Millie ruffled his ears.

'Sorry...'

'No need for that.' Guy's voice was calm and wise. 'Just to be clear,' he added. 'You're saying she kept hold of those shoes and her old phone for fifteen years – and then she got in contact...?'

It sounded ridiculous. Impossible. And yet...

'I think so.' Millie thought on it and then added. 'Yes, she did... but it isn't only her who benefits. It's me, too. She slept with Dad but he's the one who should've known better. He was twice her age. More. She was my best friend. We didn't talk for all those years but now we get to be friends again.' Millie gulped. 'You said that, too. I don't have many of those.'

Neither of them spoke for a while. Millie listened to the rustle of the undergrowth and the chirping of the birds. She thought of Nicola sitting in the woods by herself, waiting for Millie to arrive and perhaps hearing those same things. Had she hidden the shoes and phone at home, then come here? Had she sent the message from this spot and then hidden her things to retrieve the next day? Had she been home, slept in her own bed, and then come back to the woods to tie herself up in the morning?

It didn't matter, really. Those were dots around the edges and Millie had the bigger picture.

'What are you going to do?' Guy asked. 'Let her know that you know...?'

Millie thought for a moment longer. She'd done a lot of thinking since she'd been in the hall with Charlie.

'She did this for me,' Millie said. 'Herself as well – but *for me*. It's our second chance. And we all have our secrets, don't we? Like you said again. Even Whitecliff has its secrets.'

Guy had once asked her whether she'd killed her parents and, for a moment, she thought he was going to ask again. He opened his mouth and then: 'Barry! What are you doing over there? Barry!'

The dog had headed back in the direction of the Kissing Tree, where he'd stopped to poke through a pile of wood. When he lifted his head, he was carrying the same stick he'd had days before. The one that was bigger than him.

'Shall we head back?' Guy asked.

'If you want to see the spot where I found Nic, it's about five minutes that way.'

Millie pointed behind them and Guy twisted to look.

'You know what,' he said. 'I think that's one mystery I can do without seeing for myself.'

THIRTY-FOUR

Millie was standing in the doorframe, staring out towards the washing line. She didn't think there'd ever be a time where she could look at it without seeing those Converse hanging. They weren't there now, of course. She and Nicola hadn't spoken about them, or the returned phone, in two weeks. Nothing else had appeared through Nicola's letterbox, either. Nicola hadn't asked about Guy and whether he'd unearthed something new.

Not for the first time, they had jointly experienced something extraordinary – and were going to carry on as if they hadn't.

When Millie turned back into the kitchen, Jack was looking at the picture board on the back of the door.

'Is your husband going to be here later?' he asked.

Nicola was slicing cheese on the countertop and she didn't look up as she replied. 'He's at a training thing for his work,' she said. 'Not back 'til tomorrow.'

Jack exchanged a silent glance with Millie across the kitchen. A gentle raise of the eyebrows. *Oh*, it said. Millie had already told Jack and Rishi that Charlie was away for the night but he apparently needed to hear it for himself. Or, perhaps more to the point, to hear the lack of burden in Nicola's voice. Like a mother who'd unloaded triplets onto a grandparent for a night.

Nicola had told Millie she wanted to meet her 'other' friends. Her word-of-mouth hit, baked and fried lasagne, was offered up – and here they all were. Rishi was at the kitchen table, checking the mails on his phone until Jack called him across to the door.

'We've been here, haven't we?' Jack said.

Rishi crossed and peered closer at one of the photos. 'Is that Corfu?'

The knife clunked into the chopping board as another wedge of cheese hit the pile. Nicola wiped down her fingers and then headed across to the door, where she slipped in between the two men.

'That was so long ago,' she said. 'We were so young. I was blonde back then!'

'Those roots tell a different story...'

Jack giggled – and, after a fraction of a second, so did Nicola. She slapped him playfully on the arm.

'Is he always like this?'

It wasn't clear who she was asking but Millie and Rishi both answered that he was. Rishi clarified that he was worse if he'd not had nine hours' sleep, which led to a good five minutes of bickering about who slept the most, who stole the covers when they were cold, who threw off the covers when they were hot, who always had a foot outside the covers, who snored, who snored *loudest*, who fidgeted the most, why Jack always got dead arms in the night, why Rishi was always cold, and, eventually, whether they'd be better with two single beds.

Millie was still in the doorway, while Nicola was back at the chopping board. It was their turn to exchange a look this time – but there were only smiles now. There was a difference between gentle squabbling and full-on arguing.

Rishi was vegetarian, so it was a different sort of mince that Nicola used as she began to layer everything into the glass dish. That got them talking about their favourite foods (general), favourite foods (specific) and favourite-ever meals. Jack and Nicola apparently had the same taste, metaphorical and literal, in more or less everything. That led Jack to turn to Millie and ask: 'Where have you been hiding Nic away all this time? Have you been keeping her to yourself?'

'Not quite,' Millie replied.

'I don't think we need Mill any more,' Rishi said. 'Nicola is Millie two point oh. New and improved – with better cooking.' He shot Millie a filthy grin – and then they were all swapping phone numbers and setting up a WhatsApp group.

Millie stood and she sat. She listened and she joined in. She was an active part of it all but she was an observer, too.

It was the first time she'd been part of a *group* of friends as an adult. The day of the battle of the bands all those years before had been an end in so many ways. It had certainly brought the curtain down on their friendship group. They'd seen each other in smaller ways since, at weddings and funerals. But it had never been the same, especially after Millie and Nicola fell out.

And now, there was something new.

They were busy talking about ghosts, with Nicola leaning towards Jack's view that they definitely existed, when Rishi's phone rang.

The amusement left his face as he saw whatever was on the screen. 'I've got to take this,' he said.

He was halfway through the door, into the garden, as he answered with a cheery but forced 'hello'.

There was a momentary quiet and then Nicola spoke quietly: 'Charlie would go mad if I did that.'

'Did what?' Jack asked.

'Ran out of the room without telling him who was calling.

He always wants to know who it is and what they want, even before I've answered.'

It was the first serious thing any of them had said in a while. Glances were exchanged, though nobody replied.

'Rish's mum calls him most days,' Jack said. 'Usually to ask if he can help her find something online. She'll be like, "You know that song by that man your uncle likes. That one with the voice. What's it called?" Then Rish'll spend twenty minutes trying to find it for her and it'll turn out she's talking about James Blunt.' He glanced through the back door, towards Rishi. 'I think she probably just wants to hear his voice, so she makes up these mini treasure hunts to have him help her.'

The three of them watched as Rishi strode back and forth, doing widths of the garden, like a slow-motion bleep test.

'I heard they've set a date,' Jack said. Millie assumed he was talking to her.

'Who's set a date?' she asked.

Jack turned away from Rishi and frowned. 'Your ex. Alex. He and that Rachel are getting married in December. Didn't you know...?'

Millie didn't need to answer because her face said it all.

'Oh,' Jack added quickly. 'I mean I might be wrong. One of Rishi's exes handles bookings at the Grand Royal. They got talking yesterday and it somehow came up that they'd taken a wedding booking for the week between Christmas and New Year. I think Rish asked who it was, in case we knew them, and he said it was Alex and Rachel. I don't think he knew we were friends with you.' A pause. 'I assumed you knew...?'

Millie shook her head. Alex had said something about a Christmas school reunion and she wondered if he'd meant as part of his and Rachel's wedding reception? He'd also said the potential wedding was a minimum of a year away. She wondered when he'd tell her properly. Perhaps she had no right of an expectation to know? They were no longer married, after all. He'd told her about the engagement almost as soon as it happened.

'Sorry...' Jack said.

'It's fine,' Millie replied. 'I'm sure they were going to tell me next time they see me.'

She wasn't sure of that at all, though she found herself glancing up to the clock. There was half an hour until Eric would call. Those nightly check-ins hadn't ended, after all. Millie had a sense that Alex and Rachel were going to have to pick their battles, especially if they wanted Eric to start calling Rachel 'Mum'.

The dress hadn't been mentioned since Eric had told her it had been thrown out. By the time Millie had seen him the following weekend, he'd apparently forgotten about it. That might have been because they'd spent the day at the dog sanctuary. Eric and Chloe had enjoyed hours of playing fetch and frisbee with the potential rescues. After that, Eric only had one thing on his mind – and it wasn't what he was wearing. Millie had felt bad about it afterwards as she thought she'd set up her son for disappointment about his chance of getting a dog. Both Jack and Nicola had differing opinions, which, in not so many words, mainly involved telling Alex to go swivel.

Then there was Guy, with whom Millie had a different type of relationship. He was full of encouragement and advice, wanting to push her towards whatever would come next in her life. It had been a long time since Millie had felt that sort of support, from more than just a single person.

As she was lost in thoughts of Alex and Rachel's Christmas wedding, wondering what she'd do on that particular day, Rishi reappeared in the doorway. He was crying and Millie's first thought was that he must have hurt himself somehow.

He was smiling as well, though.

'Was it...?' Jack started.

Rishi nodded. 'We've been approved. We're gonna be dads!'

Jack burst from his seat to hug Rishi, then they hugged Millie, then Nicola, then Millie hugged Nicola for some reason. The Great British Hug Fest.

'Whatever you told her was perfect,' Rishi said, talking to Millie. 'How can we ever repay you?'

'Curry,' Millie replied. 'I do take payment in curry.' She turned to Nicola. 'And lasagne.'

Rishi disappeared back into the garden to call his mum and tell her the good news, while Nicola headed across to the cooker to check on the food. That left Millie and Jack alone at the dining table, where he was studiously avoiding her gaze. When he did risk a glance up, he quickly looked away again.

'You OK?' Millie asked.

'Of course. It's just, when we left you in the flat that night, I suppose I wondered what you might have said...'

'You could've asked.'

He nodded at that – but he didn't reply. The contrast in their reactions to the news couldn't be more different. Jack was sitting at the table, vaguely scrolling *The Guardian*'s website. Rishi was outside, laughing as he spoke with his mum on the phone.

Millie didn't know if she had anything more to add, not today anyway. She didn't get a chance anyway as her phone began to buzz. It was a number not in her contacts, and the only reason she answered is that it was a local 01 landline number.

'Is that Millicent Westlake?' a woman's voice asked.

Millie rolled her eyes. It was going to be some sort of marketing call. She only used her full name on official documents. 'Who's asking?' she replied.

'My name is Elaine,' the woman said. 'I'm a nurse at the hospital. I don't want to worry you but we've just had a patient brought in. He's unconscious and we're not sure what happened. We're working on him now – but the reason I'm calling is that he has your name in his wallet. We didn't know who else to contact.'

Jack must have noticed something was wrong. Either that, or the sound had bled to such a degree that he'd heard. He reached out a hand and touched Millie on the elbow.

'Who is it?' Millie asked.

There was a cough, a clearing of the throat, and then the nurse replied. 'That's the problem. *Your* name was in his wallet – but that's it. We don't know who he is. Do you think you can come in?'

Millie was already on her feet, heading into the hall. 'I'm on my way,' she said.

CHAPTER ONE

DAY ONE

Millie Westlake's foot went through the top of the feathery moss and squelched into the hidden puddle underneath. The muddy water seeped instantly into her supposedly waterproof shoes for the fourth time in barely fifteen minutes. The silt was between her socks and the sole, making her foot slide squishily around within the shoe.

The man at Millie's side slowed a pace to let her catch up. 'How are the feet?' he asked.

'Wet,' Millie replied. A pause. 'Aren't waterproof shoes supposed to be... *waterproof*?' She spoke quietly enough that the smaller group of men up ahead wouldn't hear.

'I think if the water goes over the top of—'

'I was being rhetorical.'

'Ah.'

Of the men ahead, four were wearing wellington boots, with murky splash marks pebble-dashed across the rubber. The other was in some sort of plain black shoes, that were likely wetter than hers. The ground was a sponge – and not even a fresh one from the packet. One of those grim, slimy things that live at the back of a draining board, spreading cholera and herpes.

Millie slipped her hands deeper into her pockets as the wind howled around the desolate moor. She shrank into her coat, trying to shield her neck and cheeks from the gale that fizzed around them. It wasn't raining, not yet, but the sky was a gloomy wash, and there was a general sense that it might lash it down at any moment.

As well as the five men ahead, there were another two behind. Millie and Guy were holding the middle ground, the odd ones out in their regular day-to-day clothes. Six of the seven were wearing rubbery fishing-style wading trousers. The other man was leading the line. He'd walk for a few minutes, stop, and look into the bleak distance. After a moment or two, he'd slightly change direction, and then walk for a few minutes more. Their odd little group had been on this strange, slow dance for fifteen minutes.

'What are you doing for Christmas?' Guy asked.

His question came from nowhere, still quiet enough that only Millie could hear. A distraction from whatever grim sight was to appear in the coming minutes. She suspected he was trying to take her mind off such things.

'I have friends coming over on Christmas Eve,' Millie replied. 'Christmas itself should be quiet, then I've got Eric from Boxing Day. He's staying until new year.'

Mentioning his name brought Millie's eight-year-old son's little face into her mind. She blinked it away, not wanting his image to be with her here. Not with what they were about to find.

'Come over, if you want,' she added, trying to sound cheery. 'Bring Barry.'

She thought they'd been talking quietly enough for only each other to hear but perhaps the breeze was carrying their conversation. The odd man out ahead, the one without the waders and wellies, missed a pace and then stopped to turn. The men at his side were alert and instantly on edge, hands poised next to hips, as if about to leap into action.

'Who's Barry?' the man asked.

Guy and Millie stopped together, as did the other two men behind. The wind whipped up further, somehow seeming to come from all sides.

'My labradoodle,' Guy said.

'Didn't you used to have a black lab? I remember you having him in the old office. Used to lie near the door.'

'That was twenty-five, thirty, years ago, Kevin,' Guy replied.

Kevin Ashworth nodded slowly as a hint of a frown creased onto his shadowed face. He pulled his coat higher onto his shoulders, though it slipped down almost immediately. It was at least three sizes too big for him – and clearly not his.

One of the two police officers at his side muttered something to the pair of prison guards. Millie didn't catch it but Ashworth did. He turned and scanned the grim horizon, before dipping his head and carrying on in the same direction they'd been heading.

A second later and the rest of the group was off again, stomping across the moss and slipping over the rocks, all guided by a man who'd spent the best part of three decades in prison.

It was quite the group. Two police officers and two prison guards on either side of Ashworth. Then Guy and Millie. Then, further back, two massive blokes who each looked like a cross between a Rottweiler and a wall. Millie didn't know who they were: enforcers or bouncers, something like that.

Ashworth had been locked up when Millie was barely a teenager. She'd had no interest in the news at that age – she wasn't mental – but that didn't stop everyone at school knowing his name.

His face, too.

His mugshot had been front and centre of every newspaper

and TV report for months. Kevin Ashworth was their town's Freddy Krueger or Jason Voorhees. Except Kevin was real.

And now, he was a couple of metres from her, limping along a moor in sodden shoes and someone else's coat.

'Stevie, he was called,' Guy said, shouting towards Kevin. 'That black lab was the love of Carol's life. Lived 'til he was seventeen. Nobody I know has heard of a lab living longer.'

Millie wasn't sure how she felt about Guy calling amiably to the monster ahead of them, even if the police wanted something from him. Something only Kevin knew.

She was less sure how she felt about Ashworth *specifically* requesting Guy be on the moors.

Why him?

Her own presence was less cryptic. She and Guy had somehow fallen into being something of an informal investigative duo – even if he was close to forty years older than her. Ashworth requested Guy for this expedition but Guy wouldn't do it without Millie. The mystery of whatever they were walking into had been too much to ignore.

And here they all were.

Ashworth maintained his pace but shouted back over his shoulder: 'How is Carol?'

Guy answered without hesitation, or emotion: 'She died a couple of years back.'

Ashworth stopped again and turned. So did the other men at his side. 'She... *died*?'

'Cancer,' Guy replied. 'It was quick. She didn't suffer.'

Millie had barely known Guy talk of his former wife, let alone so matter-of-factly.

'I'm sorry to hear that,' Ashworth added.

There was a silence for a moment, punctured only by the whistle of the breeze.

'It's OK,' Guy replied.

Ashworth nodded again and then turned. He led them

forward for a wordless minute or so and then stopped once more. He wiped the sweat, or damp, from his eyes and then stared across towards the trees in the deepest horizon. Everything seemed so flat and lifeless. He twisted further, towards the way they'd come.

A fair distance back was the three-way road junction from which they'd set off – and, beyond, Whitecliff. The town was out of sight, at the bottom of the hill, but the ocean was there, raging in the winter storm.

Ashworth mopped his brow with his sleeve and turned again. Millie heard his feet squelch. There was moss and heather, grass and rocks. Mud and puddles. Lots of nothing.

One of the police officers spoke: 'Are we stopping... or...?'

Ashworth crouched and touched his fingers to the damp earth. He stood again and then pointed to a large rock embedded in the ground.

'It's there,' he said.

Keep reading here!

A NOTE FROM THE AUTHOR

I grew up in the small town of Frome, Somerset, in the United Kingdom. Despite the spelling, 'Frome' rhymes with 'broom', not 'Rome'. If you are a newsreader for a national TV channel, and you ever get this wrong, be prepared to hear about it for the rest of your life.

Around seven miles outside Frome, across the county border in Wiltshire, is Longleat. If you don't know it, this is a place primarily famous for the enormous stately home. Among other things, there's also a hedge maze, Center Parcs resort, and the safari park.

As a digression, one time my primary school went to Longleat for a school trip. In the days before things like health and safety going mad, we were sitting on the grass having our packed lunches. That was when a curious giraffe trotted over, craned that giant neck down towards us, and ate my friend's lunch – including the plastic lunchbox. This was considered a massive laugh at the time and something perfectly normal. Nowadays, there would be promises of inquiries, letters to the board of governors, letters home, letters to the local newspaper, viral videos on Twitter, Facebook arguments about a lack of supervision, not to mention some sort of TikTok trend, with kids trying to feed *their* lunches to giraffes. People would probably be fired, there'd be a backlash over that, then a backlash to the backlash. The poor giraffe would be put down. Someone would dox my friend, then he and his family would have to go into hiding.

Let's just say it was a different time. The nineteen-eighties, to be precise.

Anyway, a few years on, when I was a teenager, I used to do a bit of work at Longleat. It is surrounded by vast wooded areas that stretch out and around the surrounding villages. You can walk for hours without leaving the trees. There are spots called imaginative things like 'East Woodlands' and 'West Woodlands', plus roads named things like 'Forest Road'. There's a village called 'Marston Bigot' that... OK I have no idea what's going on there.

My point is that, when I was working in those woods, places would often be identified by some of the most bizarre directions you can imagine. I'd be told something like: 'Can you head over to The Candle to look for pheasants?'

To be clear, there was no candle. It was simply a tree, in among thousands of other trees, that, from a set angle, if you squinted, looked a bit like a candle.

If not that, it could be: 'Can you shoot over to The Welly? Wait for fifteen minutes and make some noise, then we'll pick you up at The Dip.'

Again, there was no welly – but someone had lost a welly in a mud puddle there at some point in the previous seventy years and it was a story that had been passed down, long since it had any relevance. The Dip was a dip – although there were lots of dips in the rolling hills, so context was important.

Somehow, I would know precisely where all that was, so would trek twenty minutes through the woods, by myself, with zero trails, and zero markers, to that exact spot. I'd then continue in a different direction to meet the Jeep in a separate part of the woods entirely.

Thinking about it, that also sounds a bit health and safety not going mad enough, considering this was before the days of mobile phones.

Everywhere had a shorthand name and, though I wish I

could remember them, twenty-five years have passed and I can barely remember how old I am.

What I do know is that the idea for 'The Kissing Tree' came from those teenage escapades of bumbling through the middle of nowhere. I, and others who lived and worked around there, knew exactly what those vague-sounding directions meant.

I also know what it's like to have lunch with a giraffe. If you want my advice, it would be to eat quickly – because they're greedy sods.

Lastly, if you're outside the UK, it is a long-acknowledged fact that Somerset is the best county. This is a point that nobody would even bother to debate as it is so deeply ingrained in British society.

Hope you enjoyed the read. More from Whitecliff and Millie soon.

– Kerry Wilkinson, late 2022

KERRY WILKINSON PUBLISHING TEAM

Editorial
Ellen Gleeson

Line edits and copyeditor
Jade Craddock

Proofreader
Loma Halden

Production
Alexandra Holmes
Natalie Edwards

Design
David Grogan

Marketing
Alex Crow
Melanie Price
Occy Carr
Ciara Rosney

Publicity
Noelle Holten
Kim Nash
Sarah Hardy
Jess Readett

Distribution
Chris Lucraft
Marina Valles
Stephanie Straub

Audio
Alba Proko
Nina Winters
Helen Keeley
Carmelite Studios

Rights and contracts
Peta Nightingale
Richard King
Saidah Graham

Printed in Great Britain
by Amazon

21416814R00161